Liam's leaf-green eyes shone in the lamplight when he smiled at Vivie.

"Are you ready for the wildlife rehabilitator test?" he asked.

She sank onto the couch. "I have to be, or you'll shoot Button."

He regarded her gravely. "Wish you wouldn't call her that."

She hugged a pillow. "Why?"

"Because it makes her sound like a pet." Liam leaned forward and the outdoorsy, masculine smell of him filled her senses. Normally being alone with a man this late at night would terrify her. Instead, she felt alive and jittery, her stomach fluttering.

"If you pass tomorrow—"

"When I pass tomorrow," she interrupted, lifting her chin despite her nerves.

He studied her, his strong face handsome. "When you pass tomorrow, you need to start thinking like a rehabilitator. If you treat the bear like a house pet, I'll have to remove her."

The thought of it knocked the breath out of her. "Button is going to make it here." There was no way she'd let him take *her* bear...

Dear Reader,

When I was in fifth grade, my dad accepted a promotion to move to Upstate New York. I was as shocked as my classmates when my teacher traced her pointer from our location, Long Island, to the very top of the map: The Adirondacks. It looked like the end of the world and everyone, including me, gasped in horror.

Little did I know how profoundly this move would change me. I lost my city ways and became an avid nature and animal lover. I live my life outdoors as much as indoors. Cross-country skiing, snowshoeing, riding on a Ski-Doo, kayaking, canoeing, swimming, hiking, camping and, best of all, mountain climbing.

Standing on a summit is an almost religious experience. It's otherworldly to gaze at the breathtaking beauty below and imagine that this is what it must have looked like to the one who made it all. It's awe-inspiring and humbling. Suddenly a fresh perspective clicks into place, giving my soul a good housecleaning.

It's also a privilege to live so close to such an abundance of wild animals, including black bears, the amazing subject of this book. The setting and subject of this story couldn't be any closer to my heart. Please contact me anytime at karenrock@live.com, especially if you're ever visiting my neck of the woods!

Karen

HEARTWARMING

Raising the Stakes

——

Karen Rock

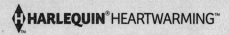

ISBN-13: 978-0-373-36719-1

Raising the Stakes

Copyright © 2015 by Karen Rock

This edition published by arrangement with Harlequin Books S.A.

For questions and comments about the quality of this book, please contact us at CustomerService@Harlequin.com.

Printed in U.S.A.

Karen Rock is an award-winning YA and adult contemporary author. She holds a master's degree in English and worked as an ELA instructor before becoming a full-time author. Her Harlequin Heartwarming novels have won the 2014 Gayle Wilson Award of Excellence and the 2014 Golden Quill Award. When she's not writing, Karen loves scouring estate sales, cooking and hiking. She lives in the Adirondack Mountain region with her husband, daughter and Cavalier King Charles spaniels.

www.KarenRock.com

Books by Karen Rock

Harlequin Heartwarming

Wish Me Tomorrow
His Hometown Girl
Someone Like You
A League of Her Own

Visit the Author Profile page
at Harlequin.com for more titles.

To Little Bit, who made my life whole.
You passed away when I wrote this book and left a
hole that can never be filled. I hope your helicopter
tail is whipping the clouds into a froth up there.
Until we meet again, I love you, my sweet girl.

CHAPTER ONE

THERE IT WAS.

Again.

A skittering sound followed by a jolting thump. Vivienne Harris huddled beneath her quilt, her mind racing as fast as her heart. Someone—or something—prowled downstairs. She eyed her window and the black night beyond it, pine branches tracing the panes like fingers. If she opened the sash and screamed, who would help?

Her nearest neighbors lived fifteen miles down her Adirondack Mountains road and were on vacation to boot. Emergency services? She'd be a headline before they fired up their engines. Besides, the only phone in her two-hundred-year-old farmhouse was downstairs, and cell service didn't exist this far off the grid. Why hadn't the intruder tripped her home alarm?

Was her mind playing tricks? Mistaking her old dog's after-hours trip to the water bowl for something more ominous? He usually slept like the dead, though, so it seemed unlikely... There was only one way to find out. She wouldn't cower in fear that her life might be in danger.

Not again.

With a clattering bang, she swung her feet over the side of her bed where they dangled, frozen. She had to move. Do something. Stop whatever darkness crawled her way. Her eyes slid to her nightstand drawer. Pepper spray. Maggie, her business partner, had gifted it to her at her housewarming party three years ago. She sent her friend a silent thank-you as she snatched the canister.

On quaking legs, she crept down her staircase. *Careful*, she warned herself and skipped over the creaky fifth step. Surprise. Her best weapon and only defense. She forced herself off the last tread and peered at the canister rattling in her hand. How much help would it be? Nightmarish scenarios looped through her mind. She'd never forget that long-ago night and the attack that haunted her still.

A snuffling noise whispered to her left. The kitchen. She inhaled the cinnamon-scented air, picturing the ten pies she'd baked tonight for The Homestead, her diner. They were up high, cooling on open cabinet shelves beyond her yellow Lab's reach. No. Scooter wouldn't be after those. Then—what?

Courage starched her spine. She needed those desserts. Loggers returned from their runs tomorrow. Hungry for a taste of home, they'd want pie. Hers.

But the phone rested on a distant end table in her living room… Where to go first?

A hard *thunk* convinced her, as did the spring breeze that fluttered her kitchen curtains and curled around her throat like an accusation. Fatigue had made her sloppy. She should have closed the window before bed. She squared her shoulders, leaped through the archway and flicked on the light, her pepper spray extended on a shaking arm.

Her eyes darted around the space, frustration washing through her when she surveyed her mostly decimated pies. Many were overturned, nearly empty or dumped on the floor, oozing into the cracked boards. Pie crust bits coated surfaces like dust.

"Darn it!" she exclaimed and advanced into the room, agitation temporarily overriding her fear. Hours of work down the drain. She eyed her half-open window. Whoever or whatever it was had to have squeezed through that.

She reached up and unhooked a skillet

from her pot rack. There was no prowler in sight but the pantry door was ajar. Maybe her trespasser lurked there. Hiding. Sweat beaded her forehead; cold shuddered through her. She forced herself onward. No backing down. The pan handle slipped in her sweating palm, and she grabbed it before jumping into the dim entranceway.

"Stay where you are!"

She stepped forward, then remembered the dangling chain in the middle of the deep, dim pantry. Nerves vacuumed her mouth dry. She slashed the air with her pot, her unsteady legs carrying her forward. Just as her fingertips brushed the metal links, a furry body swept by her calves and jetted into the kitchen, snorting.

"What the—?" A wild animal!

She pivoted, heart thumping. Where was Scooter when she needed him? She peered through the archway into the living room and glimpsed her ancient, snoozing Labrador. He was too far away to assist in her catch and release, especially now that he'd lost his hearing and slept heavily.

Shivers danced along her spine. What if it was a skunk? Or a porcupine? If Scooter woke and went after it, he'd take a mouthful of quills.

As for the creature, it skittered beneath her table, a dark thing the size of a microwave. What was it? A raccoon? Fisher? Woodchuck? Living in the wilderness made for a long list of suspects.

She crouched and slid back a seat. With her skillet shielding her face, she braced herself for an odorous spray. A high-pitched yip sounded instead.

The pan dipped and a pair of fearful, velvety-black eyes met hers. Dark fur puffed around a tiny triangular face, the petite snout ending in a quivering black nose.

A bear cub.

Her muscles loosened, her insides melting. Oh. Adorable. And frightened, despite the "terrifying" noises it emitted to scare her off. Poor thing. After eating half a pound of sweets, it should be in a sugar coma by now.

Instead, the bear cowered against the chair legs, pawing at the air. Where was its mother? The thought cooled her warm rush of affection. An angry black bear could be roaming her property. An adult—worse, a mother searching for her child. Reuniting them personally, in the dead of night, would be suicide. But other threats skulked in the surrounding forest. If she simply tossed the cub out, it might get killed before finding its mom.

She gnawed a cuticle, vacillating.

From the living room, Scooter's breathing deepened into a full-on snore. No threat to the baby animal there. She could chase it back to the pantry, lock it in, then put it outside in the morning once she called 911 and got an officer's approval. Watch for a parent to lumber along and claim it... Yes. The best compromise. Now, to grab the cub.

"Stay still little guy. I won't hurt you," she crooned.

When she stretched for it, her fingers grazed its silky pelt before the bear raced across the room. It wriggled behind her recycling bin and got stuck, its protruding rump shaking. She grinned. Despite her ruined desserts, who could stay mad at such a cute little bum?

She stole across the sticky floor. When she pulled back the plastic bin, the cub barked, then bolted for a towel-drying rack in an opposite corner, squirming on its belly to hide. A whimper rose from behind the straw and her heart broke.

How scared it must be. Motherless, hungry and now chased by a human. No living thing should feel such terror. She fingered the scar that snaked across her throat.

Maybe if she stayed still, lay down and left

out one of the demolished pies, it might come out. Either way, hounding it didn't work. She'd only terrify it more and risk waking Scooter. A yawn escaped her. First she'd clean up the mess, late as it was. She sighed. Would her ant crusade ever end?

She kept an eye on the black snout poking from behind her laden towel rack while she wiped the table, mopped her floor and rinsed out the pans. At least five pies had escaped the little marauder, including her diner's specialty—raisin. She shot a glare in the cub's direction, then softened at the sight of its nose, now resting on the floor, flanked by two paws. How had one minuscule creature created such havoc?

At least she had enough pie for the morning and lunch rushes. The rest she'd make at the diner while Maggie ran the front counter alongside the waitresses. Inconvenient, but doable. Once she got her little fur ball squared away, life would return to normal—relatively speaking. For a restaurant owner, that meant controlled chaos. She draped a wet dishrag over her faucet, closed her window and pulled off her rooster-patterned apron.

After untying a couple of seat covers, she made them into a makeshift pillow and stretched against the wall. She thought of Jinx outside on her cat prowl. Hopefully she knew enough to steer clear of a mother bear circling the property.

Vivie listened to the scratch of claws against the floor. A round eye, shiny as a brown button, peeked around a towel on the bottom rack. Holding still, she watched it roam around the room then alight on her. Her breath hitched. Friend or foe? She willed it to know she was the former.

"Come on, little one. Come out," she crooned. A frustrated breath escaped her when the cub ducked back behind the rack, grunting low. It'd be a long night…for both of them. Protectiveness seized her.

If only she could comfort it, but that would stress it more. No. Instead, she'd stay up. Wait for the half-finished pie she'd left out to tempt the cub from its hiding spot. If it emerged, she'd corral it into the pantry and get some real sleep.

Her eyes drifted closed, her lids heavy. She wouldn't fall asleep. Not a chance…

TWITTERING BIRDS ANNOUNCED the dawn. The scrape of tin proclaimed the bear had emerged for breakfast—aka her pie. Vivie leaped to her feet and, through the kitchen archway, saw Scooter lurch awake. Her dog scampered after the squealing cub, which fortunately raced for the pantry. She slammed the door shut just as Scooter bashed into its frame, unable to stop his momentum or his relentless barking.

"No, Scoots. Down."

Vivie yanked on his collar, then jammed her way inside the pantry.

"I'm so sorry!"

She met the bear's wide eyes and her heart squeezed as it scuttled backward. Its pink tongue appeared when it cried out, its head weaving, searching out another hiding spot. Luckily, most of her food was in industrial metal bins or cans. It wouldn't get into too much trouble here.

For the first time, she had a good look at it and noticed something wrong with its jaw. The lower half seemed off-kilter, swelling making it bulge sideways. Was it injured? She had to get help for this button-eyed cutie.

"I'll be right back. Umph!"

She banged into a hovering, woofing Scooter when she shimmied back through the pantry door. "Hush, boy. Outside."

At her point and shove, his tail lowered and he headed through the porch door she opened. In a flash of ebony fur, Jinx flew through the entrance. She jumped onto the table and meowed loudly, her good yellow eye narrow and accusing. The other, blinded before she'd shown up on Vivie's door, was milky white and half-closed.

"Off, Jinx. You know the rules!" Vivie's shooing had no effect. She picked up her bristling kitty and set her beside her food bowl.

Jinx whipped away and presented her long tail. She sniffed at the empty trays disdainfully.

"So it's like that, then," Vivie sighed, pouring cat food and replenishing the water. At her ear scratch, Jinx jerked her head away.

"Jinx, I'm sorry you were stuck outside." She grabbed a couple of cat treats and set them on the floor. "I couldn't let you in because of—"

A scratch sounded on the pantry door and Jinx's back arched, her tail puffing.

"Don't even think about going near there," Vivie warned. At Scooter's bark, she let him in, then went for the phone. Despite the early hour, someone had to be on emergency call.

Vivie flopped on her vintage sofa and heard a squeak. Reaching behind a fringed pillow, she pulled out a hamburger chew toy, a smile beating the frown to her face. Scooter. Would her pets ever learn to stay off her furniture?

She grabbed the phone, dialed 911 and was assured of a conservation officer visit. She hung up and dropped her head on top of her sofa. Great. The Department of Environmental Conservation…a department she'd clashed with once before. They'd probably chuck the cub into the woods, whether coyotes skulked or not. Let nature take its course.

The heck with nature. This was about surviving.

She moved restlessly around her living room, debating if she and the cub should leave before the officer arrived. But where would she go? What would she do? No. She'd stand her ground as she'd taught herself to do.

Her eyes roamed the ceiling, noting that her fan needed dusting. And was that a cobweb in the far corner? Her gaze landed on the Steinway piano she'd inherited along with her great-aunt Nancy's farmhouse. After a nomadic childhood with a marriage escape-artist mother, it was her first permanent home. The only place Vivie had stayed, growing up, where she'd felt safe.

Above the piano hung last year's holiday picture: Santa with Scooter and Jinx. Scooter's long tongue lapped the struggling man's ear while Jinx batted his hat's pom-pom. Classic. A true Harris family moment. If not for her aunt's generosity, Vivie would still be in the Bronx, fighting through the anxiety that'd plagued her since her attack. Here in the Adirondacks, however, she'd found peace. Could breathe.

Vivie turned when a loud *woof* carried from the kitchen. Scooter. She padded across the faded Oriental carpet, through the entrance-way and back into the kitchen. Across the room, Jinx leaped from the table and threw herself against the pantry door. Meanwhile Scooter dug deep grooves into the wood, barking and whining.

"Hey! Knock it off, you two!"

Jinx crashed down, then slunk under the table, her tail lashing. Scooter continued, un-hearing, until Vivie tugged his collar. She tempted him away with a bone and eventually he subsided and splayed on the floor, chew-ing.

Her shoulders sagged. She'd been up for what, thirty minutes? And it was already a long morning.

In the quiet, a small bleat sounded. High and paper-thin. Her chest constricted. Did she dare open the door and risk Jinx snak-ing between her legs and scaring the cub to death? Or Scooter muscling through? She loved her pets but they were as protective of their home as she was. If she put them out-side again, a chance she'd had to take earlier given Scooter's unreliable bladder, would they cross paths with the mother bear? Possibly. She pushed back her hair and sighed. Nothing to do but wait for the officer.

The officer… She stiffened. Possibly a man. One who would arrive soon. And she was still wearing her sleep shirt…

The doorbell rang.

Darn.

She grabbed an apron and hurried to the door. Scooter scrambled after her, reading the familiar signs for "visitor" that roughly translated, for him, into "person I must scare to death." She kind of wished he would.

She unlatched the door and hip checked a baying Scooter out of the way. Jinx's collar bell rang as the cat bolted after them. It seemed the Harris family welcoming party was in full force this morning. She stopped her eye roll before opening the door…and was glad she did.

Wow.

A powerfully built man, well over six feet, stood on her front porch. His green uniform stretched across broad shoulders and a wide chest that tapered down to a lean waist. Matching pants went on forever, ending in black boots bigger than Jinx. Too bad newly single Maggie wasn't here. Her weakness for men in uniform was legendary and vocalized often.

Reining in her wandering thoughts, Vivie finally glanced up.

A Stetson covered his hair, the brim throwing shadows that pooled beneath high cheekbones and a cleft chin.

He resembled an actor playing an officer. Not the real deal. Not the kind of man she'd meet wearing a faded nightshirt covered by a poultry-patterned apron. She flushed. It shouldn't matter…especially given who he worked for. Who he was…

"You—" she breathed. Her fingers tightened on the door handle.

"Miss Harris. A pleasure."

She gave herself a shake, determined not to be swayed by his deep voice and twinkling light green eyes. This was anything but a happy reunion, she reminded herself.

Scooter butted her leg and she stumbled forward, banging her head on the door. Smooth. Real smooth.

"May I come in?"

"Do I have a choice?"

His full lips curled at the edges. "Not if you're harboring wildlife again."

She drummed her fingernails on the molding, wishing she still had her skillet in hand.

Infuriating man. The last time she'd seen him, he'd given her a citation for leaving out leftover fresh vegetables and fruits behind her diner during last year's brutal winter.

"Some would call that protecting." She cocked an eyebrow and made to shut the door...only his steel-toed boot kept it from closing.

"That's what I aim to do, ma'am," he drawled, his confident expression making her flush hot.

"Protect what? Your promotion? Christmas bonus? It sure isn't the animals because I've heard what you people do to injured wildlife."

He leaned close, his eye flush with the open space of her door. "Is the bear injured?" he asked, his voice low but insistent.

She pictured the cub's swollen jaw and felt a twinge of guilt. It did need medical attention and help finding its mother. But could she trust him to put the animal's—not "nature's"—best interests first? What choice did she have?

"Yes," she muttered at last and slid the chain back. She paused before pulling the door open farther.

"Could you sort of come in sideways while I hold Scooter?"

"Pardon?" He pulled off his hat to reveal thick, dark hair that curled around the tops of his ears. He shooed the morning gnats away before settling the Stetson back on his head.

"The animals are a little—ah—spirited." She pushed Scooter back. Relentless dog. Meanwhile Jinx leaped on the curved arm of a nearby chair, looking ready to pounce and take out this stranger. All eight pounds of her.

"Your domestic pets or the wild animal?"

She sighed. Was there a difference? Still, she couldn't love them more. She thought of the terrified cub in her pantry, her affection including it as well. What would happen to it once this horrible man got hold of it? She eyed the officer.

"Pets." She grabbed Scooter's collar and body blocked Jinx, whose leap landed her on Vivie's shoulder. She winced, then grimaced harder as the officer slid through her door.

"Not sure if you remember my name. I'm Liam Walsh and you're Vivienne. Vivie, right?" He squatted and held out a hand to Scooter. "Come."

His firm command quieted Scooter who trotted over and held up a paw. Unbelievable. It was a trick the shelter workers had taught him, one he only did to impress. Officer Walsh gave Scooter a high five, ruffled his ears and stood.

"Nice dog."

She pressed her lips together to stop the forming smile. She would not be charmed. "Occasionally. The rest of the time, he's a stinker."

A low chuckle sounded and Officer Walsh's eyes crinkled at the corners. "Got one like that myself. A collie. Extra Pickles." Jinx flung herself between them, landing neatly on Officer Walsh's shoulders.

"You named your dog Extra Pickles?" She blinked up at him, surprised. How odd that this official, by-the-books man would name his dog something so unusual. Maybe he wasn't just a policy-spouting drone in uniform.

He plucked Jinx from his neck and nuzzled her before setting her on the floor. "Her mom was Pickles so—"

"—she's extra…" Vivie finished for him, staring.

He cleared his throat and pulled out a notebook and pen, suddenly appearing self-conscious. Her grandfather clock chimed seven times while Scooter sprawled at Officer Walsh's feet, spit shining his boots.

"The dispatcher mentioned a bear cub…?"

Vivie nodded. "Last night. It came in through my open window. Must have smelled my pies."

Officer Walsh lifted his fine nose and sniffed. "Is that raisin pie?"

She nodded, proud, despite her sour mood. "It didn't get ruined, at least."

"Your customers will be relieved."

"And Maggie, my co-owner. She's an amazing cook but hates baking. She was on vacation the week you ordered me to stop feeding the wild animals and let them starve."

His eyes narrowed on her for a long moment. "Teaching them to fend for themselves rather than relying on handouts would be closer to the truth."

"We had record low temperatures," she snapped, her anger rising fresh and raw over the year-old incident.

"And the animals best equipped to survive it, did. Natural selection," he observed with a mildness that infuriated her more. Didn't the man have feelings?

"You really don't care, do you?" she exclaimed.

"I care about doing my job." He pocketed his notepad. "I'd like to see the bear now. Since my vacation starts tomorrow, I need to get this wrapped up."

She glared, then turned without a word. Of course he'd be more concerned with his free time than the well-being of an animal.

Oblivious to his abominable attitude, Scooter and Jinx trailed him into the kitchen as if he were their new best friend.

"It's in the pantry. I'm not sure, but I think there's something wrong with its jaw."

She held Scooter's collar while Officer Walsh eased into the food closet. Jinx paced while they waited, the officer's murmuring voice coming through the thick door, indistinct, but reassuring in tone.

At last he emerged, his face grave.

"The cub's about five months old. Probably not long out of the den. Definitely the first time without her mother. Her jaw looks dislocated, like you said. Probably fell out of the tree her mother chased her into when she sensed danger. Did you happen to see any lights outside last night?"

Vivie had been so focused on baking. "I might have seen a light, but it was far away. Back there." She pointed out her kitchen window. "I guessed it was fireflies, or heat lightning. Why?"

His mouth thinned and he glanced down at her rambunctious pets. "It'll help me narrow the search area. Would you keep your animals inside while I scout the property?"

Her hand rose to her jumping heart. A large predator could be near. One who might confront the officer. As much as she disliked the guy, she didn't want him hurt. Much. Not that he seemed concerned. In fact, his no-nonsense attitude projected confidence. The pistol on his right hip heightened the impression. "Sure. I'll put some coffee on."

"That'd be kind of you." He tipped his hat and let himself out the back door. "Thanks." His reassuring smile lingered in her mind's eye, flash lightning in a pale blue sky. She shook the unwelcome sentiment away.

She untied her apron and raced upstairs. No telling how long he'd be gone, but she wouldn't wear this crazy outfit another second. Within minutes she'd whipped on a pair of jeans and a T-shirt, thrown her hair into a messy bun and dashed back downstairs.

In the kitchen, she paused at the pantry door and pressed her ear against it. Silence. Fear pulsed through her. What if the cub wasn't well? Guilt welled up inside, filling places she hadn't known existed. She should have called 911 last night instead of waiting for morning. Maybe they would have responded instead of Officer Walsh. Someone reasonable. With a beating heart.

She glimpsed his hat in the thicket behind her house and hurried to put on the coffee. He'd better take care of the cub. Protect it. Or she would. Hopefully it'd be in a good place soon—maybe with its mom—and she could breathe easier.

A burbling sound, punctuated by a hazelnut aroma, permeated the room in minutes. Officer Walsh talked on his cell outside, pacing alongside her back porch.

What had he found and who was he speaking to?

She set out two mugs of coffee and the sugar doughnuts she'd fried up a couple days ago. She eyed the creamer and sugar and left them beside her mixer. He looked like the kind of guy who took his brew black. Her diner-honed instincts were rarely wrong. At last, the back door creaked and she whirled, swallowing a bite of doughnut.

"Any sign of the mother?"

His features sharpened, his expression grave.

"Possibly. Did you hear any gunshots last night?"

Her heart swooped low. "Maybe. When I turned off my oven timer, I might have heard something. But it was faint and ended too fast for me to be sure."

"What time?"

She glanced at the cuckoo clock beside her wall calendar, trying to remember. "Somewhere between nine and nine-thirty, I think. Was a bear shot?" Her throat tightened. "The mother?"

His pen flew across his pad and his eyes, more hazel than green now that he was closer, rose to meet hers. A smattering of light freckles dotted his nose. "It's possible. There are tracks and blood a couple hundred yards east. Looks like big game. Have you seen any strange vehicles or people around your property lately?"

Her gaze swerved to the pepper spray still on her table, a ribbon of nerves moving through her stomach. She might well and truly have confronted an intruder last night. Someone armed. Again.

She held herself, hiding her shudder.

No. Not here. This remote, sleepy town was largely immune to random violence, a major factor in her decision to settle here rather than sell the house.

"My neighbor Muriel and her husband have some nephews from the Midwest housesitting while they're away. The guys are here on a fishing trip."

His eyes narrowed. "Have you met them?"

"No, just heard about it from Muriel. They're her sister's sons."

"Names?" His voice clipped, he sounded

different from the guy who'd joked about a dog named Extra Pickles and high-fived Scooter. Back was the man who'd once ignored her pleas to let her keep feeding the animals last winter.

A breeze rushed through the open window above her sink, carrying the crisp smell of a spring morning—pine sap, fresh earth and growing things. It loosened a strand from her bun and sent it fluttering across her mouth.

She handed him a mug, then lifted her own. "She didn't say. Just told me they'd visited during hunting season last fall and had come back to fish. Would you like a doughnut?" She cursed her ingrained manners, wishing she could give him the boot instead of baked goods.

"Thanks." He split one in half and dunked it in his coffee before taking a bite. "These are good." He chewed another piece, his expression intent as he stared outside.

She grabbed a dish towel and wiped up a bit of pie filling she'd missed last night. "Do you think they killed her?"

He gulped more coffee and lowered his mug, his mouth in a straight line. "I'll find out."

"What about the cub?"

His gaze swerved to hers. "I'll have to put it down if I can't find the mother."

Vivie clutched the back of a chair, light-headed and nauseous. "What? No!" How could he say that so casually?

"I've called around and our wildlife reha-bilitators are overloaded. Since the cub is too young to fend for itself, the humane thing to do is—"

"Kill it?" she stormed, interrupting. "How is that humane?" The cub's frightened eyes came to mind and she backed up against the pantry door. Officer or not, he wouldn't take the bear. Stop her from helping. It'd come to her home. Had sought refuge here.

He pulled off his hat and rubbed his fore-head. "Ma'am, I don't expect you to under-stand. But you need to trust me and move aside so that I can do my job."

"Not a chance," she ground out, wishing her pepper spray wasn't across the room.

"Please be reasonable." He raised his eye-brows, looking harmless. His holstered weapon told a different story.

Maybe she could reason with him, though she'd failed before. There had to be a way to save the cub. "How do you become a wildlife rehabilitator?"

He drew in a long breath and crossed his

arms over his chest. "Pass a certification test, then work under the supervision of a rehabilitator for six months."

Tests. She hated them. Had only ever done well on presentation-style exams in culinary school. Still, for the baby bear...anything. "And when is the next one?"

"In a week." He made a vague motion in the air with his hand. "Look. I'd be happy to discuss that with you another time, but the cub might be suffering. Please step aside so that I can take it."

She raised her voice over her drumming heartbeat. "I'll pass the test. Get certified."

He ran a hand through his hair, making the curl-tipped ends stand up. "You'd have to study hundreds of pages of online material. It's not easy. Trust me. I took it and barely finished my apprenticeship before my academy training started."

"So you're a certified wildlife rehabilitator? You could care for it."

His chin jerked. "I already have a job."

Her mind shifted into overdrive, churning up possibilities. "Not next week. You said you're on vacation. You could take her while I study for the test."

He blew out a long breath. "I don't have an

enclosure—something you'll need along with someone to supervise you."

She tried to come across as commanding, though at five-foot-three inches that was always a challenge. "You could help with both."

He shook his head, his earnest expression replaced with a wash of annoyance. "Out of the question. There are too many ifs in that idea."

She tried keeping the heat out of her voice. The DEC. Always so difficult. Especially Walsh. "Why? I'm sure you could call in a favor. Ask one of the rehabilitators to find temporary space for the cub. Then I'll pass the test and, with your help, be approved to care for it. Don't you want to do the right thing?"

Wasn't that his job?

"I do. Which is why I'm taking the bear. Now."

"Not a chance. You'll have to go through me first." She hated to sound dramatic, use a cheesy line from bad TV, but there was no other way to say it.

A crease appeared between his brows, his eyes scanning hers. Finally, he released a long breath.

"How about this—I'll take her to the vet where they'll check her jaw, give her some food and a safe place to stay, temporarily, while I continue investigating."

She considered, wishing she could trust him. But after her dealings with him before, her faith was on the short side.

"Let's try this," she countered. "I'll go with you and stay with the bear until you come back. Then we'll talk about what happens next."

He settled his hat back on, pinching the indented top. "There's no reason to get more involved, ma'am."

She pulled out her cell and tapped in Maggie's number. Someone could come by and pick up the pies. Another worker would be called in for an extra shift. The Homestead would manage without her today. She wasn't leaving the cub's side until she knew it'd be safe—from nature and the DEC.

"It's much too late for that, Officer Walsh."

She studied him for a long, heavy moment, then moved aside. If the cub's mother was dead, then she'd take on the role.

And nothing was more ferocious than a mama bear...

CHAPTER TWO

LIAM HOPPED INTO his black SUV an hour later and backed out of the vet-office parking lot, his mind focused more on the investigation than the road.

Gut instinct told him someone had shot the cub's mother last night, and the scared orphan had followed its nose to food and shelter. He cranked the wheel, heading back to Vivie's neighbors' house.

Poachers.

Had to be.

The visiting nephews might be here on a fishing trip or they might not. His fingers tapped the wheel, his jaw tight. Either way, he'd get to the bottom of it. Eight years on the job and it still surprised him how quickly people confessed when a uniformed officer knocked on their door.

He didn't expect trouble. Not from the men. The spitfire he'd left at the clinic, on the other hand…she was a handful. Just as she'd vowed, she'd followed him and the bear in a beat-up pickup, tailgating him all the way despite the winding roads. Steel lurked beneath her pretty face and expressive eyes.

She'd put up a fight when he returned for the bear. No doubt about it. Hopefully, he wouldn't find the mother dead and could release the cub to rejoin its parent. The other alternative, however...

The ugly thought lingered. He'd never been a hunter. Didn't relish killing, though he'd done his duty as a marine in Afghanistan. His mind veered from those brutal memories.

Ending a young animal's life was horrible. Yet the cub couldn't survive on its own, and without a trained caregiver, humanely putting it down might be the only option.

Unless he considered Vivie's outrageous proposal...

He punched on the radio, the music overriding his crazy thoughts. Of course he wouldn't let a novice take on such a large task, even under his supervision. Vivie didn't have a clue what it entailed.

Plus, she was already acting possessive of the cub. If he went along with her plan, she'd still have to surrender it when he released it this fall. If the jaw didn't heal properly, he'd need to find a permanent home at an animal reserve or sanctuary. Would she be able to let it go? He doubted it. She seemed like the type to get emotionally involved.

He shook his head, thankful he'd never let himself get attached to anyone or any place... not after the war. Room. Freedom. That was what he needed.

When he opened the windows, the rushing air making him want to follow wherever it led. His sister Mary Ann accused him of having wanderlust and he didn't correct her. She couldn't know what'd really happened to him in Kunar, Afghanistan. None of his family needed the extra pressure while they helped his twin brother, Niall—also an army vet—deal with losing his leg. Instead, Liam kept what had happened to him buried deep, wishing he could hide it from himself, too.

Every few years the compulsion to get out was too intense, so he relocated. He'd been investigating positions in Yellowstone National Park lately, the familiar pressure growing stronger and heavier each day. Hopefully it wouldn't be difficult to get time off for Mary Ann's August wedding if he got hired.

Mammoth fir trees flashed by as he whizzed up Vivie's road, the majestic sentinels impressive as always. A small brook wove along the roadside, its water sparkling under the strengthening sun. Cedar-scented air filled his lungs.

As he rounded a bend, a smallish home, two stories, with white siding and a red tin roof came into view. He'd passed it on his way to Vivie's this morning and noted that the mailbox number matched the address she'd given him. He pulled in behind a navy truck parked in front of a detached, single-car garage. As he eased outside, a large pit bull perked up its ears, then raced toward him, barking and straining against its chain.

"Easy, big guy," Liam murmured, pitching his voice low and firm. The dog's massive jaws snapped a foot short of his leg. Liam's eyes roamed over the thick metal links wrapped around a willow tree, an overturned water bowl and a bone the size of his calf resting beneath it. He gave the animal a wide berth and strode up to the porch, his hand automatically running over his Glock and flipping open the holster's snap. It paid to be ready in case these guys surprised him.

He rang the bell a few times, then tugged open the metal screen to knock, peering through the side glass panels. An empty living room and a narrow hall were visible. Little else. Still, with a vehicle on the premises, his suspects could be out back.

He shooed away the blackflies nagging at his ears and paced around the house, listening for voices.

Tinkling wind chimes sounded and birds called out their territory from the surrounding trees. Otherwise, silence reigned. When he rounded the house's rear corner he pulled up short, the air sticking inside his lungs.

A black bear hung from a massive maple, rope tying its paws to a thick limb. He smothered an exclamation, his worst suspicions confirmed when he noted the animal's swollen teats. A lactating female. Most likely the cub's mother. He pulled out his cell phone and snapped a couple of photos.

Had the men answered the front door, any evidence he found without a search warrant wouldn't be admissible. Yet glimpsing it while trying to contact them at the back door—that would squeak by the judge. And these guys would see their day in court.

His eyes narrowed as he turned away from the bear. He'd haul them in today. Vivie had mentioned they weren't New Yorkers. Out-of-state meant flight risk and an appearance before the bench. His lips stretched in a grim smile. Justice was sweetest when served fast.

After another regretful look at the beautiful animal, he called in backup, then marched up concrete-block steps and rapped on the door. When no one answered, he pounded on it again, using the side of his fist. He doubted the hunters would leave their prize unguarded. They were skulking inside and someone better open the door, quick, before his patience ran out.

Poachers.

The lowest life-form on the planet.

"Open up. DEC!" he ordered loudly.

At last a man swung the door open, his eyes red and puffy, dark stubble shading his sagging jaw, chin and neck. At the sight of Liam, he straightened his slouch, his lax mouth closing.

Liam flashed his badge. "Officer Walsh. May I come in?"

The man nodded, then seemed to remember he had a voice. "Uh, yeah." His eyes darted over Liam's shoulder to the bear, then swerved back. "Come in."

Liam stepped inside a small, square kitchen littered with beer cans and a nearly empty pizza box on the table. He scrunched his nose at the sour smell of cheap malt and sweat, and noted a high-powered rifle with a scope leaning in the far corner. No signs of fishing gear...

Liam pulled out his notebook and spoke,

keeping his voice neutral. Measured. "If anyone else is here, go get them."

The man dug at his ear and gaped at him.

"Now," Liam repeated, his voice harder. This wasn't a social call. Not by a stretch.

The man hurried off, his loose belly jiggling over a pair of boxers. When he returned, another man trudged behind the first, his face pinched, skin pale. In contrast to his fleshy friend, his limbs were elongated and sticklike, kneecaps nearly cutting through flesh.

"Any more weapons in the house?"

The thin man nodded, his eyes darting around the kitchen like hummingbirds. "My rifle."

"Go get it." Liam wasn't worried about these guys pulling anything on him. Besides, his backup would be here in minutes.

The guy whirled and disappeared the way he'd come.

"ID?"

"I'm Tim Favero and that's my brother Matt." Tim lumbered over to a couple of flannel jackets hanging on the backs of chairs, pulled out wallets and fished out Montana driver's licenses.

Liam scribbled down the information, then glanced up as Matt returned carrying his weapon.

"This is it." He placed his gun beside the pizza box, scattering empty cans. They clattered to the floor and rolled.

"How'd that bear end up in the backyard?" Liam stared them down. Tim lowered his gaze and Matt's mouth worked for a moment.

"Someone needs to start talking," Liam barked. "Now."

"I-it's ours," Matt sputtered, cracking his bony knuckles.

"Looks like it's been shot."

"Tim got it last night. About eight miles west of here."

Matt ducked his head at his brother's accusing stare and scratched the back of his neck.

"Could have been your shot," Tim's voice rose, accusingly. "We only had the one floodlight and we both fired at her."

An argument broke out, silenced when Liam held up a hand. "You knew it was a female right away?"

The men quieted and studied their feet. At last, Tim said, "Saw a cub run up a tree, I guess."

A sinking feeling settled in Liam's gut. No doubt about it. Vivie's cub was orphaned. Would need to be put down. He dragged his mind off the miserable thought. He had to focus on this job first. Hopefully his backup would arrive soon so he could ticket them and call the judge. Get things on a predictable, all-too-familiar track.

"You two have hunting licenses?"

Matt nodded, his movement jerky as he pulled the paperwork from their wallets.

Liam scanned the Montana paperwork, then glanced up. "You got some for New York?"

Tim shrugged. "Didn't think it was necessary. We hunt big game out there."

Liam willed the irritation off his face. Every hunter knew to get a state license. What a wise guy.

"Off season?"

The guys exchanged an uneasy glance. "No," Matt squeaked.

"So you thought you'd come to the Adirondacks and try it?"

"Yes. I mean, no," Matt's answer changed at a sharp glance from his brother. "I don't know," he added lamely, shoving back a greasy lock of hair.

"Are these the weapons you used last night?" Liam pointed at the rifles.

The men nodded. "We've got our gun permits."

Liam didn't doubt it. Still, it paid to double-check. "Let's see them."

As Tim grabbed the paperwork, a loud barking erupted. Backup. Liam breathed a sigh of relief. These guys were cooperating, but an extra pair of hands would make this easier.

"Matt. Call off your dog and let in my colleague. He'll be coming up to the front door now."

"Got it." The man smiled unevenly and stumbled away.

Were these guys still drunk? Hungover from celebrating last night's kill? Worse, had they been intoxicated while shooting near Vivie's house? The thought stabbed through him. She shouldn't be living on her own so deep in the woods.

He studied the gun permits then looked up when another officer, James Ruffalo, strode into the room, his back as straight as his pants' crease. Since they were the same age—twenty-seven—and had joined the department around the same time, they'd hung out and become friends.

"I'm Officer Ruffalo." He nodded curtly to Tim then glanced at Liam, a grim smile ghosting across his face. "Officer Walsh."

"James." Liam jerked his chin. "They're getting ticketed and then arraigned since they're out of state. I'd appreciate you taking Tim to the courthouse while Matt and I follow."

"Got it."

"We're going to court?" sputtered Tim, his body shaking in indignation, his thick face flushing red. James shot him a stern look that settled him down. Matt, on the other hand, grew paler, a thin sheen of sweat coating his forehead and upper lip.

Liam pulled out another pad and began writing. In the tense silence, James headed to the back window and whistled long and sharp at what Liam guessed was his sighting of the dead bear. Matt repeatedly cleared his throat. After a couple of minutes, Liam clicked his pen, ripped off the last slip and handed a small pile of paper to Tim.

"You're being ticketed with the following misdemeanors—taking wildlife out of season, illegally taking wildlife and taking a bear with the use of artificial light, as well as hunting without a license—a violation."

"Both of us?" Matt picked up an open beer can and drained what was left of it.

Liam nodded. "Let's go, boys."

Just as he'd hoped, they followed him and James, a textbook arrest.

If only the woman waiting back at the vet clinic would be as easy to handle…

"MISS HARRIS, WE have the results for the cub."

Vivie stood and straightened her cramped back. How long had she been sitting in that plastic chair? It felt like hours. She scanned her cell-phone screen, the time confirming her suspicions.

"How is she, Doctor Morrison?"

The pretty veterinarian smiled, the creases around her mouth and eyes deepening. "Her jaw was dislocated. Looks like she hit it hard—maybe in a fall. Hopefully it will heal properly now that I've reset it or she'll have trouble feeding in the wild. Otherwise, she's dehydrated and stressed, but healthy. No life-threatening issues."

Vivie's joints loosened and her breath rushed in, easier than it had this morning.

"So she'll be all right."

Doctor Morrison freed her gray-streaked braid from her name tag then nodded. "As long as her jaw heals well, there's no impediment to her living a long life."

None except Officer Walsh…

Vivie wondered what had kept him so long. She'd thought he'd be back in an hour or so, but was glad for the chance to delay whatever he had in mind for the bear's future. Rather than dwell on the negative, she'd spent her time studying the DEC's online material for the certification test. If Officer Walsh had been around, he might have said it was unnecessary, bursting the lovely plans inflating in her head.

"May I see her?"

The doctor nodded and gestured behind her. "Right this way. We had to sedate her earlier, so she might be a bit sleepy."

Vivie entered a spacious room with several cages, all empty except one.

Her pulse leaped at the sight of the small black animal behind metal bars, her claws poking through them.

"Hi, sweetie." She stuck a finger inside and stroked the cub's nose, making her lids lift slowly, her deep brown eyes meeting Vivie's.

Immediately, the bear jerked to her feet and pressed against the cage door, grunting.

"It's okay." Vivie imagined the poking and prodding she'd gotten today. No wonder she was disoriented and frightened. What a long ordeal for such a young animal. "Everything is going to be all right from now on. Promise."

She turned to the doctor. "May I hold her?"

The veterinarian studied her then nodded slowly. "Just for a moment. We're not supposed to let wild animals around people, but you were so good to those animals last winter." They smiled at each other, remembering when Vivie had sought medical attention for the lame critter she'd found by her dumpster.

The doctor lifted the latch and swung open the door, gently pulling out the struggling bear.

"She's heavier than she looks!" Vivie exclaimed, holding her tight when Doctor Morrison handed her over.

"Twenty-three pounds. A little underweight, actually, but within range."

Vivie inhaled the musky, clean scent of the cub, pulling her warm body closer still. She sniffed Vivie and seemed to relax. Vivie held in a laugh at the ticklish wet nose poking her ear.

The doctor stroked the cub's back. "She likes you. She gave the vet tech a bit of a hard time earlier. Hardly got her to take half the bottle. But that's understandable given her dislocation."

Vivie snuggled the bear closer, kissing the top of her head when she burrowed under Vivie's chin. "Can I try?"

Dr. Morrison appeared torn. "This is going against policy, but I'd sure like to see her eat."

A minute later, Vivie was in a rocking chair, a blanket spread on her lap, the cub on its back, pulling hard at the rubber nipple from the uninjured side of her mouth.

"She likes it!" Joy filled Vivie as she watched the hungry youngster eat. The cub held the bottle between her paws, her eyes locked on Vivie's. Too cute.

"I'm glad she's eating so well," observed Dr. Morrison. "Wasn't sure if she'd be able to do it. But she seems like a pro now. Once the swelling goes down, she should be able to try regular food."

"Of course she's a champion." Vivie smiled, feeling absurdly proud. She'd helped the bear eat. Had saved her last night. Everything about this moment felt right. Meant to be. If only Officer Walsh wasn't in the picture...

As if on cue, the tall, trim man pushed through the swinging door and came toward them, his face grim.

"Thank you for caring for the bear today, Doctor Morrison."

The older woman smiled up at him. "Always happy to help out the DEC. Any word about the cub's mother?"

Vivie tensed, guessing his news from his expression. He glanced at her, his sad eyes belying the firm set of his mouth. "She's been killed. Just finished up at the court house arraigning the poachers."

"You're sure it's her?" Vivie gasped, fear snaking through her. She contemplated the oblivious cub who'd nearly finished her bottle. Was this her last meal? If the DEC had its way, it would be.

He nodded slowly. "Positive. The men confessed to everything."

She stroked the cub's face, imagining armed strangers trekking through her woods, the vicious assault on the mother bear, the frightened orphan with nowhere to turn until it'd found her.

"So then…" She couldn't bring herself to finish her sentence.

Officer Walsh's face gentled as he gazed at her, then the cub.

"I'll be taking the bear and you can return to your diner. Thank you, Vivie, for helping today. If there were more people like you, we wouldn't have these kinds of incidents."

"I'll get the cub in its carrier." Dr. Morrison pulled the bear from Vivie and hurried away, leaving a strained silence behind.

"You're just like the men you arrested," Vivie accused when she could speak, despair and fury washing through her. "Killing an innocent animal."

Officer Walsh took off his hat, his hair

flatter than it'd been this morning, the strain around his eyes turning their color to moss.

"I'm performing a legal act. A humane one. The cub's mother is dead and given her injured jaw and age, she'll starve on her own." He touched Vivie's arm lightly and she jerked away. "I have no choice."

"You do have a choice. We could save this animal's life." She held up her smartphone. "I've been studying all day for the test. Give me this chance."

His eyes widened. "This isn't about you, it's about the bear."

Insulted, she stuffed her cell away. "Yes. An animal you're supposed to protect. I'm taking this seriously. So should you."

Silence hung between them, tight and brittle, thrumming.

He glanced over at the eavesdropping vet tech. "Let's discuss this outside."

In the parking lot, he stopped beside his black SUV, the DEC police emblem painted in gold. She craned her neck to meet his eyes, hoping for some compassion, understanding, agreement, but the emotion she'd glimpsed earlier was gone, replaced by a shuttered expression.

"I'm taking this very seriously," he began, his boots planted shoulder width apart, his hands linked behind his back. "Putting the bear down is the only sensible solution."

"Sensible or easy?" she asked, feeling violent enough to push that mountain of a man. Get him to wake up. Realize how wrong he was.

He rocked back on his heels, as if her words had shoved him.

"It's not that black-and-white. Let's say you do pass the test. I help you build a code-approved structure and supervise your apprenticeship. Are you prepared for the rigors of caring for a wild animal? Big game? She could be nearing eighty pounds before she's released or I locate a permanent home for her."

The smell of barbecue floated on the late afternoon air and her stomach grumbled. She hadn't eaten since…when? The doughnut this morning? If anything, that showed how dedicated she was to the cub. To all of her pet family.

"If she's injured, she'd be better off staying with me. Permanently. No release needed." The sun slanted over a line of birches, spinning the fine hairs on his arms into gold.

Officer Walsh's face softened. "That'd be the worst outcome…and unlikely. Wildlife rehabilitators only care for animals until they can either be returned to their habitat or placed in a sanctuary or reserve. Sooner or later you would lose her."

"Then let it be later!" she cried, pacing. She'd fight that battle when the time came. For now, she had to win this war. Convince him to give her a chance. The bear had sought a home last night and Vivie would give it to her.

"And what about your diner?" He tapped the cleft in his chin. "You're running a business. Taking care of the cub, especially in the early weeks, will be time-consuming."

"I can make my own hours. Bake desserts and do the books, the schedules and ordering from home." She leaned in, sure she could persuade him—if he had a beating heart. "That's my usual contribution, anyway, since Maggie oversees the cooking and staff. Going in and seeing the customers every day isn't necessary. Trust me, I've got this figured out."

She clenched her chattering teeth and thought of the years she'd struggled to put her life together after her own attack. Her hands balled at her sides. She couldn't—wouldn't—let this bear be a victim of circumstances beyond its control. It was a survivor, hadn't given up. And neither would Vivie.

The bell above the clinic door jingled and

Doctor Morrison emerged, lugging the over-size pet carrier. Officer Walsh reached the veterinarian in three long strides and grabbed the handle.

"Thank you, doctor. I appreciate everything you've done. Please send the bill to the DEC."

Doctor Morrison glanced between the two of them then nodded. "Will do. Take care, now."

Vivie waited until the clinic's door swung shut to speak again.

"Please give me the cub."

"We both know that can't happen." He placed the carrier atop the SUV, beyond her reach, and opened his trunk. "This is life, Vivie. Not everything, or everyone, gets a happy ending."

She almost choked. Who knew that better than her? The bear's fate shouldn't be decided on someone else's whim.

When Officer Walsh placed the carrier in the trunk, the little cub rushed to the wire grate and poked out her nose. Vivie thrust her fingers inside and stroked her fur. She met the animal's wide, frightened eyes, her heart surging.

"You can't do this," she pleaded, her voice

cracking. Was that a rifle behind the carrier? Would he use it to shoot the little bear?

"It's the kindest thing I can do for her." His low words plunged through Vivie.

She whirled, her vision blurring. "You're nothing but a cold-blooded killer."

His face tightened as he slammed the trunk and pulled his keys from his pocket.

"It was nice to see you again, Vivie. And believe me. I'm sorry about all of this."

"I wish I'd never seen you again." She collapsed against the side of her truck and watched the SUV drive away, her bear inside.

Images of the horrible deed about to unfold flashed through her mind—a nightmarish slideshow. How could she have let this happen?

She leaned her forehead against her pickup's window.

Another crime was about to be committed, and just like last time, she was helpless to stop it.

CHAPTER THREE

LIAM'S SUV BOUNCED on the backwoods road, the caged cub yipping whenever they smacked along a tooth-rattling rise. The farther into the forest he drove, the dimmer it became, small animals appearing then vanishing as he rounded a bend. Birds swooped before his windshield, chasing each other from the leafed-out trees.

Under other circumstances, Liam would have enjoyed the wild beauty around him. He glanced in his rearview mirror at the animal carrier. But this mission shattered the early-evening peace, shading it in sepia tones that matched his bleak mood. He didn't want to kill the cub. Had hoped he'd reunite it with its mother. But his time in Afghanistan and work with the DEC had taught him that life wasn't always fair.

"You get what you put into it." Jim's remembered voice sounded real enough to make Liam jerk the wheel. The SUV swerved then straightened, cold sweat slicking the back of Liam's neck. In an instant, his mind flashed back to Afghanistan and he saw his friend offering him a cigarette as they finished their outpost wall patrol.

"We're not making it out of this," Liam insisted. *His eyes scanned desert hills that hid more insurgents than their small unit could hold off. When he grabbed the cigarette, he dropped his night-vision gear.*

"Don't lose faith, kid." Jim patted his arm, his lips curling in a lopsided smile before he bent for the goggles.

"Have it for both of us, Jim."

A shot rang out and Liam ducked, his heart firing as fast as the bullet.

He reached for his friend.

"Jim?"

No answer.

"Jim!" His hands came away wet, his scream swallowed by the dark night.

The bear's bark yanked Liam back to the present and he jerked the vehicle into a wider area in the road and parked. His head dropped to the steering wheel, his breath coming hard. A dull roar filled his ears and pain burrowed deep between his eyes.

At last, heart heavy, he turned off the ignition and listened to the engine tick, then quiet.

He tossed his hat onto the passenger seat and dropped his head back. How could he do this?

How could he not?

For a moment, he imagined letting the cub go. No one in the department would be the wiser. But then he pictured it unable to find food without its mother's help, the slow torture of starving to death. Or he envisioned larger animals chasing and killing it. A much crueler way to die than a single bullet. As a former sharpshooter, he could ensure the cub didn't suffer a moment. Since the department didn't have the budget to euthanize animals, it was the only way to keep it from a painful, drawn-out death.

The bear rustled behind him, a scratching sound of claws on metal. He should get on with it. If the guys at work saw this, they'd hassle him. Call him out for acting like a wimp. They'd tell him to stop putting off the inevitable. For them, it seemed easy. Yet to him, it was torture.

A high-pitched bark sounded, startling Liam from his thoughts. The cub's stress was escalating. Delaying this did no one any good. His hands slipped on the door handle before he pushed it down. A clammy sensation crawled along his skin as he trudged

to the back of the SUV and threw open the
back door.

Killer. Vivie's accusation whispered in his
ear. He jerked, as if she were beside him. No
denying her anger was genuine. Justified?
No. She didn't understand. Had unreasonable expectations that would end badly—the
cub would likely fail to thrive at her inexperienced hands, and she or the cub could suffer
a serious, even fatal, injury if it was mishan-
dled. He shook his head. Better to face the
worst now instead of later.

The small cub's eyes met his through the
bars. It was spooked. Had a right to be, he
thought, as he hefted the carrier and a length
of rope. He forced his leaden legs to carry
him to a large maple, its trunk thick enough
to secure the bear. He looped the restraint
over its head then tied it to the base of the
tree.

An image of the mother bear hanging from
a similar maple flashed in his mind. Vivie's
comparison of Liam to the poachers had
struck a chord, but he acted within the law,
while they broke it. Their illegal actions had
started this and now he had the horrible, de-
spicable task of finishing it.

Why did it have to be like this?

"Because that's life," a voice—his, this time—whispered.

"Sorry, little girl," he muttered when he headed back for his rifle, the empty pet carrier in hand. He shoved the crate inside and grabbed his gun, his lungs sluggish in his tight chest. He did not want to do this. Would trade places with anyone in the world not to… but that was the coward's way. Passing off painful jobs because you couldn't carry out your duty.

The weight of it crushed his chest. Would helping Vivie with her crazy plan be harder than this? Could he build an enclosure after persuading a rehabilitator to take the bear for a week? It might work, though he'd be tying himself to Vivie as her supervisor until they released the bear in the fall or found a home for it. If the cub's jaw didn't heal, an animal reserve was the only option. Waiting lists for one were long, if a spot opened up at all. In the end, he and the bear could find themselves in this spot again.

He sighed, air leaving him in a long stream. The plan was improbable when he imagined all that could go wrong.

He slipped a single round into the rifle and snapped it closed. The forest seemed to hold its breath, the only noise coming from the bear—a low, keening wail.

The weapon hung by his side, seeming to weigh a ton. Vivie had fought hard for the bear. Had stayed at the clinic all day and studied up on big-game care. Her devotion was clear. Would it wane when the daily chores turned tedious? Was she one of those people who got caught up in the fantasy, then lost interest in the reality?

He thought of her deaf Labrador and half-blind cat. She seemed attracted to high-needs animals. Was her dedication strong enough to take on this life?

He shook his head, raised his weapon and sighted the small animal through his scope. Too many uncertainties…

"MR. GOWETTE," VIVIE called to her departing customer, holding up a water glass. "You forgot your teeth."

The diner's door swung shut behind the hunched mechanic and Vivie slumped against the counter. "Again." She sighed, fished out the dentures with a fork, dropped them in a to-go container and placed them on the shelf beneath the cash register. He'd be back. Had probably done it on purpose to get away from his wife—a notorious faultfinder with a voice that peeled paint.

She glanced at the cat clock hanging above the rear shelves, its black-and-white striped tail swinging in time with its eyes. Eight o'clock. The cub...

A warm arm wrapped around her and pulled her close. "Hey. It's going to be okay, sweetie."

Maggie's topaz eyes smiled into hers.

"No. It's not." Vivie's throat closed tight after the last word and tears threatened. She grabbed a dishrag from the bucket of cleaning solution and wiped the yellow-and-gold-speckled counter.

Maggie's hand dropped over hers. "You already cleaned that."

"I don't know what I'm doing, Maggie."

"You're trying to stay busy. And I get it. I'm so sorry about the cub."

Vivie ached, thinking about the orphaned bear, dead, alone in the woods, no one to care. No one but her.

"I could have given her a home." She automatically reached behind her when their laconic short order cook, Rowdy, dinged the "food's up" bell.

"Who's got the chef's salad, no meat, no cheese, no dressing?" Vivie called. A large man wearing camouflage shorts and a white tank raised his hand. "Double-bacon cheeseburger and loaded fries?" A small woman, her gray hair purple under the fluorescent lights, waved her handkerchief from down the counter.

"Right." She bustled off to one of their chrome-edged tables, the top matching the diner's counters. "Are you sure you don't want anything else on this, Pete?"

The logger shook his head, his long earlobes shaking beneath buzzed brown hair. "Watching my weight. Wife and I are renewing our vows next month, and I want to get into my old tux."

"One Heart Attack." Maggie presented their burger special with a flourish. "Will you be having anything else, Sister Mary?" she asked the retired nun, a twinkle in her eye.

"If you've got any raisin pie left, I'd have a slice of that."

"One Ministroke, coming up," Maggie called cheerfully. "I think you got the last slice."

"Good. Can't imagine a better way to meet my maker," the elderly woman joked, lifting a burger bigger than her face and taking an enormous bite. *No worries with dentures there*, mused Vivie.

She headed back to the counter, grabbing dirty plates off tables as she went. Since the loggers had come and gone, and she'd wanted Maggie to herself, they'd let the waitstaff go after the evening rush had ended.

Brett, Rowdy's nephew, pushed through the double wooden doors from the kitchen, an empty plastic bin on his hip. "I'll take those, Miss Harris," he said softly, his usual lisp barely audible.

She handed over the dishes and joined Maggie at the counter, grabbing a salt container and refilling the shakers.

"Why don't you go home?" Maggie offered. "I don't mind staying and Brett can wait tables if we get busy." She untied a scarf from her bright red hair and shook the curling mass loose.

Vivie contemplated the cozy diner, the yellow tables, the floral-patterned wallpaper covered with vintage local pictures, the spider plants that hung at each window. This felt like home—as much so as her real one. And going back meant facing the empty pantry and thoughts of the cub's fate. No. She wasn't ready for that. The extra food and water she'd left out for Scooter and Jinx would do.

"Life isn't fair, is it, Sister Mary?" She sidled down the counter and passed the woman a jar of hot sauce, anticipating her customer's usual request.

"Nope. And then you die," drawled the woman, who nodded her thanks before dumping a quarter of the bottle's contents over her fries.

Vivie shivered, imagining the bear.

"You want me to start tomorrow's goulash, Maggie?" Rowdy rested his elbows on the stainless-steel surface in the cutout between the kitchen and the restaurant, his white tank top sticking to his damp chest.

"Might as well." Maggie rolled cutlery into paper napkins and wound a self-stick wrapper around it, making a pile on the counter beside her. Vivie caught her sideways glance. "I'll be back to help in a few minutes."

"Suit yourself." Rowdy disappeared into his domain and Vivie joined Maggie, grabbing a fork, knife and spoon to help out.

"The cub's in a better place, now. Not suffering." Maggie patted Vivie's hand before grabbing more utensils.

Vivie's fingers fumbled, the wrapper sliding off the napkin. "She would have been better off with me than dead."

Melodic whistling rose from the kitchen, a heavy metal tune turned into elevator music on Rowdy's lips. Brett hustled back into the kitchen, his dish container half-full.

"The cub would have grown into a full-sized bear. You never could have cared for something that big."

"I would have tried."

"You did everything you could, Vivie. You always do. Don't torture yourself."

"I know," she said, though she didn't believe it. Not deep down. There must have been something else she could have done. Words that might have convinced the stubborn officer. It'd been a long time since she'd felt so helpless—her life out of her control. She'd thought she'd never have that desperate feeling again after making a secure home and career for herself.

"Officer Walsh sounds like a terrible person." Maggie's smile drooped a little, the closest her upbeat friend came to a frown.

"He—" Vivie dropped the napkin she'd just rolled as the bell above their glass door jingled and the man himself strode in. What was he doing here? Did he honestly think she'd put out the welcome mat? Of all the arrogant, egotistical...

He doffed his hat and smiled. "Good evening, ladies."

Vivie flicked her eyes at Maggie. Given her

friend's soft gasp, she'd been right to think the officer was her type.

"What are you doing here, Officer Walsh?" she ground out. Maggie gawked at her, then at the man nonchalantly seating himself at the counter. *Her* counter! Now she regretted wiping it. If she could give him salmonella, she would; it'd be worth the lawsuit.

"Call me Liam. I came for a piece of your raisin pie," he said lightly, his face relaxed, green eyes unnervingly guilt-free. Did the man have no remorse? No soul?

"Claimed it!" called Sister Mary, waving a dripping french fry.

The whistling in the kitchen stopped and Rowdy pushed through the kitchen door. He stopped beside Vivie and glowered at their latest customer. Brett was right behind his uncle, a similar expression on his face. No welcome for the man she'd been complaining about this past hour.

"What's he doing here?" mumbled Rowdy, the flick of his braid over his shoulder as agitated a move as she'd ever seen him make.

"Wants pie," put in Pete. He held up his empty salad bowl. "I'll have a piece of the apple with some ice cream after all, if you've got it."

"That's the spirit, Pete!" the sister called,

her mouth full of burger. "Your wife didn't marry you for your looks, anyway."

An appalled silence fell. Then Maggie's pixie laugh rang out and the others joined in, Pete the loudest. Only Vivie and Officer Walsh remained silent, eying each other.

"Guess not," Pete sputtered, still chuckling. "Better make that two scoops, Maggie."

"Coming up." She pulled a couple of pie tins from the glass case on the counter and slid pieces onto plates. She passed the apple to Rowdy. "Would you make that à la mode?"

"Sure." After eyeballing Officer Walsh, their cook headed back into the kitchen.

Maggie squirted whipped cream beside the raisin pie and delivered it to Sister Mary.

"Thank you, dear."

"You're lucky to get it. We're usually out by noon."

"Guess my years of service come in handy sometimes." She smiled at the ceiling. "Got an in with the big guy."

"More like good karma," Brett spoke up, lifting his red, wooden-bead necklace and shaking it before wiping down a table.

"You've got a nice place here." Officer Walsh scanned the room, the lights picking up auburn strands in his dark hair.

"We think so. This is my partner, Maggie Wilson."

Maggie smiled, a winsome turn of her lips that pulled in more customers than the raisin pie. "Hello. I've heard so much about you."

Officer Walsh's gaze slid to Vivie. "I'm sure. Can we have a word, Vivie? In private."

"Not interested."

Maggie laced her fingers in Vivie's and squeezed. "Hear him out," her friend whispered in her ear. "He's seems sincere."

"*Not* interested," Vivie repeated under her breath.

"You never are. That's the problem." Her partner sighed, then gave her a little shove. "We can manage these out-of-control customers, can't we Rowdy?"

A grunt sounded from the kitchen as he passed a slice of pie with ice cream through the open window. Maggie grabbed it and turned to Vivie, her eyes a warm gold. "Go outside. We'll hold down the fort."

"You have my blessing." The nun made some kind of motion in the air with her fork, then tucked back into her pie.

Vivie glanced between her so-called friends—the traitors—and grabbed her purse. After hearing the officer out, she'd want to go home. Deal with it. Officer Walsh hurried to the door and held it open when she reached it.

Outside, in the soft, spring night, it was hard to observe this handsome man and imagine his horrible deed. His hands might be clean, but there was blood on them. Crickets sang a funeral dirge in the nearby bushes, and the rushing flap of bat wings swirled the air into a living thing.

"Look. I don't mean to be rude, but I don't want to see you right now." She glowered up at him, wishing he'd leave.

His eyes delved into hers. "Vivie, the bear's—"

"Please leave. I don't need the details."

When she turned, clouds drifted away from the full moon, turning the world into a black-and-white movie. Officer Walsh—Liam—leaned against his SUV, his hat sitting low on his forehead, his face looking as tired as she felt. Maybe he wasn't enjoying this. Was just doing his job.

Despite everything, she softened toward him. "Fine. If this is some job requirement, a mandatory update to the original caller, then let's get this over with. What happened?"

She wished she could put her fingers in her ears, block out the words about to be spoken.

"The cub's at the Adirondack Wildlife

Rehabilitation Center. My friends, Steve and Wendy Reed, agreed to take her for the week."

Surprise forked through her, as electric as lightning. "I don't understand. You didn't kill her?"

His lips quirked upward but his eyes remained sober. "No. I considered what you said. We're going to save her. If you're still in."

He held out a hand and she slipped hers into it, heat flooding up her arm. Unbelievable. Elation filled her. The bear was hers. Whatever Officer Walsh had said about releasing her, or finding her another home someday, didn't matter. For now, the cub was coming home. To her home.

"I'm in, Officer Walsh." She turned on her heel and hurried away. After a few steps she stopped and whirled. "And thank you. Thank you so much. This means…" she struggled for a moment "…a lot."

His smile reached all the way to his eyes. "We might both regret it."

"Never!"

"Where are you going?" he called when she reached her pickup. "I was hoping we could talk more over pie."

"Call me tomorrow. In the meantime, Maggie will fix you up." She inserted her key and opened the door. Those two would hit it off. As for her, she had more important priorities than socializing, especially with a DEC officer. He might have spared the bear, but that didn't mean they had the same outlook when it came to caring for wildlife. Not even close.

She hopped in her truck then leaned out her open window, catching her own grin in the side mirror.

"I've got a test to ace."

CHAPTER FOUR

LIAM MOPPED HIS dripping brow and leaned on the two-by-four he'd just nailed into place. He glanced around Vivie's transformed back-yard. Soon the excavated site would hold the cub's pen. He'd poured the concrete forms yesterday—the resulting foundation walls were set a foot deep in the ground. He'd se-cure the nine-gauge chain-link fencing to them, and that, combined with the electrified overhang, would keep the little one secure.

But how to protect Vivie? She'd been hov-ering like a gnat these past couple of days. Was he sure forty feet was enough room? Was the waterfall flowing into a shallow pool a safe water supply? Did he need to cover the chain link with plywood, keeping the bear from seeing humans?

Yes to all three—especially the last one.

He hefted another piece of lumber, posi-tioned it and began hammering. Despite the nonstop studying, which had put shadows be-neath her eyes, Vivie still didn't grasp that the cub's time here was temporary. Once it could fend for itself, assuming its jaw healed, they'd release it to the forest. A return to the wild home it deserved. But he knew Vivie's attachment would grow once she cared for the bear and she'd end up with a broken heart.

He swore when the hammer smashed his thumb instead of the wood. Rubbing his throbbing digit, he glanced around the area. Above him, a maple tree in the center of the enclosure rustled softly in the breeze. He'd left it uncut, save for the branches approaching the overhang. The bear would enjoy climbing on it and swinging from the tire he'd hung from lower branches. The rest of the toys, including a rubber turtle that squeaked whenever he stepped on it, he wasn't so sure about. But like some obsessed mother-to-be, Vivie returned from work each day with new goodies to toss into the pen. She'd even had a handmade sign crafted, the name Button burned into its wood. It hung over the snug wood-sided shelter he'd built to protect the young animal from the elements.

"Looking good, Liam," a familiar voice called. He turned, ignoring the leap of his pulse at the beauty approaching him. Vivie. Her toffee-colored hair swung in a high ponytail, exposing a long, graceful neck. A back-pack hung from one golden shoulder.

"Thanks. How are things at The Home-stead?"

"Slow." Vivie perched on the concrete and held up a cardboard container. "Thought you might like some lunch."

He scanned the blue sky, seeing the mid-day sun glaring on his neck. "Hadn't realized it was that time. I appreciate it."

Once seated, he pulled out a cheeseburger and swallowed a quarter of it in one bite. Man, he was hungry. Thirsty, too. No sooner had the thought occurred than she passed him a water bottle.

"Filled it up at Cold Creek spring on my way over here."

He closed his eyes in appreciation as the pure, icy liquid splashed down his throat. It was better than any manufactured drink. No matter how much man imitated, Mother Na-ture had the best recipe.

"How's the cub doing?" he asked after an-other bite. The tart pickle and crispy bacon woke up his taste buds.

Vivie pushed back a stray piece of hair, the faintest gleam of moisture on her forehead. For late May, it was already hot.

"Saw the Reeds before I went in this morning and they let me feed Button," she said. "She's still drinking the formula since her jaw's not right yet."

He frowned. With the bear struggling to eat, he understood human contact was needed. Still, that would only make Vivie more attached. Given the light in her eyes, this seemed like a lost battle—not that he'd quit trying to make her see sense.

"Once she's in the pen, you'll feed her through a chute. Don't let her get used to humans. If she does, a successful release will be impossible."

She nodded automatically, her eyes roaming the green mountain peaks in the distance. "Do we have to board up all sides? She should be able to see nature, especially if she's going to return to it, so it doesn't seem totally foreign."

"Sounds good as long as it's facing away from you and the house. This—" Liam gestured to the partial construction "—is only a temporary home." He pointed to a patch of berry bushes bordering the forest that ringed her property. "That is her real habitat. Never forget it."

"How could I?" she asked drily. "You never let up on it."

"You wanted this." He crumpled his napkin and closed the now-empty container. "If it was up to me—"

"Button wouldn't have had a second chance," she muttered so quietly he had to lean close to catch it. Her light floral scent reminded him of their wild surroundings. For a moment, he closed his eyes and breathed her in.

"Unfair, Vivie." He stood and brushed a maple seedpod from his pants. "I've worked here every day to make this possible."

She scrambled to her feet, her expression earnest. The gold flecks in her light brown eyes gleamed. "I know. And I'm grateful every time I wake up and hear you outside. But I wish you wouldn't be so hard on me. And Button."

"I'm doing what's right. Not what's easy." He watched a couple of rabbits grazing on white-topped clover. That was the future he wanted for the cub. He glanced back at the lumber pile. Not one that stole her freedom.

Vivie nodded and picked up another hammer. "What can I do?"

He blinked in surprise. In her blue sundress, the short hem fluttering around her legs, she resembled a princess. Not a construction worker.

"Know anything about carpentry work?"

Since it was a rhetorical question, her nod caught him off guard.

"One of my stepdads had a contracting business. I can even do roofing."

"Roofing…" he repeated, imagining her slipping on an angled roof and breaking something. He shook off the image.

"You had more than one stepfather?" he asked once he'd passed her some nails and they'd begun hammering.

"Six," she mumbled around a mouthful of nails. Did the woman have no concern for her safety?

He unbuckled his tool belt and wrapped it around her narrow hips, his fingers a little unsteady when they grazed her. "You're going to choke if you keep them in your mouth. Put them in the pouch."

She spit the nails into her hand and dropped them into the pocket. "Okay, Mr. Doom and Gloom."

"I'd rather be Sir Reality Check, if you don't mind."

Her eye roll said it all. "Your reality, I guess." She resumed hammering. "Sir."

He picked up more nails and stuffed them into his jeans pockets. "So, six stepfathers, huh? Sounds rough." He couldn't deny his curiosity about Vivie. She'd surprised him at every turn.

"Yeah. I guess."

Finished with the board, they moved to the pile of lumber and carried another two-by-four to the next spot. He steadied it in place while she expertly sank nails in its base. Her aim was dead-on and the nails disappeared into the wood after two or three hits. Was it his imagination or was she smashing them harder than ever?

He knew he should leave the topic alone, but something fragile in her tone brought out his protective streak. Had she been hurt?

"Where's your mom now?"

Her hammer slammed dead center into another nail and buried it in one blow. "Don't know. Haven't spoken to her in ten years."

With her lips pressed together and her eyes narrow, all signs indicated he should change the subject, but somehow he couldn't.

"Why's that?"

"She didn't exactly leave a forwarding number when she walked out on me and her latest husband."

That sounded hard. "And how old were you?"

She stopped and gulped from her water bottle. After a long drink, she wiped her mouth and met his eyes. "Seventeen. Any more questions, Hardy boy?"

He pulled off his sweaty T-shirt. "Not really." He began nailing another board. "Just passing time."

Only he wasn't. Every moment with Vivie intrigued him. He looked forward to seeing her more than he dared admit. More than was good for his peace of mind. Like her, he shouldn't get attached…especially if he got that job in Yellowstone Park. He wondered when the résumé he'd emailed would get a response.

She moved around him and held the next piece of wood as he secured it to the foundation. "So how about you? Did you grow up with the white picket fence? Have a dog and a sister?"

"A cat and six siblings. No fence, though the Korean vegetable market on the corner had a customers-only line we couldn't cross. Especially after my sister Mary Ann filched a mango."

She considered him, something spooked in her expression. "Sounds like you grew up in the city."

He pressed the beam, testing its stability, then pounded in another nail for good measure. "SoHo. My family owns a pub there and we lived in an apartment above it. Most of them still do. Mary Ann's getting married there in August."

She lowered her hammer. "I lived in the city when I was in culinary school."

"Yeah? What part?"

Her hand rose to her neck and her voice grew faint. "The Bronx."

Before he could ask her more, she hurried on, "So all nine of you, plus a cat, in one apartment? That must have been cramped."

He forced a shrug. It had been tough, but he'd been in tighter spots... The memory of Kunar punched his throat.

"My dad died when I was seventeen, so there were only eight of us. He was a Korean War vet. It inspired my twin, Niall, and I to join the military after 9/11."

A soft hand fell on his arm and he studied her concerned eyes. "I'm sorry to hear that, Liam. Did your mother remarry?"

Spots appeared in the corners of his vision. He sat on a nearby stump and took another swig of water. "My mom has Alzheimer's. My oldest brother, Aiden, pretty much raised the rest of us." Crazy that he was telling her so much. He'd only ever opened up to his battle buddies. He stared down at the water bottle, his chest aching. Now those buddies were all gone...the nearest he could get to them was atop a mountain, where he felt closest to heaven.

Vivie plunked down by his feet and handed him a wrapped cookie from her backpack. "Aiden sounds like a great brother. Want one? Raisin oatmeal."

He bit into the chewy dessert, grateful she'd switched subjects. "Good," he said after polishing it off in two bites.

"Thanks. One of my stepdads owned a bakery. That's where I got started making desserts."

"Guess it wasn't all bad then, your childhood."

"There were worse things," she muttered, almost to herself.

He tried catching her eye but she stared at a copse of papery-white birches. Her shuttered expression made her look guarded and breakable. Something bad had happened to her. But what? He clamped his mouth shut before he could ask. It wasn't his business. She wasn't his concern…so why couldn't he stop thinking about her?

No good would come of it.

None at all.

THE NEXT EVENING, Vivie curled up on her couch with her laptop. The farmhouse smelled pine fresh from the scrub she'd given it after her own soak in the tub. Laboring outside all afternoon, alongside a gorgeous, shirtless DEC officer no less, had been sweaty work. Not that she should be working herself into a lather over chiseled abs. This was the guy who'd almost killed Button.

And spared her, a voice whispered in her head. Would another officer have given her, and the cub, this chance? She pictured Liam working every day this week in her backyard. He never complained. Didn't seem to tire. Always showed up. It was a far cry from a lot of the men she'd known growing up. Still, she felt better keeping an eye on him, seeing him follow through on his promises.

She should have used the extra time preparing for her certification test, but she'd studied him instead. It made no sense, but she looked forward to working, eating and talking together. Learning about his childhood made her see the man more than the uniform.

She lifted her mug of mint tea and sipped. Her eyes glazed over as she reread, for the third time, question number two hundred and sixteen on the New York State Wildlife Rehabilitator certification practice test. This was hard. Much more challenging than she'd imagined when she'd vowed to pass it.

For the first time, doubt set in. The test was tomorrow and she'd still missed too many questions. What if she failed? Her heart stumbled to a halt. Without a home, would Button be put down after all? The bear's temporary spot at the rescue center expired at the end of the week. Vivie was all she had.

Vivie gripped the mug handle. She couldn't let Button down. The cub had kept going after the shooting, dislocated jaw and all. She hadn't quit, and neither would Vivie.

She answered several more questions, relieved when she missed only three. Progress. For a reward, she tossed back a handful of chocolate. This had to work. Button deserved a safe home.

Didn't everyone?

The thought brought her up short. Once, she wouldn't have asked that question at all. Would have assumed that personal safety was a guarantee. Her mind flashed back to her last year in culinary school, the sudden hand over her mouth as she walked home from her late-night cooking job. How her masked attackers had tortured and tormented her, then left her for dead.

She shuddered and pushed away the thought. The journey to recovery had taken her too far to go back there.

When a sharp knock sounded on her front door, Jinx leaped from her lap and slunk under the piano bench. Vivie wished she could curl under there with her, but made her feet take her to the door. After the attack, her support group, Reclaim the Dark, had helped her think like a survivor. Not a victim.

She would not live her life afraid.

She eased open the door as far as the chain allowed and body blocked Scooter.

Liam's leaf-green eyes shone under the porch light. "I was coming back from a rescue call and thought I'd stop by. See how you were doing with your studies."

"What'd you rescue?"

His mouth pursed. "Another heron caught in a fishing line. It'll be touch and go for the rehabilitator tonight."

"That's awful." She unlocked the chain and let him in. Scooter leaped, putting both paws on Liam's stomach.

The officer caught them in his hands and smiled down at the rambunctious dog. "Shall we dance?" he asked in such a formal tone that Vivie laughed, her mood lifting.

"I think he might need some breath mints first."

"Thought that was you."

She swatted Liam's arm. "My breath is

minty fresh, thank you very much. Would you like some tea?"

He shook his head and sat on her side chair, his size dwarfing it. "Are you ready for tomorrow?"

She sank onto the couch. "I have to be, right?"

"Right."

"Or you'll shoot Button."

He regarded her gravely. "Wish you wouldn't call her that."

She hugged a pillow. "Why?"

"Because it makes her sound like a pet." Liam leaned forward and the outdoorsy, masculine smell of him filled her senses. Normally, being alone with any man this late at night would terrify her. Instead, she felt alive and jittery, her stomach fluttering.

"If you pass tomorrow—" he continued.

"When I pass tomorrow," she interrupted, lifting her chin despite her nerves.

He studied her, his strong face handsome. "When you pass tomorrow, you need to start thinking like a rehabilitator. If you treat the bear like a house pet, I'll have to remove her."

The thought knocked the breath out of her like ice water. "Button is going to make it here."

She pictured the nearly finished enclosure, how the sides facing the house had been boarded up, the back open save for the fence. Would she only ever glimpse the bear through the feeding slot? How would she let Button know she wasn't alone? It was important to have support after being attacked.

Liam nodded at her laptop. "Are you studying now?"

She nodded. "I'm not getting the material," she admitted.

"Want me to quiz you?" Jinx had jumped into his lap and was kneading his stomach, purring like a race-car engine. He didn't seem to notice the holes she'd punctured in his shirt as he petted her. When she turned and began shredding his pants, he pushed her tail from his face.

"That's okay. I'm fine on my own." He was acting kind, yet he was still a threat to Button if things didn't work out. How to focus on the test with so many warring thoughts?

"So do you know whether or not all incoming wildlife should be treated with antibiotics to ward off infection?" he pressed, the fur in front of his mouth fluttering with every word.

Jinx's purring filled the room as Vivie wrestled with the question. She'd seen it on the practice test but couldn't recall the answer, so she went with her gut.

"Of course. It's better to be proactive." She tucked her jiggling foot underneath her opposite leg.

Liam pulled a protesting Jinx away and shook his head. "Wrong. Antibiotics are only effective against bacterial disease and some types of parasites, but not viruses. Plus, they have side effects. Misuse of antibiotics can cause development of resistant bacteria. Oral antibiotics can destroy delicate gut microbes, leading to diarrhea. Some types of antibiotics can cause fatal enteritis in some species. Antibiotic treatment should be given only after careful examination of an animal's condition and consultation with a veterinarian."

When he sat back, a smug look on his face, she remembered to close her mouth. "Do you have this whole manual memorized?"

Liam studied his hands, a wry flip to the corner of his mouth. "I have a photographic memory."

Her eyes narrowed. "So you probably only had to read this once to know it, right?"

He nodded, abashed.

"Some people have it so easy," she mumbled to herself. He had looks and brains, yet somehow she couldn't resent him for it. The opposite actually, she thought, a blush creeping up her neck as she took in his strong jaw, dimpled chin and the width of his shoulders in his close-fitting T-shirt. He must have taken off his uniform shirt in the SUV...

"Why don't you give your eyes a rest—I'll read the questions and multiple-choice answers to you."

Her traitorous heart leaped. That sounded good...too good...

"Why would you do that?"

His soulful eyes met into hers. "Because despite what you think, I'm on your side."

She peered at him, sideways. "I want to believe that."

"Do you think I want to put down the bear?"

"Button," she contradicted stubbornly.

"Do you believe I would willingly harm her?"

She thought about his hard work this week, laboring during his vacation to make an enclosure that met code.

"No," she admitted. "But you will if you feel you have to, and that's as bad."

"Yes," he agreed, his voice low and level. "It is. So will you save me from doing something I don't want to do and let me help you pass this test?"

She blinked at him in surprise. She hadn't thought of it from his point of view. That he'd want her to succeed as much as she did. They might have different opinions on how best to raise Button, but they both wanted the bear alive. She could get behind that. She eyed Liam. If she wasn't careful, there was a lot about this man she could support.

Vivie handed him the laptop and Scooter threw himself across Liam's boots as if settling in for the evening.

"I was on question two hundred and sixteen."

His scrutinized her over the screen. "How many of those did you get right?"

"A hundred?"

He glanced at her wall clock and settled deeper into the chair. "Guess I will have that tea. This is going to be a long night."

CHAPTER FIVE

"STOP CHEWING YOUR NAILS. It's not hygienic and besides, what will Officer Walsh think about those cuticles?"

Vivie yanked her finger from her mouth and glanced at the diner's cat clock. Officer Walsh? Cuticles? Like any of that mattered. Okay. Maybe it did, a bit, she admitted to herself. She'd thought about him way too much lately.

But Button was most important—and her certification test results. She'd taken it yesterday and had spent a restless night going over every question she knew she'd gotten wrong.

"And staring at the time won't make it go faster," Maggie added, swiping a washcloth in wide circles along the counter.

Vivie dropped onto a stool and twisted back and forth, her sandals sliding along the metal base. "I know. But the test was hard. If I didn't pass…"

Sister Mary waved a squirt bottle of hot

sauce. "I put in a good word for you, Vivie. You passed."

She smiled at one of her favorite regulars. "Wish I could believe that's enough."

"Of course you passed it," their waitress, Lauren, reassured her. She patted Vivie on the back as she bustled by, carrying a laden tray one-handed. A family of five let out a cheer when she stooped and passed out shakes and burgers.

"I'm not sure," Vivie groaned. In fact, the more she thought things over, the more she was certain she'd failed. Mastering recipes, graduating culinary school had been do-able. She was a visual, hands-on person and watching and repeating what she saw got her through. But reading and memorizing… Not her thing. What if she failed Button? "It'll be midnight in six hours. Maybe they'll post the results."

Maggie broke a daisy from one of the bud vases and tucked it behind Vivie's ear, smoothing her hair. "I think when they said 'results Tuesday,' they meant more like 8:00 a.m., sweetie."

Vivie dropped her head to the cool countertop, her heart beating fast. She needed to know. Now. Spending time with Button at the rehab center the past week had made her more protective than ever. And the cub's excitement when she caught Vivie's smell, that wriggling body, made her melt.

Holding Button as she fed her had filled Vivie with peace. Finally, she wasn't focused on healing herself; she was helping another. If only she hadn't struggled through her studies. Vivie pictured Liam in her living room until 3:00 a.m. the night before the test. He'd drilled her like a sergeant, not leaving until she'd gotten at least seventy-five percent right. Without him, she wouldn't have had a prayer, Sister Mary or not.

He'd done more to help than she'd have ever imagined. Beneath that official, practical, tough persona was a kind, caring man. He didn't want to hurt Button. Wanted Vivie to succeed. Yet it was hard to reconcile that with the threat he presented. He couldn't be both ally and foe. Yet how to see him any other way?

A forty-foot enclosed structure now took up the clearing behind her house. Everything about it was built according to code. Its inspection had been expedited and preliminary approval granted through the DEC thanks to Liam.

He was Button's savior, and her possible executioner.

Vivie shivered, imagining the sweet bear harmed. If only she had her test results.

The bell above the door jingled and a group of firemen entered. Across the room, Lauren madly scribbled on her pad as she took an order from an elderly couple who kept changing their minds.

"You want them, Maggie?" Vivie nodded at the concentrated testosterone overflowing one of their booths.

Maggie shook her head, her hand rising to her chin. "Have you seen the size of this pimple? No way."

"Seriously?"

Maggie heaved out a sigh. "Don't want to meet my potential husband with Mount Vesuvius on my face."

Vivie grabbed some menus and studied her friend. "Why are you so convinced you're marrying a guy in uniform?"

"Would you believe a psychic told me?"

"Unfortunately, yes." Vivie rolled her eyes then headed to the loud table.

"It was at a fair. In person. Not one of those hotlines," Maggie called after her.

"Much more credible," Vivie answered before reaching the firemen.

"How are you fellows tonight?"

Even seated, they were nearly at eye level with her.

"Tired. Been working a forest fire on Spruce Ridge," the eldest in the bunch answered. "Could we have some water?"

"Sure. Have you got it contained?" Spruce Ridge wasn't near her property but she hated thinking of the animals caught in a smoke-filled, burning forest or neighbors worried for their homes.

"It's unusual to see a fire this early in the season, but we had a mild winter and dry spring. This one's small and we'll have it out in a day or two," the man said, his voice hoarse. It sounded as though he'd been shouting for hours. Maybe he had. "If we don't get some rain later this summer, the whole place could be a tinderbox."

"Let's hope not," Vivie answered before turning on her heel and hurrying for the water pitcher. Back at the table, she filled up the glasses, took an order large enough to feed their entire station and headed to the kitchen window.

"Rowdy, hope you're ready to get slammed."

Her cook stopped chopping onions, tears streaming down his face, and nodded. "Whatcha got?"

She handed him the long slip and leaned on

the wide ledge of the pass-through window. "So, no sunglasses today?" It was their trick to keep the onion juice from getting in their eyes when dicing.

Rowdy shook his head and brushed at his damp cheeks. "They fell off in Loon Lake while I was kayaking this morning."

She imagined the isolated spot, the haunting calls of the loons as they swam with their offspring on their backs. What she would give for that peace of mind. She wondered what Liam had been doing this morning. Was he responding to emergency calls? Helping with the fire…? Concern shivered through her, taking Vivie by surprise.

"That's too bad. Want these?" She took her pair of black-and-white polka-dot frames from her purse beneath the counter and held them up.

The sizzle of meat hitting a hot grill sounded as Rowdy placed the last of the burgers and turned. One side of his mouth lifted. "Don't think I could pull 'em off."

Maggie nudged in beside Vivie. "Sure you could, Rowdy. Own your masculinity. Real men wear polka dots."

He grabbed handfuls of cut potatoes and tossed them into the deep fryer. "Not this man."

"I'll wear them," put in Brett as he pushed by his bosses and entered the kitchen. "It's all about who you are on a spiritual level. Doesn't matter what society expects you to be…it's your inner being, man."

Rowdy grunted and flipped the burgers.

Brett loaded some dishes into the washer and shrugged. "You should get your chakras checked. Maybe you wouldn't be allergic to tofu anymore."

Maggie nudged Vivie. "Don't see that happening."

"Not in this lifetime," Vivie whispered back, and the women turned, hiding their grins.

Automatically, Vivie's eyes flew to the clock. Only fifteen minutes had passed? This waiting would kill her.

Another ring of the bell had her glancing at the door. Liam strolled in, exchanging a nod with the firefighters before sauntering to the counter.

His army-green T-shirt and khaki shorts fit him too well for her comfort. Vivie forced her eyes away. Her slamming pulse, however, didn't cooperate, making her feel slightly dizzy as he drew close.

"Hey, Officer Walsh," chirped Maggie. "We're all out of raisin pie but we've still got some strawberry rhubarb if you'd like a piece."

Sister Mary waved her fork. "Beat you to it again, Officer."

Liam smiled at the elderly woman then slid onto a stool, his gaze on Vivie. "Strawberry rhubarb sounds good. And a cup of coffee. Black, thanks. How are you, Sister?"

She scratched at her white stockings and adjusted her head covering. "Itchy. Had to garb up for another retirement party this week. Forgot how uncomfortable uniforms are. Right, Officer Walsh?"

He nodded politely, though Vivie had to admit, he wore his as though it were tailor-made for him.

Maggie finished scribbling and bustled off, leaving the two of them alone. Vivie eyed Liam, noting the slight droop of his broad shoulders, his pale lips. Her self-consciousness turned to concern. "Long day?"

Weary eyes rose to hers. "Been helping out with a forest fire."

"You don't think it'll come near my house, do you? Threaten Button?"

He lifted the mug, and his eyes closed as he gulped the strong brew. Absurdly, Vivie was glad she'd made a fresh pot a few minutes earlier. She wanted to please him. Crazy.

"No. Wind's going in the opposite direction."

"Good. Plus, my neighbors come home next week. I wouldn't want anything to happen to their house while they're away." She moved aside as Maggie returned with the pie. "Still can't believe their nephews are so bad. Muriel and Pete are the nicest people. They were the first friends I made after I moved into my aunt's house."

"And I was your second after you stopped supplying me pies and finally agreed to become my partner!" piped up Maggie.

"That's because you wouldn't quit pestering me."

The friends grinned at each other. Vivie remembered the day she'd finally taken the chance and gone all-in with the money her aunt had left her. At the time she'd been nervous, but she'd never regretted the decision. She'd gained a business and a work family.

When Rowdy rang the pick-up bell, Maggie loaded the firemen's plates on a large tray. "I'll take these over."

"What about Mount Vesuvius?" Vivie couldn't resist teasing.

"It erupted a few minutes ago." Maggie pointed at the flatter red spot on her chin, then headed away, her hips swinging as she neared the boisterous men.

Lauren whizzed by, scooped up some baskets of chicken strips and fries, and grabbed a bottle of vinegar. "These snowbirds are going to kill me. Do we even have an early-bird special?"

"No. But we have the senior discount. If that's not enough, I'll talk to them."

Lauren nodded, grateful, and returned to her section.

"It's busy, tonight." Liam put down his fork. "And this is excellent."

"Thanks," Vivie eyed the pie, noting the overly browned edges, the way the crust hadn't flaked when he'd cut into it. Last night's baking had been a disaster because her mind was still full of the test and not on measurements, rolling or oven timers. A certain officer had also stolen a few of her thoughts...

"Do you think they're dangerous?" Vivie asked, imagining the men close to her house. Moving to the isolated Adirondacks had made her feel safe. She didn't want that faith shaken.

Swearing rose from the kitchen and Vivie automatically flipped on the radio. A smooth Sinatra tune covered up what sounded like someone burning alive back there, Rowdy's usual noise for a scorched pinky.

"I'll check on the drama queen," Brett called, then rolled his eyes before striding through the swinging door.

She waited for Liam to stop chewing, trying not to stare at the firm set of his square jaw. Polka-dot sunglasses would have no effect on his manliness

"No. Not dangerous. They were cooperative. Though it turns out they were wanted in their own state for ripping off a convenience store." Liam studied her. "The troopers will probably stop by to ask you a few questions."

She nodded, a jerky motion, as fear soured her gut. The last time she'd talked to the police, she hadn't been of much help. No, she'd told them, she'd never seen her attackers' faces, hadn't recognized their voices, hadn't noticed anyone follow her as she'd walked to the subway after finishing the graveyard shift. They'd struck as unexpectedly as a thunderstorm on a sunny day, turning everything dark, a gray filter that'd cast a pall over her life for four years.

Only the Adirondack's crisp blue skies, navy waters and deep green forests had returned the color to her life. She'd remembered to breathe here. Had carved a safe path from home to diner and back again that gave her the security she needed.

"You okay?" He squinted at her over a forkful of pie.

She gave herself a small shake. "Yes. Guess I'm just worried about the test results."

He chewed slowly, his eyes faraway. "If only you knew someone with a password into the DEC system. Someone who could find out those results so that you wouldn't have to—"

Vivie lunged across the counter and grabbed his muscular forearms. "Can you find out if I passed?"

He nodded, his mouth curling. "I could, since I saw the test administrator enter the scores a half hour ago."

She snatched her purse and raced around to his side. "Let's go." With a hard tug, she got him on his feet.

"Maggie, I'm taking off," she called. "Liam's getting my test results early. Are you okay to close?" She was already halfway to the door, Liam in tow.

"No problem." Maggie let go of one of the fireman's suspenders and straightened. "Call me as soon as you know."

"Me, too!" piped up Lauren who gathered the departed family's tip and stuffed it into her apron's pocket.

"I didn't pay for the pie," Liam protested as Vivie shoved him out the door.

"It's on the house." She pointed to his SUV. "Follow me."

He shook his head. "My place is closer."

She caught herself before she nodded. Fear unfurled in her, a shadow deepening the cracks that'd remained even after she'd put herself back together.

"N-no. I'd prefer my home." Home was safe. It was what she knew. Where she was comfortable. That was as far as she'd let that line of thinking go.

He cocked his head and shrugged. "Okay. Meet you there."

She nodded and got in her pickup, wondering at her initial response. Had she almost agreed to go to an unknown place…alone… with a man?

With Liam?

LIAM PUNCHED IN his password and tried not to focus too much on the woman pressed against his side. Her long caramel hair brushed his shoulder and gave off a wildflower scent.

"What if I failed?"

He found the right tab and pulled the mouse over it. "Ready?"

She shook her head then said, "Yes."

Another click brought up a list of names. They scrolled to hers and he read off a number that made her leap to her feet and got Scooter barking.

"I did it!"

He logged himself out and set the laptop on the couch before standing.

"I knew you would."

Her mouth twisted. "Then why did you stay here until 3:00 a.m. the other night?"

He felt his mouth turn upward in return. "That's how I knew you'd pass."

She laughed, the sound reminding him of a spring-fed brook. "At least you're honest."

"Ah. Something nice to say about me for a change." It bothered him, more than he dared admit, that she distrusted him. He wanted her to like him. Plain and simple. Only it was much more complicated than that.

"My mother always taught me, if you can't say something nice—"

"Change the subject," he finished for her and they cracked up.

"When can I get my bear?"

Her wide eyes reminded him of late Adirondack autumn, all golds and browns. "She's not yours, Vivie. You can't think that way."

"Technically, she is my bear. For now." She

pointed to the laptop. "That said so. Can we go now?"

He peered at his watch. It was nine o'clock. Getting late, but he could see the urgency in her face. That need to please her, to help, rose up inside. Again.

"Let me get ahold of the Reeds."

Her foot tapped as he picked up her the receiver of her ancient phone, dialed the number and spoke with the rehabilitators.

When he hung up, she studied him eagerly. "Sounds like a yes to me. Should we take my truck?"

"No. The bear will be more secure in the SUV."

Outside, she hesitated before getting into the SUV. "Never thought I'd ride in a DEC vehicle. Throw eggs at it maybe…"

"Yeah. Especially mine."

Her delicate profile scrunched as she slid in beside him and he started the engine. "Not if you were in it…maybe. You shouldn't have stopped me from feeding the starving animals. Many probably died because of that."

His grip tightened on the wheel. "They couldn't get reliant on humans or be protected when that wasn't nature's way. We can't control the world. Keep everything safe."

She moved restlessly beside him. "You

believe everything is fated—even horrible things? That when terrible stuff happens we have to just—just accept it."

He nodded slowly. Her voice wobbled a bit on the edges and he sensed a deeper issue at work than a simple philosophical debate. Towering pines whizzed by as they cruised the back road.

"You can't stop the bad in the world." He thought of his long, tense nights at his besieged outpost in Afghanistan. How he'd been powerless to leave, to prevent the insurgents from killing his friends the moment they ventured beyond its walls...or patrolled them.

"But you can try to prevent it!" Her voice rose and she gnawed the sides of her nails.

He thought of that terrible, hopeless feeling he'd had during the war. The waiting and wondering when it would be his turn to die. Since the insurgents had outnumbered them, and their inexperienced commander had refused to call for help, it'd felt like waiting in line, cuing up for death. How he'd dreaded it. Hated feeling trapped. No matter how guarded they'd remained, they hadn't been able to stanch the bloodbath.

"No. You can't," he said as evenly as he could manage around his clenched jaw.

"Only a fool would think that way."

"Could you stop the cub's mother from being shot?" He knew it was a low blow, but he needed Vivie to see that life wasn't some fairy tale and that Button might not have a happily-ever-after...or *any* after if things didn't work out.

She subsided against the seat and sucked in a harsh breath. "I didn't know that was going to happen."

"Even when you do, you can't always stop it," he muttered under his breath and turned on the radio. They drove in tense silence until the familiar sign for the Adirondack Wildlife Rehabilitation Center appeared. He turned onto the long dirt drive, bumping along it until a rambling, cedar-sided ranch house appeared.

Before he could turn off the engine, Wendy and Steve Reed appeared, giving them a cheery wave from their small porch.

"We've got Button crated for you. She's a darling and we're going to miss her." Wendy's eyes shone in the dimming light.

Steve put an arm around his wife and pulled her close. "Always gets a little emotional when it's time to say goodbye."

Liam felt a sharp nudge in his ribs and glanced away from Vivie's knowing look. "Thanks so much for fitting her in this week."

Steve nodded. "We're just glad it worked out." He turned to Vivie and held out a hand. "Congratulations on passing your test, Vivie. There's nothing in life more rewarding then helping an animal rehabilitate. It's not easy and will take an emotional toll. You'll have to work hard not to get attached."

Vivie shook her head. "How do you do that?"

Wendy stopped blotting her nose. "It's tough. Keep telling yourself you're doing this for their good. Not yours. Your needs don't count. Neither do your feelings, so best to try to keep them out of it."

Steve gestured to the scaly Scotch pines swaying at the edge of the compound. "That's their world. We aren't supposed to take them from it."

"But if we're keeping them safe…"

"Safe isn't the same as living," Liam interjected. He'd been safe inside that outpost, relatively, but he'd felt as dead as those who'd tried escaping.

"It's better than the alternative," she snapped.

He rubbed his jaw. She didn't have a clue. Someday she'd have to face reality and stop seeing life as some sort of fairy tale.

"Where's the bear, Steve?"

He followed the man past a raptor enclosure, stopping to admire a clutch of young
snowy owls, before reaching the crate.

A snort sounded from its depths and he
squatted in front of the caged front, surprised
to see how much the cub had bulked up in
a week.

"She's put on some weight since you last
saw her," Steve said, sounding proud. "Can't
take all the credit, though, since Vivie came
out here a couple, sometimes three times a
day to feed and check in on her."

Liam shook his head. Was that dedication
or desperation? It was hard to tell with Vivie.
No doubt she had attachment issues. Still,
more and more, he found it charming. Her
big heart drew him. He sometimes wondered
what it'd be like if he were in it. Most important, he hoped it never got broken.

He squinted at the long-time rehabilitator.

"Do you think Vivie will be okay with letting the bear go in September?"

They turned when bats emerged from a
barn, their dark wings flapping against the
purple sky.

"Let's just say, I'm glad I'm not a betting
man."

Liam hefted the crate and headed back.
"Fair enough."

He wasn't a betting man, either, but he could read the odds. They were not in favor of this working out.

How could he protect Vivie and Button? On top of that, how could he keep from becoming even more embroiled in this whole thing?

CHAPTER SIX

LATER THAT NIGHT, Vivie tossed and turned in bed, thinking of Button in her new enclosure. The little bear had cowered against one of the boarded-up walls after going inside. Since Liam insisted Vivie leave the rear entrance, she didn't know if the cub got braver. Wandered around a little bit. Maybe played with the toy turtle Vivie'd gotten her.

Vivie rolled over and stared out her window at the wisps of cloud floating across the full moon. Did Button watch the same scene? Wonder about her safety? Or was she asleep, plagued with nightmares of her attack? It was a fanciful thought, but Vivie believed that animals dreamed. Scooter's sleep woofing and leg scrambling suggested he'd chased many a rabbit while unconscious. While napping, Jinx sometimes sprang into the air without warning, sprinting nowhere in particular.

And what did Liam dream about? Practical things like paperwork or clearing trails, she supposed. Nothing romantic, especially not about a woman who opposed and challenged him at every turn. And why was she thinking about the handsome officer again, anyway? She flopped onto her stomach and buried her face in her pillow.

Animals. A much safer topic for her peace of mind. They had more in common with humans than many imagined. The orphan outside, alone on a dark night, tugged at Vivie's heart.

At a howling gust of wind, she sat up. Her covers pooled in her lap and the draft blew across her bare shoulders. Was the gust unsettling Button? Would she be even more afraid?

Vivie had to go check on her. It was that simple.

And that complicated.

Liam would never sanction it. As much as she wanted to see the cub, a part of her rebelled against letting Liam down. He'd gone out on a limb for her. Wasn't it only fair she follow his rules?

He'd given many warnings before leaving. According to him, Button could rarely see Vivie…a glimpse at best during the weekly enclosure cleaning. Interactions of any kind were a definite no. As for feeding, a critical point in Vivie's mind, that had to be done by shoving food—even leftovers from the diner, according to the DEC—through the feeding slot.

She trudged to the bathroom for a drink and ran the tap, waiting for the water to turn cold. Ironic that the bear was not allowed to become used to humans, but could eat people food.

The DEC's logic didn't make sense. How could a bear survive in the wild if it never saw another living creature? Didn't interact with its future habitat? Wouldn't recognize or know how to forage for the food it'd need?

Of course, given Button's off-kilter jaw, there was a chance she wouldn't return to the wild and would stay here. Vivie understood that releasing her when the time was right would be best, but a part of her longed to keep the cub safe. To guarantee that no harm would come to Button ever again.

A faint cry from outside made Vivie jump to the small window facing the back of the property. Was Button okay?

She tossed her hair into a ponytail and slid on sandals. The heck with DEC policies; she had to check on Button. As long as Liam didn't find out, she'd keep her certification. She didn't want to lie to him, so she wouldn't. She'd simply leave out certain details. A part of her suspected that even if Liam knew, deep down his kindness might let him understand that she only did what was best for Button. At least, she hoped so.

She shrugged on a robe and ran downstairs. At the back door, inspiration struck and she doubled back for honey. Maybe it'd soothe Button. Who didn't need comfort food when stressed?

Outside, she tightened her belt against the crisp early-summer air. Sycamore trees put on a puppet show across her back lawn, the moon behind them acting as flashlight. An owl called to her right and a flurry of wings sounded as it flew from her spruce tree for the deeper forest beyond. Moths and june bugs still stirred and they circled her flashlight the moment she flicked it on.

The enclosure's wooden sides came into view and she skirted them, heading for the back of the pen. She listened for more distress cries and blew out a relieved breath in the quiet. At the open chain-link section, she flicked her light around the enclosure searching for Button. At last she saw a small black ball in the same spot they'd left her hours ago. Vivie's heart broke. Poor baby.

Vivie unlocked the heavy padlock and clicked it closed behind her, repeating the process on the second door before slipping inside. A light wind rose and tossed her ponytail in front of her face. Button lifted her nose, a snort escaping her when she caught sight of Vivie.

"Hi, Button. How are you doing, sweetie?" she called, approaching carefully. The cub had been spooked on the ride home. Vivie didn't want to cause her any more distress. Before closing the distance between them, Vivie scooped up the plastic turtle. Button rose to her feet and butted her head into Vivie's calves.

She squatted down and stroked the young bear's trembling back. "It's okay. This is your new home now. You're safe here." But she listened to the sounds of the forest and wondered if they only brought back bad memories for Button, the way the bustle of city life had done to her.

Button placed her front paws on Vivie's shoulders and snuffled her neck. The ticklish feeling made Vivie laugh. She wrapped her arms around the cub, resting her cheek on top of the bear's soft head. "See. All's well here. And you're not alone. I'm sorry you don't have your real mom anymore, but I'm going to do everything I can to be the next best thing."

She sat back and Button rested her head

in Vivie's lap, her large eyes on Vivie's face. She pulled the jar of honey from her pocket, unscrewed the cap, and held it out to the cub. It wasn't exactly a honeycomb, but Button could figure it out.

After some sniffing and some pawing at the glass Button stopped and stared up at her, a question in the tilt of her triangular face. Why weren't Button's instincts kicking in? Maybe she needed to be shown. Steeling herself, Vivie reached in and withdrew sticky fingers, putting them to the bear's muzzle.

Button's tongue flashed, lightning quick, over Vivie's hand again and again as she grunted deep in the back of her throat, a satisfied sound that warmed Vivie. Finally, real bear food for Button. The swelling in her jaw had gone down a fair bit over the past week, and she managed to slurp up the treat without much difficulty.

When the cub finished, she scrutinized Vivie expectantly.

"You can have more," she urged, holding out the jar, but the bear simply stared, dark eyes reflecting the stars above.

"Do you want me to take a turn?" Vivie dipped her fingers into the jar, brought them to her mouth and licked. This time, when she extended the container, Button grabbed it away, scooping up honey and shoving her paw in her mouth.

Vivie did her best to get the honey off her hands. Why hadn't she thought to bring a hand wipe? She eyed the small waterfall and pool. It was her best option, but she hated to leave Button. Then again, the orphaned animal was now nosing into the jar and completely oblivious. She'd be okay for a few minutes.

Wandering across the grassy space, she imagined Button growing to love her new home. Would she feel protected? It was essential, she'd learned from her support group in the Bronx, after such a violent incident. She eyed the dark woods beyond the enclosure. Danger lurked there, but in here was security. Hopefully Button would come to learn the difference as Vivie had.

Soft fur brushed against her legs as she lowered herself to the water's edge. "Hey, Button. Want a drink?" She shoved her hands into the streaming water and rubbed them together.

Button dropped the plastic turtle from her mouth and lowered her muzzle to the pond. Vivie could hear her tongue lapping up water delicately and quickly, like a hummingbird's wings.

She ran a hand along Button's curved back, ending on her sweet puff of a tail. The cub was so cute. And so helpless. Suddenly Vivie was fiercely glad she'd made this clandestine visit. The heck with the DEC. She knew what was best for her bear and this was proof. How long would Button have stayed huddled against the wall if Vivie hadn't come outside?

When Button finished drinking, Vivie walked over to the cedar shelter, inhaling the fresh hay that covered its floor. She crawled inside and Button followed. The cub turned in a circle then nestled in a soft patch of shavings close enough for Vivie to pet her warm body, the rubber turtle squeaking in her mouth. At last the animal's breathing evened out and her chest rose and fell slowly, filling Vivie with contentment.

Finally, the cub had let down her guard. Relaxed. Vivie would never let her feel afraid again. Vivie's eyes started to droop when a bell sounded and a cat-sized shadow leaped inside.

"Jinx, no!" Vivie made a scooting motion that her wayward cat pretended not to see, milking that one-eye condition for all it was worth. The little scalawag.

Her cat tiptoed close to the bear and extended her nose to the cub's nose before twitching away. Button jerked awake and scrambled to her feet, her fur puffing as far out as Jinx's.

"No fighting, you two," Vivie warned. She kept a firm hand wrapped around the bear, not wanting her feisty cat to get torn apart. But true to form, Jinx's retreat was only temporary and she slunk closer, extending her nose again until it touched Button's. For a moment they stared at each other and no one, including Vivie, breathed.

At last, her cat turned tail and stalked away, stopping briefly to bat at Button's ball of a tail. Nice.

Button lay down again, but kept an eye on the lingering feline who circled, at one point rubbing her cheek against Button's side. The bear jerked but otherwise remained still, now fascinated with this small fearless creature.

Jinx stopped her cat-and-bear game, finally, and sidled closer, stretching out to full-body length alongside Button and Vivie. The cub lifted its head to observe the other animal, then lowered it. She fell into the kind of deep, instant sleep only a child managed.

Relief swept over Vivie. Jinx had been surprisingly sweet, other than the tail batting. And Button had accepted the cat. It was all she could ask for.

Given her past issues, animals were the only creatures to put her completely at ease. Talking to men, even joking around with them, was one thing. Allowing one close, dating, left her feeling vulnerable—something she'd sworn she'd never be again. Strange that she'd felt so comfortable with Liam all week, though.

She pictured his easy smile, the light in his eyes when he laughed. He'd charmed her rather than scared her…and that frightened her even more. A romantic relationship wasn't possible. No need to stir up old terrors by taking a risk on love. Better to content herself with all the riches she had: a home, her diner, her pets and friends.

Her fingers smoothed both animals' fur, a strange longing winding through her. This was all the companionship and love she needed, wasn't it?

Liam came to mind again.

There wasn't a chance she might want him in her life, too, was there?

THE MORNING SUN lit the tent like a Chinese paper lantern.

Liam rubbed his eyes and stretched in his sleeping bag, waking to the loamy forest smells of spruce, damp leaves and rich, dark soil. He'd camped last night, wanting to spend his last day of vacation outside. Being indoors made him antsy and brought on nightmares that left him sleepless and shaking. Roughing it gave him a break from the haunting memories that stalked him.

He pulled down the entrance's zipper and stepped into the cool morning air. A hint of mountain laurel was carried on the breeze, ruffling his tarp.

The Adirondacks.

How often, as a kid growing up in the city, a soldier surrounded by sand, had he wished for green? He eyed the majestic elms filtering the light into a golden web, the lacy boughs of a northern white cedar and the moss-covered rocks strewn about his makeshift campsite. Was there a better color?

Only soon he'd be leaving it for the rocky canyons of Yellowstone National Park. He'd gotten a call to come out for an interview next week. Strange that it didn't give him the happiness he'd expected. Did Vivie have something to do with that?

Lately he'd been finding excuses to see her every day. Needing to check in. Hear her voice. See her face. If he wasn't careful, this beautiful, feisty woman would make it hard for him to escape. Go where the wind called him. And after Kunar, he'd vowed never to feel trapped again.

He tossed a couple of logs on last night's campfire and struck a match to the kindling, his mind turning to Button. If Yellowstone hired him, how soon would he start? When he left, would he find someone to take over Vivie's supervision? If he couldn't...

He pulled off his T-shirt and sprinted for the river flowing past his site. Without hesitating, he plunged into the icy water, purposefully keeping his mind blank. Wasn't that the best part of the wilderness? You could think as much or as little as you wanted. No one to order you around, no responsibilities except for your own survival.

He broke the surface and shook the water from his eyes, fighting the current that tugged at his feet. On the opposite bank a mother and fawn emerged from the trees. When they spotted him, they bolted back into the forest, white tails flashing. He swam in the swift water. Had this been even three weeks ago, when spring runoff was at its peak, he wouldn't have attempted it. Spots like this pinned down grown men. And if there was one way he wouldn't go, it'd be getting stuck in one spot again. Ever.

He pulled himself up onto a rocky out-

cropping and swung his feet in the water,
watching minnows dart around his toes. The
strengthening sunshine warmed and dried
him. From the firm, dark brown earth around
him sprang fern fronds, wood vetch and sage.
For a moment he longed for his old guitar,
wanting to serenade this beauty.

After a hasty cup of campfire coffee, he
took down his tent, packed up his SUV, and
headed for Vivie's house. She'd been warned
of unexpected visits. And though 7:00 a.m.
was early, as a diner owner, she should be
up. Plus, he'd like to be there for Button's
first feeding. Not that he didn't think Vivie
capable. The way she'd pitched in this week
had impressed him. He'd seen her stubborn,
sentimental side before. Been on the bad end
of it more than once. But this dogged, determined nature of hers caught him off guard.
There was more to Vivie than met the eye.

He cranked up the radio and lost himself in
an old rockabilly tune, not trusting his mind
to linger on her much longer.

Twenty minutes later, he pulled up to her
farmhouse and rang the bell. After waiting
a couple of minutes, he pushed the button
again, his wave through the side panel window getting only a barking Scooter's attention. Where was she? Her pickup was still

here, so if she wasn't in the house, she must be out back. Had she fed the cub? He strode around the side of her home and eyed the enclosure. No Vivie. He squatted beside the feeding slot and pushed it open, peering inside. No signs of food, either.

Worry gnawed at him. There had to be a logical reason for her disappearance, but he couldn't shake the feeling that something was wrong. Then he saw it. The distinctive, brown-striped hide of a timber rattlesnake, a rare species reintroduced to the Adirondacks over a decade ago. It was especially uncommon at this high elevation, but clearly not impossible. Not when he could see it coiling right outside of Button's shelter.

Had Vivie seen it and run? Would Button know enough to stay inside? He sprinted to his SUV, grabbed a lidded bucket and a pinning hook, and raced back. When he unlocked the first door of the double-entry opening, he froze, watching in horror as Vivie appeared at the small shelter's entrance. If her descending foot didn't stop, she'd step square on the poisonous snake.

He dropped his gear and waved his arms, not wanting to startle the snake with a loud noise, but needing her attention. What the heck was she doing in the enclosure in the first place?

Luckily, she heard him jangle the second padlock and stopped moving at his frantic gesture. Her wide eyes followed his pointing finger down to the snake beneath her foot.

She recoiled, her face stiff and pale. He breathed easier when she disappeared inside again. A few slow steps got him closer to the sunning snake. He'd wrangled a few snakes from garages and beneath back porches. But this was his first deadly reptile, one whose poison could bring down an adult deer.

Another couple of strides nearly had him in striking distance when he heard the distinctive rattle. The snake's angular face lifted and its lidded eyes focused on him. They were staring each other down when Button appeared. His pulse jumped for the innocent animal. Before he could react, a burlap bag flew from the building, smothering the snake. Vivie hurtled after it.

The fool! Did she think her actions would stop such a vicious predator? Taking advantage of the snake's disorientation, he sprang into action, grabbing it with the U-shaped end of his metal rod before it slithered free. It hissed as he held it at arm's length, its body and head whipping from side to side.

"Go inside. Keep Button away," he ordered Vivie. She shook her head and grabbed the bag, approaching him.

"I mean it, Vivie. Back off."

"You'll never get it in the bag without my help."

He had to admit he'd grabbed the snake at a bad spot, far enough down that it could bite if he came at it straight on. Worse, in his hurry, he'd left the bucket on the other side of the gate. If he let go, however, it would slither off the grip. Still, he wouldn't endanger Vivie.

"I'll manage," he ground out, his arm straining to keep the snake steady as it lashed and back and forth.

"Not without me," exclaimed Vivie who tiptoed behind the snake and slid the bag beneath its tail.

"Let it go," she said, a quake in her voice.

"No. You won't be able to keep it in that. It's too flimsy. You could get bitten."

"So could you." When she brought the bag over the snake's midsection, it twisted her way, assessing this new threat. If it managed to turn and face Vivie, she could well and truly be attacked.

Nothing for it.

"Drop the bag!" She let it fall, and Liam

released his grip on the rod then pounced on the writhing burlap, unable to tell where the head was. He grabbed the top, hoping he'd guessed right.

"Get that bucket back there. Quick," he directed. But Vivie had already anticipated him and returned with it.

"Slide it under the burlap, but be careful not to touch the sack. Got it?"

She nodded, appearing composed despite the tremble in her fingers. Brave woman. An overconfident risk taker, too, he reminded himself. One who had defied his direction to leave the bear alone.

In a moment too short to process, they had the snake secured and the lid snapped over the top of the bucket. He wiped his damp brow and peered at her.

"What were you doing in here?"

Her small chin lifted. "Making sure Button's first night was safe." She pointed to the bucket. "Looks like I made the right call."

Left over adrenaline flowed through him. "We both know you broke the rules."

"And if I hadn't, then Button might be dead. But I guess you wouldn't mind that, would you? Since you don't think she's going to make it, anyway."

He recoiled. Sure he had his doubts. But

he hoped the bear would survive. Thrive, even. He'd worked all week to give her this chance.

"If you don't follow procedure, there's a good chance she won't be rehabilitated."

Button's small black face appeared. Beside her, to his dismay, stood Vivie's cat.

"And your animals can't come in here, either."

Vivie sat in the building's entranceway and put an arm around both creatures. "What if I don't agree with your rules?"

He snatched up the bucket handle, incensed by her close call and Button's brush with death.

"Then you'll need to deal with the consequences," he snapped, instantly regretting the words at her harsh intake of breath.

But what did she expect? Policies were in place to protect, not hurt. He eyed the container as he shoved it inside the back of his SUV.

So why was he starting to doubt that now himself? If not for Vivie, Button would have been bitten or dead by the time they'd discovered her. He probably wouldn't have peeked into the enclosure and seen the snake if Vivie had been in the house. Was it possible some rules needed to be broken?

And was the professional distance he'd tried keeping from Vivie one of them?

CHAPTER SEVEN

"ORDER UP! *STILL!*"

The kitchen bell dinged again and Vivie turned, meeting Rowdy's stern gaze, or—as Maggie dubbed it—the "hairy eyeball." Vivie hustled to the pass-through window and grabbed a meat loaf platter and a casserole of macaroni and cheese.

"Sorry, Rowdy. Preoccupied I guess."

"I guess," grumped her taciturn cook. He whipped back to the hissing grills, his pinky swathed in a massive amount of gauze.

Vivie wove through the diner's packed tables, her mind returning to Button. It stung that she hadn't gotten more than a glimpse of the cub in over a week. Shoving food through a slot, listening to the bear scrabble against the spot, made her heart ache. Vivie wanted to be in there, spending time with Button, but how could she do it without incurring Liam's "consequences"? She'd hoped to save a life. Was she ruining it instead? Button must be lonely and miserable.

It should comfort her that at least Button was safer now that Liam had attached boards to the lower part of the chain-link. No more snake visits. But still, Vivie was beginning to wonder if safe was enough, despite Liam's assurances.

An involuntary smile crossed her face as she pictured him hauling lumber and nailing boards within an hour of catching the snake. He was a man who took care of things. Looked after his charges. Despite his stubborn insistence on following the letter of the law when it came to Button, she liked that Liam took his responsibilities seriously. He had good intentions. Just wrong instincts.

She wove through the crowded restaurant and overheard snatches of excited conversation about this weekend's Woodsman Lumberjack Festival. Sam and Randy Trudeau, the area's most renowned trackers and hunters, would be giving workshops alongside a famous outdoor skillet cook and an author autographing his bestselling travel memoir.

Most anticipated of all were the wood-carving and lumberjack competitions.

"I hope they have one of those big wooden bears," said a young boy. He reached his hands overhead and clawed at the air, roaring. At his father's raised eyebrow, the kid subsided and nodded his thanks as Vivie set his food on the table. "I want to learn to carve one someday. Can I have a chain saw?"

His father returned Vivie's smile, then picked up his fork when she set down his meat loaf. "Better leave that to the experts, champ." The dad ruffled his son's hair then squirted ketchup on the boy's plate.

"Is this your first time going to the festival?" Vivie asked as she grabbed their bread basket.

The boy's head bobbed. When he set down his milk, a white film coated his upper lip. "Mom never liked to go camping. But now we're divorced, so Dad says we can come whenever we want."

Vivie's gaze flicked to the man, then dropped. She wished she hadn't glimpsed the pain in his eyes.

"The lumberjacks will be competing in greased pole-climbing and log-throwing competitions," Vivie babbled to fill up the awkward silence. "Plus, fly fishermen will take you out on Tupper Lake and teach you their tricks if you're interested."

The kid bounced in his seat. "Cool. I wish it started today."

"I don't like waiting, either. Have fun, you two." She left the pair, reminded, in a way, of her own childhood. How often had she and her mother eaten in diners when they'd moved? Too many times to count. In some ways, it'd come to feel like a refuge. A temporary haven they'd fled to when another of her mother's disastrous marriages fell apart.

Fingers snapped in front of her nose. "Yoohoo. Orders to take, water glasses to fill." Maggie's uptilted nose wrinkled as she studied Vivie. "Sorry I had to call you in today."

Vivie shook her head. "Margaret's still on maternity and Lauren called in sick. Goes with the territory of owning a diner." She spotted another group at the front door and hustled over to seat them.

Settling them in a booth, she passed out menus and filled water glasses. Then she cleared plates off another table, took a dessert order and placed a bill on a fourth table.

Phew.

She preferred the quiet of baking in her kitchen at home. Being around a lot of people filled her with unease. It unsettled her to feel so many eyes on her, to bump into customers before she saw them, to have her arm tugged unexpectedly. The sensations made her insides curl.

When a hand fell on her shoulder, she jumped.

Maggie's concerned eyes searched hers. "Hey. You okay?"

"I don't know." She thought about confiding in Maggie about her assault. They were close friends. It seemed wrong that Vivie had never shared this with her. But, somehow, talking about it outside of her support group felt dangerous. As if she'd summon her assailants by mentioning them. Moving to this rural area had felt like a clean break and she wanted to keep it that way. Separate lives. No bringing her menacing past with her.

"Maybe I'm just being anxious," she said, kicking aside the darker reason for her unease. "I haven't seen Button all week and it's stressing me out."

They shuffled aside when a customer asked if they were in line for the restroom.

"So see her, Vivie. She chose you. There's a reason for that. Don't forget it."

"I can't risk it. I'm lucky Liam didn't take her after the last time."

"He's been fair, Vivie. You have to give him that."

Vivie nodded, glad that of all the DEC officers, this one had dropped into her life. She no longer saw the heartless officer who'd ordered her to stop feeding winter wildlife. He had been understanding about Button. Given her chances when others wouldn't. And then there was that special way he made her heart twitch whenever she caught sight of him.

"You like him, don't you?" Maggie's small, bow-shaped mouthed curved. "You're turning red."

Vivie jerked, stung. "What? No. Not that way. I mean, he's okay. It's just that...well—"

Maggie wrapped her in a tight hug. "Hey. Don't get worked up. You've got a lot on your plate right now and no need to add Officer Walsh to it. Speaking of whom...there's Liam now."

His tall frame filled the door. The third time this week. Her pulse raced as she took in his angular face and the strong, proud way he stood as his eyes roamed the room.

Had he suddenly developed a liking for pie or was he seeking her out? Not that it should matter. Yet Maggie, who knew her well, had her thinking. Despite their differences, she looked forward to his visits.

Maggie strode off and Vivie watched Liam amble her way. With each step he took she became more self-conscious. If Maggie could read her strange feelings, could Liam, too?

"Hi, Vivie. Thought I'd grab a coffee and some pie before heading back out."

She struggled to return his lazy smile, not

sure if she'd come across as too eager, too happy, or what.

"There's a spot at the counter. I'll send Maggie over to take your order."

His gorgeous eyes studied her. "Are you handling these tables?" He pointed to her station and the man flagging her down with a menu.

"Yes," she admitted.

"Then I'll take a spot there." Liam stretched his impressive body, all female eyes swerving his way. "My back's bothering me and I'd rather have a booth."

"Suit yourself." She turned and marched to the red-faced customer.

She took the irritated patron's order and, as if on autopilot, refilled drinks and delivered meals as her mind turned over her current conundrum. Liam behaved as though their week together had made them friends. As for her, she just needed his cooperation to keep Button safe. But was she lying to herself? Despite her misgivings, she couldn't deny his effect on her.

"What's it going to take to get some service over here?" Liam joked when she passed him for the fifth time.

She drew in a deep breath and stopped by

his table. "Apple or cherry? It's all we have left."

"Cherry. How's Button?"

At his question, she softened. Maggie's accusation had gotten under her skin, making Vivie read way too much into Liam's attention. He was her supervisor and had asked about their charge. Professional responsibility. Nothing more. Weird how, instead of feeling relieved, she felt let down.

She straightened his napkin basket and said brusquely, "Can't say since I haven't seen her much. Good, I guess. Safe, thanks to you."

His smile flashed, making her head swim. "It was a team effort. We make a good pair."

At that, she backed away and knocked into a kid raising his glass of chocolate milk. Darn that Maggie. Her teasing suggestions had wormed under Vivie's skin.

"I'm so sorry!" she exclaimed, mopping up the mess. Her cheeks heated as she felt Liam's eyes on her. She was all elbows and thumbs around him now. Time to get a grip.

No matter how he seemed to affect her, he still stood in the way of getting Button what she needed—companionship and real survival skills. Somehow she had to convince Liam to see her side of things. When she got home tonight, she'd locate other rehabilitators, see what alternatives existed.

There had to be another way.

LATER THAT EVENING, after scouring the internet for a couple of hours, Vivie finally found what she was looking for—Dr. Phillip Vogel, a wildlife biologist and rehabilitator in Maine. He was an acknowledged expert on reintroducing orphaned bears into the wild and his methods made sense to her in a way the DEC's instructions didn't.

She stayed up past three in the morning, reading everything he'd published online, her mind turning over his approach. According to Vogel, young bears needed to be trained in the woods, not left to grow up isolated in an enclosure. Rehabilitators needed to take them on foraging missions where they showed cubs the kinds of things a mother would—most importantly where to find food when it came in season. Otherwise, he argued, the bears wouldn't have the skills they needed to make it on their own when released. They'd grow used to handouts and would search for easy feeding opportunities, including campsite and dumpster raids, putting them in human contact, anyway.

She clicked through picture after picture of

the small, grizzled man in various poses. In one he wore a bee suit and plunged his hand into a tree nest as a cub watched. Another picture showed him with an overturned log, dangling an insect over his mouth while his charge did the same. She shuddered. Maybe she could fake that part.

Before logging off, she sent him an email, asking for advice. Button deserved a real chance at survival if released and Vivie would find a way to give it to her.

If only she could convince Liam to go along with it, or at least not interfere.

THE NEXT MORNING, Liam clicked off his phone and caught his smile in the rearview mirror. What was that about? He'd just called Vivie to tell her he'd be stopping by on his day off. Nothing special. Not enough to make him grin like a thirteen-year-old boy at his first school dance. Yet something about her voice, the energy that pulsed through it, made his foot press on the gas harder than it should. He'd grown used to seeing her. That had to be it. Nothing more.

He wouldn't let it be more.

After slowing his speed, he forced his mind onto practical thoughts. Tomorrow he'd fly to Yellowstone for his interview and he needed to make sure Vivie could hold down the fort on her own. He'd be away for three days. So far, other than that lapse on the bear's first night, she'd been a model rehabilitator-in-training. He should have nothing to worry about, but her impulsive nature and big heart could lead her down the wrong path without him around.

He paused to let a logging truck pass before turning onto the route to Vivie's house. Of course this had nothing to do with him wanting to say goodbye. Visit her one more time. Yet somehow the idea of not seeing her for three days left him with an empty feeling he couldn't shake. It worried him. Was he enjoying his time with her too much?

He suspected he was and it needed to stop. No denying she charmed him more every day. Their fiery debates, her compassion for animals and her courage when facing down a deadly snake intrigued and drew him.

But if things went according to plan, he'd be in Yellowstone soon. He wouldn't let himself regret leaving anything behind, even these strange new feelings for Vivie, his possible attachment. Attached meant stuck and stuck meant no escape. The thought filled him with dread, the sandy winds of Kunar howling in his ear.

No. He'd make a short stop at Vivie's house, ace his interview tomorrow and keep a professional distance from now on.

A few minutes later he pulled up to her white-sided farmhouse and parked in front of the detached garage. Scooter bounded out, his bark loud and friendly.

"Hey, boy," he scratched the dog's ears, then leaned down to rub Scooter's belly when he flopped in the dirt and squirmed. "Full of it today, aren't you?"

The front door squeaked open and Vivie stepped onto the porch. Her caramel-colored hair waved softly around her pretty face and covered the straps of a white lace tank top. Her jean shorts showed off long, tanned legs, and he looked away when he caught himself staring.

"I'm glad you phoned," she called. "I was just on my way out to the Woodsman Lumberjack Festival." She hefted a stack of white boxes and tottered down the steps. He hustled to her side and took the containers from her. The fresh-baked smell of apple and cinnamon wafted from them.

"Are you selling pies?"

She headed back up the stairs and grabbed another stack. "No. They're for the pie-eating contest. Last year, Sister Mary cleaned house, so my money's on her."

"You bet at these things?" He slid the boxes inside the back of her truck.

"Haven't you ever been to one?" The bright sunshine picked up the lighter strands in her hair and the gold flecks in her brown eyes. As she put her stack down, her bare shoulder brushed his arm, making his flesh heat. Overhead, tufts of clouds drifted across the blue sky where wheeling falcons rode air currents.

"No. Heard about it, though. Is it fun?" He usually avoided touristy things like that, but something about the way the subject made her eyes dance and her face relax intrigued him. Charmed him, if he was honest.

"A lot of fun. You should go," she urged over her shoulder as she headed back to the house.

He hurried after her, picking up another bunch of pies. "Are you asking me on a date?"

When the boxes in her arms tilted, he steadied her, his hand lingering on her elbow. She had the softest skin…

"Excuse me?" Her wide eyes met his, a strange, spooked expression in them.

"Bad joke." He kicked himself for the stupid comment. It was obvious she didn't want anything romantic with him. He didn't want it either, he reminded himself. So why did her negative reaction bug him so much?

They labored side by side, filling her cargo bed in awkward silence. At last, without an inch of space left, he slammed the tailgate shut.

"Guess you're all set."

"You can come if you want," she blurted, studying her nails. "To the festival with me." When her eyes lifted, he caught that wary expression again. It filled him with a curious need to protect her, but from what?

"Okay," he agreed, then instantly wished he hadn't. He had stuff to do before his trip. Packing. Paying some bills. Boarding Extra Pickles. Yet all of that faded into the background when he imagined a day with Vivie. One where they weren't arguing about Button for a change.

Speaking of …

"How're things with Button?" Was it his imagination or did a flash of guilt appear in her eyes?

"Good. I think—if my feeding slot views count."

He pulled his baseball hat off and sweat trickled down the back of his neck. Today would be a hot one. A good day to be in the deep forest.

"Then you're doing your job, Vivie. She can't get used to humans."

Vivie squinted up at a couple of ravens alighting on a nearby oak. "Did you know that a bear's sense of smell is seven times keener than a bloodhound's?"

Liam slapped at a mosquito and stared at her, puzzled. "They have the strongest sense of smell of any animal. Why?"

She reached down to pick a dandelion and twirled it in her hand. "Doesn't matter if Button sees me or not. Either way, she knows a human is feeding her. I'd call that interaction. Wouldn't you?"

He found himself staring after her as she hopped into her pickup and started the engine.

AFTER DELIVERING THE pies to the contest station, Liam wandered through the festival with Vivie by his side. The smell of roasted meat and wood smoke hung in the cool air. Locals and tourists wandered amongst booths where artisans displayed their crafts, gardeners sold homemade relishes and a syrup producer passed out maple ice cream and candy. A puppet show captivated a seated group of children while their parents stood behind them, laughing at the old-school Punch-and-Judy-style routine.

A high-pitched chain saw buzz grew louder as they neared a section of animal wood carvings. Shavings snowed around one of the sculptors who demonstrated his technique to avid fans. Vivie edged to the side of the thick crowd. They glimpsed a majestic eagle, half-finished, its wingspan nearly six feet, its head cocked, eyes sharp and knowing. Liam took in the feather detail on the wings and body, the scales on the talons gripping a tree branch. Hard to believe a chain saw created things like this. Liam couldn't take his eyes off the artist as he whizzed around the piece, his helter-skelter white hair pushed back by a red bandana.

"Amazing," Vivie whispered.

The sculptor's chain saw flashed as he lifted it and slashed into another section of the statue, each movement deft and sure.

"It is." Without thinking it through, Liam slipped his hand into Vivie's and tugged. "Let's go see some of the finished ones."

Her hand felt small and fragile in his and he fought the urge to squeeze tight and not let go.

He forced himself to drop her hand. She was getting under his skin in the worst way. Her wide eyes met his and pink rushed to her cheeks. Was his touch affecting her the way hers impacted him?

"A bear!" She pointed to a sculpture of a life-size grizzly, not native to their area. "It looks terrifying."

"They can be. Some have killed humans."

Her small features creased. "But black bears don't kill people."

"It'd be very unusual. Usually they're more interested in eating what's in your cooler than in eating you."

She let out a soft sigh, the floral scent of her perfume as fragrant as the wildflowers springing around their feet.

"Strange that people hunt them."

"They do it for sport. The thrill of the kill."

"Are you a hunter?"

"Some of my friends are, but not me."

Her sudden smile took him by surprise. "Good."

They grinned at each other until a small boy bumped into them, his father in tow.

"Hey. That's the lady from the restaurant! And see, Dad. There's a bear."

The father nodded politely at Liam then gave all of his attention to Vivie.

Moved by some irrational need, Liam stepped in front of him. He held out a hand, his grip extra firm before he released the guy.

"I'm Jack," the man said, shaking out his hand. "And you're Vivie. I remember from your name tag."

She nodded. "Glad to see you two made it. Your son's enjoying the fair."

Jack angled his body, facing Vivie directly and shutting Liam out. "He's had a rough summer."

"I overheard about your divorce," Vivie said, her voice too warm for Liam's peace of mind. "Sorry about that."

The man adjusted his safari-type hat, giving Vivie a sorrowful gaze that irritated Liam. Please. The guy was appealing to Vivie's sympathies. Hitting on her.

Possessiveness forked through Liam, electric and sudden. He slipped his hand into hers and met her startled glance. A grin spread across his face. He was glad he'd staked his claim—even if he had no right to it.

"We should get in line for the author before he sells out of books," Liam said. "Nice to meet you, James."

"It's Jack," the man protested as Liam tugged Vivie away.

She pulled herself free after several steps. "Hey. What was that about?"

Liam forced a casual shrug. "Thought you'd want a copy of the book. That guy climbed all forty-six of the high peaks after turning fifty. Inspiring."

She stepped over a jutting rock and scrutinized him, one eyebrow raised. "If you say so."

He put a hand on her arm and stopped her, curiosity filling him. "Haven't you ever climbed a mountain?"

A shuttered expression stole over her face. "I don't get out much. With the diner and all..."

"You must get days off. And you can't live in the Adirondacks unless you've been on the top of one. It's like, like—" He grappled for the words to describe the awe that struck him when he viewed the world from extreme heights. "Knowing what it must have felt like to create this place."

His eyes tracked a balloon that scuttled along the tree line.

"You should come with me. I've got three more to climb before I make my 46er status."

They joined the line for the scribbling author. "I'm not sure." Her uncertainty made him all the more determined. Maybe if Vivie could better appreciate the wilderness around her, she wouldn't be as reluctant to see Button released when the time came.

"Look. I'm going away for three days, but

when I get back we'll climb Mount Marcy. The hike in leads to a waterfall and picnic area at the base. You'll have time to change your mind there before we climb. What do you say?"

Her teeth caught her bottom lip. "We'll see. How far away are you going?"

He nodded, suspicious of the sudden light in her eyes. Was she planning something with Button? A break with policy?

"Out West. But you still need to follow protocol. Nothing changes."

A kid pulling a carved wooden truck on a string careened into them, pushing Vivie into Liam's chest. His hands slipped around her waist and for a breathless moment they froze, staring at each other. He imagined what it would be like to bend down and cover her lips with his. Would they be as soft as the skin of her shoulder? Softer? She moved away from him slowly and his hands fell to his sides. "They're starting the greased pole–climbing race. We should go." She hurried to a row of upright logs that rose twenty feet in the air.

Trying to shake the image of kissing Vivie out of his head, he caught up to her and put a hand on her arm. "Vivie. You heard what I said, right?"

A horn blew and a wild cheer rose from

the group surrounding the climbers. Men slipped and shimmied up the greasy poles, some using belts for extra leverage, others relying on brute strength. What a spectacle.

"Vivie?" he repeated, needing to hear that she wouldn't do anything that might endanger the cub or herself. His memory of the snake's visit was still too fresh.

She turned and her eyes skimmed past his. "Yes. I heard you."

Suddenly a clanging bell rang out and a man whooped atop one of the poles. The rest slid down, some waving their hands and jeering while others pounded the winner on the back.

"Do you want to go back for the book?" He glanced at the shortened line.

Her hands fiddled with the lace hem of her tank top. "No. Maybe it's better to experience things firsthand than read about them."

She contemplated him for a long moment before turning and heading to a small hill where men hefted logs to toss.

Once again he found himself hurrying after her. Playing catch-up.

Would he and Vivie ever be together...on anything?

CHAPTER EIGHT

Dear Ms. Harris,
What a delight to receive your note. I'd be happy to discuss your situation on the phone at your convenience.
Best regards,
Phillip Vogel, PhD

VIVIE COPIED DR. VOGEL'S contact information from below his electronic signature and powered down her computer. Jinx wove in and out between her legs, fur tickling Vivie's ankles. At last her cat stopped, hunkered down, then sprang onto her lap. She butted Vivie's stomach, arching her back and purring the instant Vivie stroked her.

"What do you think, Jinx? Should I call Dr. Vogel?"

Jinx's good eye closed in bliss, her body now sprawled across Vivie, her nails digging into Vivie's thigh.

"I take it that's a resounding, 'don't care.'" Vivie scooped up her cat and resettled both of them on the couch. She eyed her watch, then the phone. Eight in the morning. Early, but most were up at this time. If he didn't pick up, she could leave a message. Maybe get a call back from Dr. Vogel when he had free time later today. With Liam away, this might be her only chance to connect with Button. Last night, when she'd dropped food through the slot, the cub hadn't come over, and glimpsing her curled up, listless, beneath the tree had filled Vivie with sadness.

Determination made her reach for the phone and dial his number. After four rings, a phlegm-filled cough sounded. She pulled the receiver from her ear until the noise died down.

"Hello?" a voice rasped.

"Dr. Vogel, I'm so sorry to wake you. I'm Vivienne Harris. I was planning to leave a message, but you picked up and now it seems I've woken you and—"

A deep rattling chuckle came through the receiver. "Miss Harris. A pleasure. And please don't get worked up on my account. I've been up for hours with the ferrets. A hobby. You had a question about rehabilitating your orphaned cub?"

Vivie tucked her feet beneath her and settled into the plump cushions. The story

poured from her now that she had a knowl-
edgeable and sympathetic ear.

"And Button doesn't even come to the food
slot anymore," she finished, her voice shaking.

"I'm sorry to hear that, my dear." The gur-
gle of a coffeemaker sounded through the
phone line. She glanced into her kitchen,
wishing she'd thought to start a pot. Jinx kept
up her relentless kneading, working Vivie's
empty stomach like fresh dough.

"Is she—she—giving up?" Vivie choked
out, imagining all that Button had lost. What
would give her the will to go on if she only
had herself for company?

A long sip sounded followed by an *ahh*.
"No. Not that. Not yet, anyway. But you've
called me just in time. Much longer without
contact, and her social skills would be completely lost."

"What do I do? The DEC will take her if I
don't stick to their rules."

"Then you need to show them that you're
right."

She shoved her tangled hair from her face
when Jinx began to bite the ends. "They
won't believe me."

"But they'll believe the results. Follow my
rehabilitation plan whenever you're sure you

won't be discovered. If the officer in charge catches you, remember the media is a powerful tool. A cub about to lose its life because a well-meaning rehabilitator didn't follow the rules is not a headline the DEC wants to see. Trust me. Hopefully it won't come to that, but I'll come and support you should a protest be necessary. I do have a way of attracting national attention." He cleared his throat, sounding pleased with himself.

She couldn't help but find him endearing. Warmth filled her. Here, at last, was the support she wished she'd gotten from Liam. "Thanks, Dr. Vogel. I have one more question if you have time."

"Of course."

"What if I don't release Button? She has a dislocated jaw that's healing slowly. She eats, but strangely—from the side of her mouth. Wouldn't she be safest, and happiest, if she grew up used to the enclosure and me?"

He sputtered for a moment and she wondered if he'd swallowed wrong. "Dr. Vogel?"

Scooter scratched at the door then turned to glare at her. She held up a finger, hoping he could wait to go out.

"Yes. Sorry about that. I was taken aback by your comment, Miss Harris. The jaw will need to be watched, but never forget that the animals' natural habitats, not ours, are their homes. Being safe does not guarantee quality of life."

She thought of the carefully constructed world she'd made for herself, far from the danger that'd nearly killed her in New York City. It'd brought her happiness, but lately she'd felt less satisfied. Dividing her time between home and the diner, rarely venturing elsewhere, closing out others—even Maggie to an extent—wasn't really a fulfilled life.

Yet she couldn't imagine her life without those protective limitations. She remembered the electric feel of Liam's hand in hers at the Woodman's Lumberjack Festival. It had felt good. Right. But she wasn't ready for a relationship...might never be ready. Not when it meant making herself vulnerable. Especially with Liam. He'd slipped past her guard so easily that it petrified her.

"Miss Harris?" The scientist prompted her.

Gently dislodging her cat, she carried the phone with her, unlocked the front door and let Scooter out. Before she could shut it, kamikaze Jinx streaked through the narrowing crack. Two pets down. Her mind returned to Button. One to go...

"Yes. I see your point."

"But you don't completely agree."

"I—" She hesitated, not wanting to lie to this kind man. "I guess I don't. She can have a good life here and never want for anything, not have to struggle for survival with a misshapen jaw."

She eyed the coffeemaker through the kitchen archway, wishing her phone cord reached it. Why had she gone with a vintage replica over practicality? A cordless would have meant caffeine.

"A good life for whom?" Dr. Vogel's voice was soft but pointed, and Vivie felt herself flush. Was he suggesting she was thinking selfishly? He must know the challenges that Button could face on her own in the woods if she had a handicap.

"For both of us," she replied, though she acknowledged it sounded more like a question than a statement. Was she less certain than she thought? Surely she would never let Button go unless she was completely sure the cub had every chance of thriving.

"I see." She heard the sound of a match being struck, and after a few exhales, Dr. Vogel's voice returned. "Vivie, your heart is in the right place. Why don't you begin with bringing native food to her enclosure? Demonstrate the right kinds of things to eat.

Maybe hide things and show her how to find them."

Her tight shoulders relaxed. That she could do and it'd give her an excuse to spend time with Button...if she wasn't caught.

"Okay."

"So what's on the menu for today?" Dr. Vogel asked, a smile in his voice.

Her head drooped, knowing what eating season it was according to Dr. Vogel's website.

"Bugs."

LATER THAT MORNING, after delivering her baked goods and checking that Maggie had a full staff, Vivie entered Button's cage.

She caught no sight of the cub and peered into the small wooden shelter. It touched her to see Button's small, dark sides heaving as she slept, the rubber turtle in her mouth. Good. It'd give Vivie time to clean up the enclosure before she tried her feeding experiment.

She peered at the gray sky, the green trees muted to olive and khaki without the sun. Still, it was a pretty spot. Would Button grow to love it or yearn for more if she stayed here for good?

Vivie walked the enclosed area, scooping

up scat and dropping it in a bucket. To her dismay, she saw that none of the other toys she'd bought had been touched. What had Button's long days been like in here? She peered at the three boarded-up walls, the other now half-covered. If she was stuck in here alone, she'd go insane. How had Button coped?

A grunt behind her made Vivie whirl. At the doorway to her shelter stood Button, the rubber turtle dangling from her mouth. Her heart swelled when the cub leaped down and galloped her way. She skidded to a halt, but crashed into Vivie's legs, anyway, knocking her down. Dirt flew up around them.

"Hey, Button!" Vivie sat up and held out her arms, hoping the bear would crawl into her lap. Instead she sniffed Vivie's feet, casting a wary eye over her and jittering away at any slight movement she made.

Poor thing. Her time alone had cost the cub. Button's fur was matted, her size a fraction smaller, and she'd lost her playful, adventurous spirit.

Vivie kept herself very still when Button moved higher up, snuffling along Vivie's rib cage and even her armpit. At last, the cub reached its front paws up to Vivie's shoulders, her nose inches from Vivie's.

She kept her expression calm, despite the

pain she felt beneath those sharp claws. Button needed to get to know her again and, in
an instant, Vivie vowed that separations like
this week would never happen again. She was
Button's pet mom—or wild animal mom.
Time to start acting like a caregiver instead
of a DEC policy enforcer.

She was here for an animal, not a bureau-
cratic institution. If Liam caught her, then
she would call in the press. Raise the alarm
with animal lovers everywhere. She'd find a
way to keep Button safe from predators. How
sad that her number-one danger was humans.
Vivie shuddered. She could relate.

At last, Button's wet nose found its way
to Vivie's ear and, unable to hold back, she
hugged the cub. Button's warm belly pressed
against Vivie and shook. From fear, relief or
both? she wondered. Vivie pressed her cheek
against the bear's as a tear slid down her face.

"I'm sorry, Button," she whispered. "I'm
not leaving you again. Ever."

As if she understood, the cub settled on her
four paws, picked up her turtle and showed
it to Vivie.

"Is this your friend?" She gingerly reached
out and touched the heavy-duty rubber. "She
seems nice." When Button opened her jaws,
the slimy toy slid across Vivie's palm. "Thank

you." Then inspiration struck as she eyed Button's dull coat. "You know what turtles really love? The water."

She jumped up and ran to the small waterfall and pond, tossing in the turtle then leaping after it. The shallow, cold water nearly knocked the wind out of her, but she kept her composure. This was supposed to be fun, so she splashed around with the turtle, making it zoom across the rippling surface.

Button galloped after her and stopped on the pond's edge. She leaned in for a drink, but otherwise watched Vivie cavort. The bear's angled face practically shouted, "You look nuts, lady!"

And maybe she was, but Button needed to see all of the fun things to do in the enclosure. This could be her home for life. As much as Vivie understood the bear should learn to fend for herself if released, her first priority was making Button love it here.

Vivie floated the turtle close to Button. When the cub reached out a paw, Vivie zoomed the toy farther out so Button had to stretch until—

Sploosh.

A wave of water erupted around Vivie as Button hit the water. Her paws scrabbled through the liquid, her face dipping below the surface. Before Vivie could reach her, however, Button steadied herself and blew a stream of water from her mouth, the gesture so comical, Vivie laughed. The cub reached her turtle, scooped it up in her mouth then made for the rocks where she pulled herself up and regarded Vivie.

"Did you like that?"

Button lowered her head to the water then slid, on her belly, into the pond again.

Vivie bounced back a few steps. The cub was still small, but it didn't pay to get that close to a splashing bear with its claws out.

Button circled, her chin touching the water, small nose pointed skyward.

"Feels good, right?" It was a humid day and the gnats were already out in full force.

Now that Button seemed settled, Vivie got out of the water. She watched avidly as the cub played a game with the turtle. Button pushed it beneath the surface then snatched the toy with her mouth when it rose, shaking it as if she'd caught a fish. She missed more often than she succeeded, her jaw working awkwardly, but she pranced a bit with every "catch."

Cute. Practical, too. She'd need to be able to catch fish if returned to the wild. Fear snaked through Vivie as she imagined a hungry Button struggling to catch enough trout. An upcoming vet visit would tell them more about Button's jaw. If it'd healed properly, she'd be released in September. If her mouth didn't work effectively, however, Vivie would need to think of a strategy to keep Button permanently. Only a little over eight weeks to figure it out...

She got to her feet and paced, her mind turning over possibilities. Minutes later a dripping Button joined her, disrupting her thoughts. Button followed Vivie and they stopped at the tree with the rubber tire.

"Have you tried this yet?" She peered at the unblemished swing and guessed not.

Vivie swung herself up onto a tree branch and Button followed her, scrambling up the trunk. Vivie clambered up a few more branches and sat inside the leafy fortress. Below, Button's black face appeared and, in a moment, the bear joined her on the thick limb.

"It's nice up here. I used to have a big tree like this in a backyard once." Vivie puzzled over which of her mother's marriages that'd been, which house that'd never really belonged to her. She sighed and studied the area. It didn't matter, she supposed. This was her home now, one that could be Button's, too. If the bear wasn't fit for release by Vivie's

judgment, no one could take Button away.
Vivie smoothed a hand down the bear's back.

Not even Liam.

LIAM HOPPED OUT of his SUV a couple of days
later, his pulse speeding too fast for just a routine visit to a rehabilitator.

But this wasn't any wildlife caregiver, a
voice whispered, it was Vivie.

He'd cut his Yellowstone trip short for reasons he couldn't even explain to himself. He'd
planned to camp out one of the days, take in
the sights. Instead, his mind had returned to
the Adirondacks and the woman and bear in
his charge. Had he rushed here out of a sense
of responsibility or something more?

He was heading around back when he
heard noises. A squeal turned his brisk walk
into a sprint and in seconds he'd reached the
cage, jerking open each door and bursting
into the enclosure.

To his shock, Vivie sat inside holding a
wriggling centipede over her mouth. Button
watched then scooped insects from one of the
rotten logs Vivie must have dragged inside.

"Liam!" Vivie scrambled to her feet, a hand
splayed across her chest. Even in the over-
cast morning, she seemed to grab the light.

Her hair tawny, her skin gold. "What are you doing here?"

"I should ask the same," he ground out, his ire rising that, once again, she'd gone back on her word. Or had she even given it to him at the festival? She'd heard him. He remembered her acknowledging that much. He should have pressed her further. Gotten her vow.

Button raced behind Vivie and poked her face around Vivie's back to watch him. Did he intimidate the cub? Good. Or at least, it should feel right since she needed to be afraid of people who might shoot her. Still, he didn't like frightening the young animal.

"Let's continue this inside." Without a backward glance, he strode out of the enclosure and headed for Vivie's house, pausing to toss the ball Scooter dropped at his feet.

Vivie closed the kitchen door when she joined him, her expression defiant.

"I thought you weren't coming back until tomorrow." She gestured for him to take a seat, but he stood by her pantry instead, his hands clenched behind his back. By all rights, he should confiscate the cub now. Vivie had proven more than once that she wouldn't follow the rules.

"I'm sure you didn't. What were you doing inside the enclosure again?"

She pulled out a pitcher of iced tea and poured them each a glass. When she passed him one, he noticed her steady hands. Shouldn't she be nervous? Scared of the consequences? He hated thinking of it, yet she looked calm.

After a long drink, she lowered her cup. "I was feeding Button."

"But not through the slot."

"She can't learn to eat the right things that way. I need to teach her."

His drink sloshed when he gestured. "Animals act on instinct."

"The larger the mammal, the more dependent they are on a parent. Bear cubs stay with their mothers for two years sometimes. I read that on Dr. Philip Vogel's website."

Philip Vogel? How had she heard of the animal behaviorist? Liam had picked up a book by the doctor a few months ago but hadn't gotten around to reading it yet. "You're not her mother."

"I'm the nearest Button's got." Her eyes darkened, the lighter flecks disappearing.

"Not anymore," he forced himself to say. "I'm taking the cub. Today."

Her face paled. "Not happening."

He stared at her, admiring her tenacity, despite his frustration. "You're a danger to her well-being."

"And shooting her will be taking such better care of Button."

His mouth fell open before he caught himself. He hadn't planned on harming the bear. Had hoped Wendy and Steve might agree to take it for a couple of days while he figured things out...but Vivie was right. The chances of finding a refuge on such short notice, or at all, were very slim. Ultimately, he would probably have to put Button down; the thought rolled through him, heavy and dark.

"Better than letting her walk right up to a hunter and get shot."

"Sounds like the same end, either way," she fired back, her hands curling as she leaned on the table. Color returned to her face, the blood brightening her cheeks.

She had him there. But still...these were his department's methods. Not to be questioned... or should they be?

As if sensing his indecision, she pulled him to her living room and tapped on her keyboard, bringing up Dr. Vogel's home page. The cover photo, him dangling an insect over his mouth as a cub watched, mirrored Vivie's earlier action.

"I spoke to Dr. Vogel and he's had more

success reintroducing bears to the wild than any other rehabilitator in the country."

"Or luck."

"Not luck. He's a scientist who's researched animal behavior, particularly that of bears, for decades. He promised to come here, accompanied by every media outlet he can get hold of, if you try to take Button."

Her words shoved him like he'd been slapped. "Are you threatening me?"

"Aren't you threatening Button?"

"No. I'm doing what's right."

"And so am I. Why don't you help me instead of blocking me?"

He scrutinized her askance. Did she think he'd go against his department's regulations? He'd lose his job. Then again, he had just been offered one in Yellowstone. And their rehabilitation regulations resembled what he saw on Dr. Vogel's web page. His current employer didn't have all the answers. Maybe—just maybe—Vivie had a point.

"If I help you with this plan, and that's a big if, it means we'll be working together to achieve the bear's eventual release. Do you support that?"

She swallowed, uncertainty flickering in her eyes for the first time since he'd arrived. "I can't promise that until I'm satisfied her jaw is no longer an issue. But I know it's important to show her the kinds of food she'll need to find if she's forced back into the wild. And shoving them through a slot won't cut it."

"Neither will sitting in her enclosure and having a picnic." He raked a hand through his hair. "Vivie. If you plan to follow Dr. Vogel's methods, you can't do them halfway. Otherwise you're just playing house with a pet."

"No I'm not," she snapped. Her desk chair spun around and she glared up at him.

"Think about it. You're sharing meals, playing, napping together...not the actions of someone raising an animal to be wild."

"But I don't want her to be—"

He raised an eyebrow and waited for her to see how unreasonable she was being.

A long sigh took the air right out of her. "Fine. Then what do you suggest?"

"I'm not agreeing with Dr. Vogel's methods yet. I'll need to talk to him. Read more. But if we do this, I need your full commitment. We'll take Button into the wild and show her how to find her food and other survival needs. Expose her to what life as a bear is like, not life as a house pet."

She studied him for a long time. "I'm not sure I can do that."

He swallowed hard, wishing she'd accept

this olive branch. Did she know how much he risked by even contemplating her crazy scheme? "And why is that?"

"I don't like leaving home."

"If you're worried about more poachers, they're rare and never this close to towns. It's highly unlikely we would encounter any."

She shook her head, her eyes wide. "I don't like leaving home."

He stared at her. Confused. "You go to the diner."

"That is home," she said quietly. "And the Woodsman's Day is something Maggie took me to long ago to deliver the pies...but that's it except for the supermarket and the vet's."

Suddenly he realized they weren't talking about Button. This was personal. Something kept her from leaving her carefully constructed habitat. What? He turned over possibilities, but held himself back from asking.

Like Button's enclosure, if her world was this narrow, she needed more. By getting Button out into the wild, he might help Vivie, too. He wondered why that mattered to him as much as it did.

Feeling warm, he reached up and pulled the chain on her ceiling fan. "I could take Button on my own, but she'd do better with you near."

Vivie bit her lower lip, her jaw tight. "How far would we go?"

"In search of food? Hard to say. Could be miles." He wasn't going to sugarcoat it. Maybe, if he made this difficult enough, she'd change her mind and back down. But somehow he didn't want her to. Despite his training, he recognized the sense in Dr. Vogel's approach.

The clock chimed and they studied each other, tension stretching between them.

At last she nodded.

"For Button, I'm in."

CHAPTER NINE

THE ROSE AND LAVENDER sky held the promise of a beautiful June day. Vivie zipped up her sweatshirt against the morning breeze and shivered with nervous anticipation. After four days, Liam finally had time off to take Button out with her. She eyed the clouds drifting across the lightening horizon and wondered. Everything seemed too perfect for something to go wrong, but her mind ran over every possible danger.

Number one—what if Button ran away? Dr. Vogel had assured her, during last night's chat, that the cub might venture, but she would always follow the person she saw as a mother figure. Number two—what if they encountered something bigger than Button, a male bear that might attack? Dr. Vogel had tried to ease that concern, too. Black bears weren't typically aggressive.

Typically. Vivie chewed on the inside of her cheek, her fingers pressing tight against the sides of her legs.

And most scary of all—what if there were poachers camped out there? Shooting at anything that moved? Liam had assured her they were rare, but worry still filled her.

Liam's tires crunched along her gravel driveway and she stepped off her porch. Now or never. Dewy grass clung to her ankles as she headed to meet him. Hopefully the strengthening sun would dry the woods before they got too far.

Goose bumps rose on her arms. How much distance would they travel? The terrifying notion had kept her up most of the night. But she had to do this for Button. Another part of her couldn't resist the idea of spending a day with Liam. Deep down, she knew he'd keep them safe.

The officer's handsome face appeared as he emerged from his SUV, his dark hair set off by a light blue T-shirt. He also wore shorts that stopped above his knees and his hiking boots looked much more practical than her sandals. He smiled when he caught sight of her and a glow, like a struck match, flared inside. Was he happy to see her or eager for this adventure?

She fought the urge to jog over, not wanting to appear as excited to see him as she felt. Instead, she meandered, breathing in the fresh wildflower- and pine-scented air. The trees resounded with waking birds, their tweets and calls breaking the hush. Scooter bounded out of some brush and a quail squawked skyward. Her dog's square head swiveled from side to side and his tail drooped. Poor buddy. Since he couldn't hear, he'd lost the element of surprise. She eyed her galloping pet as he neared, wondering if he'd ever had it. For a gaming dog, he lacked—er—game.

"Hey, Scoots!" Liam hunkered down and held up a large rawhide "bone." Quail forgotten, Scooter's ears pricked forward and he nearly knocked Liam over when he grabbed for the treat.

"Sit!" Vivie gestured with her hands until her pet looked over, then signaled for him to get down. She didn't want Scooter losing all of his manners around company. Although the more time she spent with Liam, the less he seemed like a stranger and the more he felt like a—a…well, there was no need to label Liam. But the word *enemy* no longer seemed to apply.

Especially for her rambunctious dog. With satisfaction, she watched her Lab drop his butt to the ground. His sweeping tail cleared an arc of pine needles and pebbles. Overhead, a towering red maple rustled crimson against the bruised sky.

"Good boy," crooned Liam, even though Scooter couldn't hear him. He stroked her dog's head and lifted his eyes to hers, their sparkling delight setting off that strange fluttering sensation in her stomach. He was so good with her animals. Showered them with attention when others dodged their exuberant affection.

It'd been a long time since she'd noticed a man this way. In fact, after the assault, it'd been a hard road to feel at all comfortable around men again. But something about Liam, as angry as he made her at times, cut though her guard. Strangely, he made her feel safe.

She eyed the woods. Would that keep her from having a panic attack once she lost sight of her home—of civilization? It'd be humiliating to make a fool of herself. Plus, she might scare Button.

Liam reached into his SUV, donned a backpack and sauntered over to join her.

"Ready for this?"

No, she thought. But she nodded, anyway.

One side of his mouth lifted. "Good. This should be fun. I finished Dr. Vogel's book last night and, since it's berry season, we'll forage for them with Button today."

Sounded harmless enough. "Okay. Should I put Scooter inside?"

Liam nodded. "Probably a good idea. He might chase after a porcupine or do something else that could take our focus off Button."

She headed to her front door and pulled it open. Once she caught Scooter's attention, she gestured for him to go inside. "Button won't go after anything like that, will she?"

Scooter brushed by her, bone in mouth, as Jinx leaped over his back and raced across the yard to some distant bushes. The life of a pet owner. Never dull...

Liam pulled out his water bottle and uncapped it. "No. Bears are more opportunistic. If we see a dead animal she might get interested, though."

Luckily he was too busy drinking to notice her shudder. She didn't want him thinking she was squeamish, not up to the job. Though, for her, this "introduce Button to the wilderness" venture was just an excuse to spend time with the cub. She didn't really believe they'd release the bear.

"After you put on proper foot gear, let's get Button. Sandals won't cut it on a hike." He stowed his water and walked to the enclosure. Minutes later, boots on, she joined him at the pen. They had a devil of a time trying to get Button outside.

"See?" Vivie gasped. She leaned against the fence holding her aching sides. "She likes it in here. Doesn't want to leave."

Liam shook his head, his jaw firm. "She just doesn't know what she's missing. Go outside and call her."

Vivie eyed Button. She crouched beneath the maple tree, her eyes large and her mouth open as her sides heaved. Poor, stressed-out cub.

"Maybe we should do this another day."

"I have tomorrow off, too, but it won't make a difference. It's now or never."

With a sigh, Vivie headed for the gates and called for Button. Luckily, the cub had dropped Turtle during their chase and Vivie grabbed it before leaving the pen. She waved it overhead.

"Button! Come on. Want to play with me and Turtle?"

Liam stayed motionless at the opposite end of the space and Button warily took a few steps toward the exit.

Vivie swam Turtle in the air. "Look at this. Turtle likes it out here. You will, too. Come on."

Button gave a couple of short barks, then

galloped across the grassy area and stopped at the fence's opening.

"Come on, girl. We're going to have a fun day berry picking."

Button stepped outside and turned her head from side to side, each paw placed as carefully as if she walked on hot coals.

"See. It's not so bad," Vivie soothed. A part of her wanted to scream, "No. Go back where it's safe," but she'd promised Liam.

The metallic click of the shutting door startled the bear. She whipped around, spotted Liam and backed toward Vivie. Once the bear was in reach, Vivie rested a hand on the Button's trembling head. "It's okay. He's a friend." *One who almost shot you*, she added silently. *Who might still do so...*

Best to remember that.

Liam reached into his backpack and pulled out a bag. "Want some?" When he extended a palm full of raspberries, Button's nose flared, inhaling the strong, sweet smell.

Button peered at Vivie, back at the berries, then up at Vivie again.

"Let's check out what Liam brought us." Vivie closed the distance between them, plucked a piece of fruit from Liam's hand, and dropped it into her mouth. The tart sweetness made her suck in her cheeks.

"Yum. Good," she forced out. Liam's twinkling gaze met hers and she couldn't resist smiling. It was hard to remember every strike against him when he stood so tall and handsome, his face kind, gestures thoughtful.

Button nosed Liam's palm and her pink tongue flashed. In seconds, she devoured the treat and sniffed frantically for more.

"Like those, huh?" Liam stroked her head, then moved away. "Follow Vivie and me and we'll help you find more."

With that, he turned on his heel and headed through a gap in the thick tree line that surrounded Vivie's backyard. Button shuffled close to Vivie and waited. Vivie peered at the dense foliage, feeling a quiver of fear spread from the pit of her stomach all the way up her spine.

She'd wanted a house on an isolated property but, until now, had never wanted to explore the surroundings. Seeing Button look so excited, however, gave her courage. They'd have a good day together.

Her gaze lingered on Liam's vanishing back. *Together* being the most important word of all.

LIAM FOLLOWED VIVIE and Button as they ascended a dirt path in the forest. Everything smelled of fresh leaves, blossoming flowers and green wood. Bees hummed and wasps droned, filling the fragrant stillness with their murmur. But what captured his attention most was the beautiful woman wandering ahead. Her dark blond hair fell full and long across her shoulder blades. Her back nipped into a narrow waist, her hips flaring just enough to make his hands itch to span them.

He forced his eyes away. He had no business admiring what he couldn't have. He'd been offered the Yellowstone position. Although he hadn't given them his decision yet, accepting the new job was a foregone conclusion. Three years in one spot was enough. After meeting Vivie, however, his need to leave had stopped its persistent clamor. Was it because he felt responsible for the bear, or something more personal? Was he developing feelings for Vivie?

He listened to her steady chatter as she talked to Button, liking the easy rise and fall of her voice. It soothed the restlessness in him. When he was around her, something tight inside him relaxed for the first time since he'd left Kunar. While she drove him crazy over Button, he knew she wanted to do right by the animal. As a conservation officer, he had to admire that about her, even if she was sometimes misguided.

He stepped over a fallen tree and his boot landed in a muddy patch before snagging on a tree root, pitching him to one knee. Vivie's boots, he noticed, remained dry, her feet firmly on the ground. With luck, the rest of today's excursion would go as smoothly for her.

If all went as planned, the foraging missions would help Vivie accept Button's release this fall. When he'd explained that to his boss, and let him know about Dr. Vogel's media threat, his supervisor had given his grudging permission. They could break policy as long as Liam was present during the outings and he kept this to himself.

With everything in place, Liam was ready to experiment. After reading Dr. Vogel's compelling arguments, he actually looked forward to trying his techniques.

He swatted a nagging horsefly. The buzzing insect reminded him that he'd forgotten the repellent. "Wait, Vivie!" He caught up to her and pulled out a canister. "Hold out your leg."

She peered at him beneath raised brows. "Excuse me?"

He shook the bug spray. "For ticks."

"Oh." She extended a sweetly curved calf and he took his time spraying the back and front of each leg.

"You've done that part three times now," she said, a hint of laughter in her voice.

"Right." He coated himself then stowed the can. "Safe now."

She wrapped her slender arms around her waist and shivered. "I hope so." Suddenly her eyes got big and she turned in a circle. "Where's Button?"

"She won't have wandered far. I'll find her." Fear raced through him. Focusing on the bear was his priority and he'd dropped the ball.

"Button!" hollered Vivie as she sprinted farther up the trail.

Liam began to follow then stopped, reason returning. The cub was small but would leave a noticeable trail. He scouted the area, found a bent brush and a paw print on the side of the path and tracked, working slowly so as not to miss the route she'd taken.

"Button!" he heard Vivie shout again, fainter now. At that rate, Vivie would make it up to Poke-O-Moonshine's peak before she turned back. Still, he didn't want to call out to her in case she accidentally walked through the trail he followed, disturbing signs of the bear's passage.

A bit of black fur dangled from a low branch and he headed in that direction. It surprised him that the bear would wander this far. Yet Button was a wild animal. Predictions rarely panned out. He pushed through more brambles, following faint paw impressions and bent branches. A scrabble of claws on stone told him he was closing in.

Just as he caught site of a round, black rump, it disappeared again into a meadow and he pulled up short.

The trees rimming the grassy spot held still under the blue sky, their limbs outstretched to receive the sun's rays. Flowers unfolded like red, white and yellow stars on shrubs and bushes on the clearing's edge. Small birds twittered and clung to the tall, waving grass, taking flight as Button tramped past. She headed, if Liam wasn't mistaken, toward a raspberry patch.

"You found her," gasped Vivie beside him, the hand she placed on his arm warm.

"She followed her nose." He nodded at Button who stretched up on her back legs and nosed through the red clumps dangling from a bush.

"Wow." Vivie waded through the grass and

Liam followed, studying the ground ahead of her in case any snakes lurked. It was unlikely they'd find another timber rattler, but it paid to be careful.

"You found this on your own, Button!" Vivie plunked down on the grass by the bushes and began pulling off the plump berries. Her eyes closed when she put a couple in her mouth, her expression blissful.

Liam couldn't stop staring at her delicate features, his eyes tracing the curve of her cheeks, the fine arch of her brows and the narrow point of her chin. When she wasn't mad at him, she was gorgeous. And when she was, she got even cuter. But her beauty had nothing to do with why he looked forward to seeing her. There was no easy answer for that. Or at least, not one he'd let himself nail down.

"This is heaven," she sighed as he dropped his backpack to the ground and sat beside her. They glanced at each other sideways, eyes skidding away from meeting.

"Close enough." He watched Button stick her face into the bushes, the grunts and sideways chomping making him smile. Although the fruit fell out of her angled mouth as much as it stayed inside, she gobbled plenty. "Hungry bear."

Vivie opened her eyes and stared at him,

her expression languid. "I'm glad we did this."

He nodded and tossed back a few berries. Being with Vivie felt as peaceful as his solo campouts and hikes. Usually he wanted to get away from the world, from people. But not her...

"Why haven't you hiked up here before? Tourists travel from around the world to access the kinds of trails you have in your backyard."

Her open expression grew pinched. "Not really much of an outdoors person."

He pondered her love of animals and wondered if that could be true. "You moved up from the city. Why'd you leave?"

She rolled onto her stomach and laid her cheek on her crossed arms. "I inherited the house from my aunt and wanted to get away. Something different."

Her short answer sounded truthful, but he sensed she held back. What did she hide? A troubled relationship? Financial problems?

"The Adirondacks are a far cry from city life. Wild. Rugged."

"Yeah. Remote, too. I like that."

He strained to hear her muffled words.

"Makes sense since you isolate yourself, so much."

She sat up, her nostrils flaring. "Excuse me?"

He shrugged and dropped some berries into his plastic bag. "You don't get out much. Like you said...it's either work or home. Even the festival was a diner-related thing."

Her gaze dropped after a moment and she nodded. "True. I just like going to places I know."

Her voice reminded him of a bruise, tender and wounded. It made him reach for her hand and turn it over in his palm. "Why is that?"

Her fingers grew cold. "Let's drop it."

But he couldn't.

"If something's bothering you, I'm a good listener." Anything Vivie had to say, he was all ears. Especially if it was about this strange aversion to leaving her "safe" spots.

She lowered her head, hiding her expression. "I appreciate that, Liam." She squeezed his hand, then let go. "But it's in the past."

"Is it?" He knew he shouldn't persist, but Vivie's thinking was distorted. Whatever she'd tried leaving in the Bronx had followed her, anyway. She needed to see that.

Vivie held her hair off her neck, fanning the air with the ends, her eyes fixed straight ahead. "Can we switch topics now?"

He heard the slight tremble in her voice. She'd been pushed far enough. Before he left, though, he hoped she'd open up. It wasn't his business, but it felt that way. He wanted to help.

"How many berries do you think Button can eat?"

She turned to him with a small smile, sadness lurking in her eyes. "Who knows? She's already gone through this whole section, but a lot of it's on the ground."

"No signs of slowing down, either."

They both watched the greedy cub. Button kept one paw on Turtle, dragging her friend along as she trailed beside the bushes. Her rooting and chewing showed no signs of letting up, her determination to eat despite her stiff jaw impressing him.

"Can she get sick from too much fruit?" Vivie plucked wild daisies and buttercups along with pink-topped clover. She brought the fragrant bunch to her nose and tipped her chin to the sky.

His pulse picked up when she suddenly handed him the wildflower bouquet.

"She might get tired, but sick? No. And what are these for?" His voice sounded gruff.

"Just wanted to thank you for going along with this." She poked his arm with another flower. "I hope I'm not putting your job in jeopardy."

He shook his head, staring down at the flowers. When was the last time someone gave him a gift? His sister Mary Ann always sent a card on his birthday. Christmas? Only kids hung stockings. For some reason, this simple gesture touched him, as did her concern for his job. "I have permission, so all set."

She blinked at him, clearly surprised. "They're okay with you not following policy?"

"It's more like they're not okay with Dr. Vogel and his entourage descending on us. Plus, as long as I'm with you, my boss felt there'd be no harm."

"Hope he's right," she muttered, her chin lowering again.

He lifted it with a gentle finger and gazed down at her. "You're always safe with me."

For some odd reason, her eyes welled and a tear clung to her lashes.

He brushed the wetness away with his thumb, his hands lingering and cupping her face.

"I'm never safe," she whispered, her voice so low he had to bend closer to hear.

"I'll protect you," he found himself saying, a gallant and reckless offer considering his planned move. Still, a fierce urge to reassure her filled him. A need to kiss her full lips followed.

He captured them with his own, tasting berries, and something sweeter still. He buried his hands in her silky hair and brought her close, an insatiable hunger taking hold. The wildflower smell of her enveloped him and her mouth tantalized his. He nibbled on her lower lip, loving her soft exclamation of pleasure. Or was it surprise? She was early-spring sunshine, a spring-fed pond, a mountain peak and everything that'd ever made him glad to be alive.

Without warning, she jerked away and sprang to her feet, backing away until her legs brushed the bushes.

"What's wrong?"

Her face had lost all color and she looked as if she might faint. She shook her head, her hand rising to cover her mouth.

Regret snuffed out his elation. He shouldn't have moved so fast. Or at all, darn it. "Did I offend you? I'm sorry. Blame it on a beautiful day. A lonely bachelor. A stupid one."

Button appeared at Vivie's feet. She stretched up on her hind legs, put her paws on Vivie's sides and pressed her face against her caregiver's stomach. If Button wasn't a wild animal, he'd think the young bear sensed

Vivie's mood. Was trying to console her. He'd comfort Vivie, too, if she didn't seem ready to bolt.

"I'm an idiot, Vivie." He got to his feet, feeling like a consummate jerk for kissing her without any signs she'd welcome it. But for a moment, when she'd kissed him back, it'd seemed as though...

He shook his head. Women had the final say when it came to what they wanted. He should have been more sensitive. Not given in to impulses. "Please. It won't happen again." And he meant it. She was upset. Had a right to be. If he had any sense, he'd know kissing her was wrong for him, as well. Soon he'd be across the country. His attraction to Vivie was irrational.

"Vivie, talk to me."

She stumbled away, Button sticking by her side, the cub's turtle dangling from her mouth.

He ducked in front of her, unwilling to let the moment end badly. "What can I do?"

She wiped her nose and met his gaze. "Just stay away." Without another word, she returned to the trail.

It took all of his willpower not to chase after her. He'd follow at a distance instead, staying far enough behind to ensure she got home safely. But it wasn't enough. He wanted things back to normal again. If that was possible.

Strange that she'd said the same words he repeated to himself whenever Vivie came to mind—*stay away*.

Yet the more time he spent with her, the harder that became. His emotions for this complicated woman deepened every day. He could deny it all he wanted, but he cared about her.

The job in Yellowstone came to mind. He wouldn't put off his decision any longer. As soon as he got home, he'd let them know. Escape before his feelings lashed him down forever.

Vivie was right.

Except for when it came to Button, he'd stay away.

CHAPTER TEN

VIVIE MOVED THROUGH The Homestead on autopilot, replacing ketchup bottles, refilling napkin holders and sliding their daily specials sheet inside menus. Her body moved, but her mind remained locked in place, replaying her humiliating reaction to Liam's kiss.

He must think her crazy...or crazier, since she hadn't given a great impression from the start. After yesterday, though, she wondered. Since he'd kissed her, he must like her. Did she dare admit that she felt the same way?

She pictured the amused and exasperated way he looked at her, how he challenged and called her out, and his thoughtfulness at the most unexpected times. Something about him drew her. Made her want to be near. Still. They would never be on the same page about Button. Worse, her reaction to his kiss proved she wasn't ready to be that close to a man. Even Liam.

It'd taken years to see herself as a survivor. To make peace with what had happened.

But Liam made her restless, dissatisfied with the careful way she picked through life. How much farther from her comfort zone did she dare venture? Button and Liam had shaken the world she'd constructed, and she chafed at its parameters now.

A large man in a plaid shirt waved her down, breaking her from her thoughts.

She wove through the tables to a booth by the window. Sunlight streamed through the half-open blinds, glinting off the gold specks in the Formica top. "Hi, Pete. How was the vow renewal? Did you fit into your suit?"

The logger snorted. "My eldest boy did. Got mine tailor-made in Malone." His blue eyes sparkled. "Gray pinstripes."

She nodded, impressed. "Bet you looked handsome in it." She reached for her pad and flipped it open. "Ready to order?"

Pete pointed a thick finger at the menu. "Still wondering about this apple-fritter French toast."

She patted his shoulder. "You don't like fruit or anything French… Are you a hundred percent sure this time? Okay without hash browns? Eggs?"

"But the whipped cream…"

"How about I bring you a side of it with your lumberjack breakfast?"

He sighed, closed his menu and handed it to her. "Sounds good. And I'll have orange juice this time. No, cranberry. Wait. Make that apple."

Vivie's pencil point broke on her last scribble and she peered at him. "How about coffee?"

Pete smiled, his missing left canine giving him a devilish look. "Exactly what I wanted. You always know."

She tightened her slipping apron and turned. "Yes, I do," she called over her shoulder.

At the kitchen window, she flagged down Rowdy.

"Got some hash browns ready to come out," he growled from the deep fryer.

"Take your time," she soothed. No sense making her short-order cook any more short-tempered.

"Don't mind him," put in Brett. The kitchen door swung behind him as he carried in a dish bin. "He and his old lady are fighting over the cat again."

"Darn woman wants Buttercup declawed," Rowdy muttered, pulling the basket of dripping golden squares out of the oil and dumping them into the warming tray.

"It's pretty common," Maggie interjected, sidling up beside Vivie. She stuck a slip on their swiveling order holder and spun it to face the kitchen. "Got Freddy Mercury's nails removed last winter."

"Is he an outdoor cat?" Rowdy brushed past Brett and yanked off Maggie's order slip.

Maggie pursed her lips, their dark red shade harkening back to a 1940s movie star, her yellow polka-dot head scarf adding to the effect. "Nope. I let him out once and he scratched to come inside five minutes later. Spent the rest of the day licking his fur clean. He'd rather bully my dogs inside than catch birds."

"Without claws, Buttercup will be terrorized out there."

Brett spoke over a high-powered water stream aimed at the dishes. "When it's your time, it's your time."

Rowdy swatted the air. "Knock off that karma crap."

"Have you tried aromatherapy? It's relaxing and maybe you'll stop smelling like motor oil and goat cheese." Brett didn't even try to hide his grin.

Maggie giggled. "Better get back to my station." She hurried off when some kids began a syrup-flinging war.

"Got a special order, Vivie?" Rowdy studied her over Maggie's slip. His face was creased and weatherworn, the miles his Harley traveled reflected there.

Vivie handed him Pete's order. "Lumberjack, eggs over hard. Oh. And a side of whipped cream."

Rowdy's droopy lids rose. "A side of what?"

"Cream. A big swirling heap of it. Maybe sprinkles on top. The rainbow kind."

Rowdy turned, muttering. "I'll see what I can do."

Vivie glanced out the window and spotted a familiar black SUV pulling in to the parking lot. Her stomach clenched. Liam? It'd been a few days since their kiss, but she still didn't feel ready to see him. At least, not in front of others.

The bell chimed as she shoved open the front door, the late-June air heating her face. Above her, a large ash tree shook leaves that whispered in a mild breeze. The soothing sound didn't lull her jangling nerves, though. If anything, her pulse accelerated as she reached Liam's vehicle.

A wailing guitar riff ended when Liam shut off his CD player and turned to the door. His expression flickered when he glimpsed her: surprise, pleasure, wariness. No regret, however. It seemed as if kissing a woman in the woods was something he took in stride.

His window lowered and he peered at her. "You haven't returned my calls."

"I asked you to stay away."

His eyes didn't waver and finally, she dropped her gaze. "I've kept my distance, but tomorrow's my day off and I need to schedule a visit. Do you want to take Button out?"

She caught a lock of hair and wrapped it around her finger. What did she want? If she were honest, she'd missed seeing Liam these past few days. Spending time together would be nice. On the other hand, the thought of being alone with him in the woods terrified her. What if he tried to kiss her?

As if reading her mind, he said, "I won't kiss you, if that's what you're worried about."

She opened her mouth to deny it but couldn't.

At last he nodded, solemn. "If I could take it back, I would, Vivie. But I promise I won't do it again. Okay?"

She needed to hear this, so why did she feel let down?

"You still seem unsure," he persisted. "I could duct tape my mouth. Maybe stuff a sock in it. Any preferences?"

She laughed and instantly the tense mood broke, leaving things feeling normal again.

"I was thinking of one of Scooter's tennis balls, but the sock would do."

Liam chuckled. "Deal. How about we hike farther up Poke-O-Moonshine, find more logs for Button and get her some insect protein?"

Vivie nodded, her breathing coming easier. "Sounds appetizing, though I'll pack a separate lunch for us."

The SUV's engine started. Liam leaned an elbow out the window. "Raisin pie?"

"Two pieces."

"Four."

"Deal."

They grinned at each other for a moment and then, with a wave, Liam backed out and drove back onto the road.

Vivie watched the vehicle until it disappeared. What was it about Liam that made her trust more than she ever thought she could?

"THERE'S A GOOD PILE!" The next day, Liam pointed at some rotting wood alongside the trail and waited for Vivie and Button to catch up. He straightened his slouch, not wanting to look tired. He'd spent a restless night wishing away the hours until morning. But now that it was here, he felt more unsettled than ever.

Kissing Vivie had been dead wrong. Yet she'd felt right in his arms. Perfect. The lingering sensation of her burned in his memory. It made him want more.

"Come on, Button," Vivie called and he turned in time to see her slip on a mossy rock. He steadied Vivie then released her, alarmed at her petrified expression. Why did his touch frighten her so much?

"Thanks," she mumbled, pushing her hair behind her ears. For all her rugged gear, she appeared more feminine than ever. And delicate. He'd take care not to scare her. Wouldn't let any harm come to her. Despite her strength and fierce personality, she brought out a protective streak he hadn't felt since Kunar.

He squatted by the logs, the forest's gloom a cool blanket around him. "Check this out, Button." The bear, now the size of a chow chow, loped closer and buried her nose in the pile. Liam turned one over for the cub's inspection. When it revealed a smorgasbord of wriggling insects, Button pounced with an eager snort. She snatched the log and rolled on her back, bringing it to her mouth like a Popsicle. Her tongue darted and her jaw moved in that side-angle way of hers as she tucked in to her bug buffet.

Vivie pressed a hand to her stomach. "Glad someone gets to eat. How long have we been hiking?"

He checked his watch. "Two hours. Let's sit."

She settled on a large rock the winter had heaved high out of the ground. Although there was plenty of room beside her, he picked a smaller rock and pulled out a bag of trail mix.

"Want some gorp?"

She nodded, her light brown eyes brightening. "Any chance there's chocolate chips in it?"

"Is that a rhetorical question?"

Her laugh warmed him, as it always did, and he passed over the bag. After scooping out a handful, she gave the bag back. Her head tipped skyward as she chewed and he couldn't tear his eyes away. She matched the natural beauty of their surroundings. Eclipsed it.

"I'm glad we did this," she said with her eyes closed.

A shaft of sunlight pierced the green canopy and fell across her chin and neck. With a jolt, he noticed a faint white scar encircling her throat. A mark like that looked deliberate. A battle wound. What had she survived— barely?

He held his curiosity in check. There'd be a better time to ask. "I'm glad, too. So is Button."

They watched the cub snatch up another

log and lick its length. Breathy grunts escaped her as she gobbled up everything that moved.

"Dr. Vogel's right. This is good for her."

"She'll be prepared for her release this fall." He held out the snack, but Vivie ignored it, her expression stricken.

"Button won't be ready. Her jaw—"

"She'll know how to handle herself and she's finding her own way to eat," Liam assured Vivie, wishing these outings would change her mind. After another few weeks, he hoped she'd see things differently. Would agree that Button belonged here. Not in a cage, watching life instead of living it.

"You won't take her without my permission." Vivie's gaze swerved to meet his.

"Button belongs to New York State. The DEC makes that call." He scraped some brown lichen from the rock with the back of his boot. Too bad he couldn't eliminate this festering issue between them as easily.

"That's not how I see it," she snapped.

"Your feelings don't matter in this case." He popped the top off his water bottle and drank. There was no way to sugarcoat this harsh truth.

She shot to her feet, startling him and Button. "They never do." Leaping from the rock, she stomped up the trail, rounding a corner so that he could just make out the bright red of her backpack.

Button dropped her log and raced after Vivie, her paws throwing up dirt clouds behind her. When Liam joined them, Vivie's arms circled the cub, her face buried in the bear's side. "Not going to let you go, sweetie," he heard her murmur. "Your home's with me."

He opened his mouth to object, then closed it. No point in debating an issue with only one possible outcome. Even Dr. Vogel wouldn't launch a demonstration to prevent a bear's return to the wild. Even one with a malformed jaw, as long as the animal could care for itself. In fact, the expert would advise Vivie against stopping nature from taking back one of its own.

At least Liam would still be around for the release. He'd spoken with Yellowstone a couple of days ago, accepted the position and received his official start date for the fall. The woman leaving the job would be delivering her child at the end of September and planned on joining her husband in Alaska. He'd been relieved to hear he'd have this extra time with Vivie and Button, to help with the rehabilitation and to ease the bear's transition into the wild.

Yet deep down, he knew other reasons motivated him. Plain and simple, he liked being around Vivie. Wanted to spend more time with her. He avoided lingering too long anywhere or with anyone. Somehow, however, this impulsive, determined, caring woman made him want to have her and his freedom.

He cleared his throat and Vivie peeked up, her cheeks damp. "Ready to go?"

"Yeah. How much longer?"

"Another thirty to forty-five minutes to the summit. Can you make it?"

Her jaw set. "I've come this far."

"Yes." His eyes searched hers. When he thought of the narrow range she roamed—home and diner—it impressed him how far she'd traveled for Button's sake. "You have."

After gesturing for her to take the lead, he followed, keeping his pace moderate. He wouldn't lose sight of her. Not until their time together ran out…and, even then, he doubted she'd ever completely disappear from his thoughts.

AN HOUR LATER, Vivie stood on the flat stone shelf at the top of Poke-O-Moonshine. Wind gusts brushed back her hair and billowed her shirt but she barely noticed. Instead, her hungry eyes drank in the wild beauty around her. Over two thousand feet below, a lake curved and light sparkled on a navy surface that contrasted with the deep green forest surrounding it. In every direction majestic peaks rose, some with trees springing from their sides, others with sheer rocky cliffs. It stole her breath.

The air was pure and exhilarating. When she inhaled, it was as if her lungs couldn't expand far enough. Wind blew the white clouds dotting the bright blue sky, casting shadows on the mountain sides.

"Clear view today," Liam spoke beside her.

Button nudged her leg and she reached down to stroke the bear.

"I'm guessing that's Lake Champlain." She pointed at the distant water body, vast and wide. World-class fishing derbies descended on it every year, some of the fishermen also finding their way deeper into the forest to explore the rivers that fed the lake.

"Right. And that's Mount Mansfield." Liam gestured to a distant peak across the lake in Vermont.

"I've never seen anything like this." She pulled on her sunglasses against the bright sunshine. "It's incredible."

Liam's wide smile matched hers. "Unparalleled."

"Is this one of the three peaks you have left to climb?"

He shook his head. "No. But you're welcome to come with me when I do. We'd talked about Mount Marcy."

She stared at him for a long moment, willing herself to refuse. Being this far from home should panic her, but somehow, seeing the world from this distance had the opposite effect. It filled her with electricity. As if she'd been zapped from a stupor and brought back to life.

All of the dangers and troubles below seemed smaller, more manageable, from up here. It was humbling and uplifting at the same time. Her body felt light, and she wished she could float with the birds gliding on the air currents, soar above all that had or ever would hurt her.

"Vivie?" Liam's eyes traveled over her face, his tender expression overwhelming her. "If this hike's too much, we can go back."

"No," she blurted. Now that she'd reached the summit, she wished she never had to return to the world below. "I like it here. It feels safe."

She sat down and Button, growing larger by the day, muscled her way onto Vivie's lap.

Liam lowered himself beside her, his profile as rugged and compelling as her surroundings. "That's important to you, isn't it?" he asked. "Safety."

She peered up at him then back to the young bear drifting to sleep across her legs.

"Isn't it to everyone?"

Liam's piercing stare stirred up feelings she wished he'd leave alone. "You take it pretty far. What happened to your neck?"

Her hand rose to her scar and pressed, remembering the gush of blood she'd tried to staunch before she'd blacked out.

She shook her head, beyond words, memories crashing over her, knocking her flat.

"Did someone cut you?" His harsh voice broke through the dismal fog swirling inside.

"Yes," she managed, closing her eyes, wishing she could blot out the images flashing through her mind.

"And that happened in the Bronx?"

"Yes."

"You were attacked."

She willed herself to steer the conversation into safer waters, but floundered instead, unable to resist the swift and unexpected pull to tell Liam. For so long she'd tried keeping those parts of her life separate. Bronx—danger. Adirondacks—safe. Yet the poachers passing so close to her house had shaken her confidence that she could have a before and after.

Liam's calm, solid presence reassured her. Maybe up here, where it felt like nothing bad could touch her, it'd be okay to open up. She wiped her clammy palms on her shorts and began.

"I was raped."

His swift inhalation blanketed her with the familiar shame.

He turned toward her, but she glanced away, unwilling to see his expression. "I was coming home from a graveyard shift at a restaurant." Her voice wobbled and her heartbeat slipped in and out of rhythm as she pushed herself to continue. Maybe Liam would understand her better. See her real reason for rejecting his kiss. Know why Button's safety meant everything to her.

"You were alone." His hand settled next to hers, the brush of fingers steadying her. "Is this okay?"

She nodded, every moment like a grenade she held. "A man bumped into me as I passed an alleyway. A second dragged me farther in and covered my mouth."

All of the silent, unreleased screams, built back up in her throat.

An angry exclamation beside her made her jump.

"They—they—used me. Attacked me like

I wasn't anything to them. Nothing." Despite herself, her voice cracked. How long had it taken her to feel as if she was something again? Someone who mattered? Had value? Until her support group, she'd spent months falling through the gaping hole the men had ripped in her heart, her soul. Unable to think. Feel. Function.

A hand brushed her wet cheek. "You're everything, Vivie." Liam's voice splintered at the edges.

Her gut clenched. "The men argued about what to do—after. Debated how to get rid of me. I heard them, Liam. I heard them and they didn't care." The words tore from her, black poison falling from her lips. "Even when they cut me here." She drew a finger across her throat. "And left me to die."

"I'm sorry, Vivie. I know that doesn't cover it, not by any stretch, but I am. More than I can say. And your attackers weren't men. They're monsters. Tell me they're behind bars."

Vivie's heartbeat was cannon fire, burst after burst shuddering through her. "The woman who found me didn't see them. Since it happened so fast, in the dark, I didn't get a good look, either. None of the forensic evidence turned up anything in the data systems."

Vivie recalled the glare of the clinical white light in the hospital, the long night getting stitched, scraped, probed and prodded. It'd been nearly as invasive as her assault. An extension of her trauma. And for what? Her hands curled at her sides. Nothing.

"So they're still out there," Liam stood and paced in front of her. "Those sons of—"

"I thought moving up here would make me safe."

He stopped and studied her, his eyes in shadow. "Thought? You don't believe that anymore? Is it because of me? That kiss?" When he squatted in front of her, his anguished expression touched her.

"No. Just knowing men like the poachers came that close shook me up."

His thumb glided over her knuckles then withdrew. "I won't let them or anyone harm you."

Certainty rang in every word, bolstering her. Why had she mostly kept her rape to herself? Opening up was terrifying, but it hadn't torn her apart.

How much of that was because of Liam? Thoughtful, considerate, patient man.

Gingerly, he held her hands, capturing them in his large palms. Unlike the kiss, this touch settled her rapid-fire heart. Had sharing her secret made her trust him more? Let him close?

"Your attack is the worst thing that can happen to any human being, Vivie. It's incredible that you've come through so strong and determined."

Strong? Determined? After everything she'd confessed, she thought he'd see her as weak. Light pierced the dark within. She'd braced herself to be judged, blamed...the kinds of things she'd done to herself when she'd tried making sense of it all. Instead, he'd comforted her. Given his support. Wanted to protect her. He saw the best in her and it meant everything.

"Thank you, Liam."

His brows met over his nose. "I didn't do anything, though if I could get my hands on those lowlifes..."

She squeezed his hands, loving the feel of his fingers tightening around hers. "Thank you for listening, for bringing me up here, for not judging me."

"Judging you?" he exclaimed. "The only people who deserve judgment are your attackers."

"I didn't want people—you—to think of me as a victim."

He stared at her for a long moment then

shook his head. "Vivie, you're the toughest woman I've ever met."

His words poured into her. Liquid sunshine.

"Want to go home?" he asked.

She shook her head and stared into the vast space around her. "Not yet."

This is what she missed by staying within the boundaries she'd marked for herself. Up this high, that invisible fence tumbled and set her free. Nothing could reach or harm her when she stood atop the world.

She eyed the winding highway below.

Soon they'd climb down to earth, however, and reality would return with a vengeance.

CHAPTER ELEVEN

"WE'VE GOT FIRE moving fast along Black Brooke heading east. Copy?"

Despite being off duty, Liam grabbed his walkie-talkie and pressed the side button. "How far from Route 9? Over." He gripped the steering wheel tighter as he thought of Vivie. She could be in danger. Button, too.

"Ten miles with wind at twenty-five knots eastward. We've got… Copy?" The whirr of chopper blades drowned out most of the reply and Liam pictured the responders flying over the forest, assessing the situation. The small blaze they'd been monitoring the past few days had escalated into a serious threat. His chest squeezed when he imagined its proximity to Vivie's house.

"You've got what? Over."

He yanked his SUV into a hard U-turn and sped toward Vivie's home. Had she woken yet? Smelled smoke? He needed to see for himself that she was safe.

The intercom crackled. "We've got boots

on the ground but the blaze jumped the fire-break. Calling in more assistance. Advise homeowners at higher elevations of voluntary evacuation. Not encroaching on populated areas, yet. Copy?"

"Copy," Liam repeated, his mind racing. "Over." Trees whizzed by, and a deer and her fawn scrambled across the road ahead of the fire. But what about Button? Stuck in the enclosure, she'd be trapped. He had to get them out. Fast. Voluntary evac or not. Forest fires were capricious beasts. You took them lightly at your own peril.

Since Vivie's house was one of the highest on this route, it put her in the most jeopardy. He had to let her know. Warn her.

He jerked to the side of the road and dialed her number. When her answering machine picked up, he left a hurried message, hung up and left the same urgent words on her cell voice mail. Where was she? She'd already survived so much and now another threat loomed. How would she react to this news?

He rushed through ten stops along the way, advising occupants to head into town. His stop at Vivie's neighbors' revealed they'd returned from their trip. They expressed deep regret about their poaching nephews.

At last, he closed the distance to Vivie's house and swerved into her driveway.

Scooter galloped in front of Liam's front bumper, barking, his long tail swinging. Liam threw open his door, hopped out, and sprinted to Vivie's porch accompanied by the old Lab. The faintest hint of smoke carried on the morning breeze. Had the fire crept closer than the report suggested? At his pounding, she opened the door an inch, peered at him, then undid the chain and let him inside.

She brushed wet hair back from her cheeks, her face soft and unguarded. He breathed in the freshly showered scent of her. His contrary heart wanted to pull her into his arms—or throw her over his shoulder—and get her out of here. Take her away…with him.

"Liam. Why are you here so early? What's wrong?"

"I left messages but you must have been showering. There's a forest fire. About ten miles east and heading in this direction. We need to get you and the animals out."

Her face paled. "Is Button in danger? My house?"

A breath escaped him. One he hadn't known he'd held. "It's possible. How fast can you grab some things and meet me in front? I'll load up Button."

Her eyes darted around the room, lingering on pictures and knickknacks. "Where will you take her?"

"Wendy and Steve's. They'll let Scooter and Jinx stay, too."

Her eyes widened. "Jinx hasn't come back from her night prowl."

He imagined how wound up he'd be if he couldn't find Extra Pickles. His heart went out to Vivie. But this was a time to think, not feel. "Animals know when there's danger. She's probably on the back porch already." With Vivie on his heels, he hurried to the kitchen door and flung it open.

No cat.

"Did you see her when you pulled in?" Vivie's voice rose. She peered out the side window above her sink and twisted one of her earrings.

"No," Liam admitted. "But we can't focus on her yet. Let's get you, Button and Scooter to safety. She may turn up any minute. Get ready and I'll be back in ten."

Her forlorn expression lingered as he pushed through the oppressive air to Button's enclosure. The early-July heat could explain the temperature, but it was unusual this early in the morning. He suspected the fire contributed. They had to get out. It'd be hard for Vivie to leave without Jinx, but she had no choice if the cat didn't turn up soon. Something about the still, expectant air made bumps rise on his arms. The blaze was closing in. This might be a voluntary evacuation, yet he sensed it'd be mandatory soon.

It'd been a dry summer, little rain to stop him and Vivie from taking Button out on his days off these past few weeks. He'd noticed the harder, crisper edges on the leaves, the baked ground that cracked beneath brown grass, and the low water levels in the streams. Even the muddy forest trails had dried up. He'd wondered when and where a fire would start. Hadn't been surprised at the one that'd popped up a couple of days ago.

Still, he hadn't worried about it coming this close to Vivie. Her property bordered on Catfish Creek, and the Ausable River flowed just a couple of miles west. A fire fierce enough to jump bodies of water had the makings of a natural disaster. One that wiped out homes and destroyed lives... All things were temporary.

He grabbed the bear-sized carrier at the front of the boarded enclosure, loaded it in the back of his SUV, then went back for the cub. Hopefully she'd come easily. The smell of smoke was becoming pervasive, strengthening by the minute.

Button ran to the fence when he unlocked the first door, restless and agitated. Her instincts must be alerting her to the encroaching danger. As she stretched upward, her paws grabbed hold of the chain links, her height now about equal to Scooter's.

Their foraging expeditions had done her good. Her coat was glossy and black, her nose glistened and her eyes shone. When he slipped through the first entrance, she snorted impatiently. She dropped to all fours and paced, her turtle in her mouth. It'd lost a couple of flippers, been licked nearly colorless, but remained her favorite toy.

When he stepped inside, she rushed him, wrapping her front paws around his thighs and burying her head in his side. His hand rubbed beneath her chin and soothed the trembling animal.

"It's okay, Button. I'm getting you out of here. Follow me."

He beckoned and headed out the first opening, but she scraped the ground and grunted, shaking her head from side to side. Her fear was obvious. How could he convince her it was safer to leave than stay? Suddenly he was in Kunar again. He could smell explosives, sweat and blood. They'd tried to escape their besieged outpost, but been repelled back to "safety" where they waited. For rescue or ambush, whichever came first. He shook himself out of the memory. It'd been an agonizing cat-and-mouse game, one almost all of his buddies had lost.

But he wouldn't lose Button. Or Vivie. He reached into his pocket for a granola bar he'd brought for breakfast.

He tore off the wrapper and poked the granola bar through the steel fence. "Hungry, Button?" He glanced at his watch. He'd been out here seven minutes. No time to waste.

The cub lifted her snout and sniffed. She took a tentative step forward, then another and another. Just when her lips fell around the bar, he jerked it out of reach.

"Over here!" He waved it beyond the exit and she stared at him then back at her sleep spot. "Smells good, right?" He brandished it like a magic wand, hoping it'd call her to him.

Suddenly, she charged out of the cage and he sidestepped her and closed the first door behind her. Only then did he notice she'd dropped Turtle inside. The anxious bear turned from the granola bar and rammed the closed entranceway. She stuck her nose under the door and sniffed, clawing at the gate. He checked the time again.

Nine minutes.

The air felt heavy and the blue morning sky had grayed somehow, as if the color had leached from it. He couldn't squander more moments. Yet would the bear cooperate without Turtle? He watched her paw desperately at the lock. Bears were one of the smartest animals in the world. And the most stubborn.

Kind of like Vivie...

He chucked the granola bar through the second exit and muscled Button out of the way as he slipped back into the enclosure. In a stride, he grabbed the toy, jerked open the door, and blocked Button from racing back inside.

"Here, girl." The bear gently mouthed the turtle then raced outside for the granola bar.

Priorities...

He scooped up Turtle and let another precious moment pass while she ate. When Button finished, he held out the toy. "Follow Turtle," he called and headed for the SUV, peering over his shoulder. For a second, she huddled against the enclosure then chased after him.

Vivie met them at the SUV. "Have you seen Jinx?" She'd swapped her shorts and tank top for jeans, a tee and a long-sleeved plaid over-shirt with her heavy boots. Work clothes. She appeared ready to battle the fire herself. His adorable warrior.

"She hasn't turned up. I'm sorry, Vivie, but we've got to go. Will you help me with Button?"

"Of course."

Relieved she wasn't overreacting, he tossed Turtle into the carrier and when the bear stretched up to reach for it, he and Vivie hefted Button the rest of the way inside. He rammed the bolt home, lifted Scooter into the back beside the carrier and slid in the suit-cases Vivie had placed by his feet.

"All set. Let's head to the Wildlife Reha-bilitation Center, drop off the animals then stop by the diner if you want. Okay?"

Vivie shook her head and backed away. "Not without Jinx. I'm sorry, Liam. I'll catch up with you when she returns."

A mixture of frustration and fear snaked through him. "Be reasonable, Vivie. Jinx may have hightailed it out of here at the approach-ing fire. There's a good chance she's not com-ing home at all."

A frightened sound escaped Vivie and he regretted every syllable. "I mean she'll come home. But not until it's safe."

Vivie raised damp eyes to his. "What if there is no home left? Where will she go? I'm not leaving."

"You need to evacuate."

Her small jaw jutted. "Is it mandatory?"

He leaned his head in his window and listened to the firefighters and dispatchers squawk over the speaker's emergency channel. After a moment, he turned. "Doesn't look like it. Yet. But it will be soon."

"Then you can't force me to go. Take the animals and come back if you want. Or go to whatever emergency station you're assigned to. I'll be fine."

He hooked his thumbs in his belt and faced her. Why was it always this way between them? On opposite sides of nearly every important issue. "This is my designated area and you're my responsibility."

"And Jinx is mine." Her hand fell on his tense arm and her eyes implored him. "Please Liam, take the animals. I'll be fine."

After a minute, he nodded reluctantly. They were wasting time by standing around arguing. "I'll be right back."

He reversed toward the road. Fire trucks screamed along it. For a second, he paused and took in Vivie. She seemed more petite than ever as she stood beneath her red maple, a hand to her mouth as she called her cat.

His heart expanded as he took in the brave woman. She reminded him of his battle buddies. No man left behind. He felt the same way. When he returned, she'd come with him, Jinx or no Jinx.

No *woman* left behind, he thought as he quickly shifted gears. Especially not Vivie.

TWENTY MINUTES LATER, he swung into her driveway, leaping out as soon as the SUV stopped rolling.

"Vivie!" he shouted. No answer.

He knocked on her door then thrust through it, too impatient to wait. He needed her out. Now. The evacuation status hadn't changed, but the firefighters had lost ground according to reports. The blaze was creeping closer to her home.

Her house echoed with his calls and suddenly a flash of black streaked by her front window. Jinx. He bolted outside and scooped the cat off her porch, striding to the SUV. With the cat secured in his front seat, he marched to the back of her property. Was she searching for her pet? Venturing into the woods? His pulse streamed, fast as a melting river, when he rounded the back corner. A group of deer bounded in front of him and, in a leap almost too fast to register, disappeared into the woods away from the fire. A raccoon trotted by, its offspring following in a swift line behind it. It seemed everyone was running. All but Vivie.

He spotted her at the far edge of her cleared property with, of all things, a shovel. A trench stretched five feet to the left of her and she leaned on the handle, mopping her brow.

"What are you doing?" he demanded as he joined her. She contemplated him, fatigue and strain clear on her face.

"Digging a firebreak. If the fire comes this way, I want to redirect it past Button's enclosure and the house. Give it another path to follow."

"Vivie, leave that to the professionals."

"You think they're going to care about one property? This is my home. I'm not letting it go without a fight."

"They'll do everything they can to save your house."

"And so will I." She rammed her shovel into the ground, stepped on its back edge, lifted and tossed the dirt behind her, repeating the process as he watched, speechless. This took stubborn to a reckless, dangerous level.

"You'll never get enough of this cleared

in time." He breathed in the smoke-filled air and watched a flock of blackbirds wing by overhead.

"If you help me, maybe we can get the western corner done. If the fire's coming from there, it might work."

His jaw tightened. Opposition at every turn. "You can't predict something like that."

"But I can try," she ground out, hefting another chunk out of the earth.

He studied this resolute woman, knowing he could easily toss her into the SUV and drive off with her. Yet her story of being attacked held him back. Manhandling would frighten her far more than any fire. He'd been careful to keep his distance as they'd grown more comfortable the past few weeks. He wouldn't risk destroying the fragile peace that had unfolded between them.

Voices came across the radio on his belt. He listened for a mandatory evacuation order or a worsening of the blaze and heard neither. It wouldn't hurt to indulge Vivie a little now that Jinx and the other animals were safe. Speaking of which…

"I found Jinx."

She dropped her shovel, spun and threw her arms around him. "Thank you. Where is she?"

He laced his fingers behind his back, striving not return her embrace. Her silky hair brushed his chin, her hug the best thing he'd felt in a long time. Still, she reacted in the moment. Wouldn't get this close to him if her thinking wasn't muddled.

When he forced himself away, a hurt, then confused expression crossed her face. "In my car. Ready to go when we are."

"I'm not ready." He wasn't surprised to hear her say it.

"I'll get a shovel." He pointed to her toolshed. The sooner they got this over with, the faster he'd get her to safety. "In there?"

She nodded and returned to her digging, her cheeks pinker than before. Was she embarrassed she'd hugged him? Mad at herself? Both? Either way, he couldn't dwell on it.

An emptiness drummed inside him at the thought. Despite his resolve not to get attached, he had. The more time they were together, the less appealing his move seemed. But his growing feelings would only make him feel trapped. Plus, she'd made it clear she wasn't interested.

He shook off the unwelcome thoughts, grabbed a shovel and joined her. Time to work, not think. And doubting himself wouldn't help anything. He'd made the decision to leave and he'd follow through.

An hour later, they'd nearly dug around the entire backyard and halfway along the sides. With any luck, the fire would follow that trail and bypass her home. He eyed the tall trees. A spark from one of them, landing in the enclosure or on Vivie's roof, would render all of this pointless.

"We did it," she gasped, leaning on her shovel. Dirt and sweat streaked her face, yet she was more beautiful than ever. She was a survivor, capable of a lot more than she gave herself credit for.

"Ready to go?" He shoved his damp baseball cap into his back pocket.

"Almost. I want to wet all of this down."

He glanced up at the slate sky, knowing ash, not clouds, blotted the sun. "Not a bad idea. Where's your hose?"

"I've got one on either side of the house." She headed to the left before he could respond.

"Mandatory evacuations called for all areas—" He shut off his radio. After watching her work doggedly, without complaining, she deserved every chance he could give her. Mandatory usually meant they still had thirty minutes or so and he'd give it to her.

He raced to his car, got a quick update from

the station to ensure the time window was right and returned to find her dragging the hose across her backyard. He hurried to take it from her, pulling it the rest of the way, before running for his. When he returned, she aimed the nozzle at Button's enclosure, wetting the area down. He aimed his water at the ground before the firebreak, working his way carefully along the line, saturating it so that the dirt squished up, muddy and thick, around his boots.

When he glanced at his watch, it shocked him that almost an hour had gone by. The fire smelled closer than ever and the forest crackled faintly around them. Were they too late to get out? If he'd put Vivie in danger, he'd never forgive himself.

He joined her by the house and aimed his hose with hers at the roof. Water soaked the shingles, dripping off the edges and running down the sides. Another jet across the toolshed soaked it, as well, and he clicked off the latch, stopping the stream.

"Time to go, Vivie."

Her arm fell to her side and she wove on her feet. "Is it enough?"

A plane flew low overhead, dumping orange powder not far from the property. He shivered. The blaze was almost on them.

"It has to be."

She nodded and the hose dropped to the ground. He led her to the SUV, opened the passenger door, and helped her inside. Her head flopped back and rested against the upholstery. "What about my pickup? I should drive it."

"Not this tired and with emergency vehicles all over the road. Your insurance will cover the truck if it comes to that."

He jogged around the front and slid in the driver's seat. More fire trucks roared by and stopped a few hundred yards up the road. His gut tightened. This was it. Showtime. If he stayed here a moment longer, Vivie would witness her home, and everything she held safe and dear, crash around her.

He wouldn't let that happen. But before he could reverse, a flame, orange and bright appeared on the northwest corner of her property.

"There it is!" she screamed, pointing. Jinx leapt on her lap and pushed her head under the hem of Vivie's shirt. "Please, no—"

He turned on the engine and backed away from the encroaching fire. If the blaze reached the other side of the road, they could be penned in.

"I want to watch!" she cried, but he accelerated onto the road, roaring away from the fire and all of the misery it would leave in its wake. Vivie might not agree, but it was for the best.

When he pulled up in front of Maggie's house, he struggled to speak. How could he express feelings he didn't understand? He and Vivie had fought hard together, their common purpose tightening the bond they shared. She was a warrior and his heart somersaulted as he glanced at her stoic face, her strength and spirit beautiful. If only he could hold her. Kiss her. Reassure her that she would get through this. She wasn't alone because he'd stand by her.

Suddenly her friend ran outside and yanked open the door on Vivie's side of the SUV.

"I heard about the fire and tried reaching you. When you didn't pick up, I drove out there but some fireman turned me away." She pulled Vivie into her arms, lavishing her with the affection Liam denied himself. "I was scared to death. I'm so glad you came here. You're going to stay, right?"

The woman held Jinx and guided Vivie away, leaving Liam to stare after them. He ached to follow. Make sure she'd be okay. But he had to check in on the responders. See what he could do to lend a hand. He'd helped

Vivie, and now he'd turn his attention to others in need.

Before they reached the stoop, Vivie ducked out of Maggie's arms and raced back to the truck. His pulse sped when she stood on tiptoe and pressed a kiss to his cheek through his open window.

"Thank you, Liam."

He touched his face, marveling at the sensations washing through him. "I only did what anyone would do to help."

Her eyes searched his and he struggled to breathe under her scrutiny.

"No. You always go above and beyond. And you're not just 'anyone,' either, Liam. Not to me."

Before he could respond, she bolted back to Maggie and disappeared into the house. For a few moments, his truck idled in the driveway as he sat, lost in thought. His chest swelled when he replayed her words. In his large family it'd been hard to stand out, especially as a twin. Being a marine had taught him the value of blending in, working as part of a team, not an individual.

Vivie, however, noticed him. Made him feel unique. Not the kind of person who slipped in and out of people's lives without making an impression or leaving one. For once, he wondered if he might be missed when he left for his new job. Strange that, instead of the thought making him want to bolt, it had the opposite effect.

He backed onto the subdivision's road and decided he'd head out toward Wendy and Steve's place after he'd worked with the fire department. They'd probably settled Button into the small holding enclosure, but he needed to be sure everything had gone smoothly and that the fire wasn't a threat. Vivie would want that. Plus he needed to get Scooter and bring him to his owner.

Another excuse to see Vivie?

Maybe.

It was growing harder to stay away. So much so, that he was over fighting it. He wanted to be around her as much as possible before leaving. If his time with her didn't have an expiration date, would he be so willing to give in to his feelings? Probably not.

Luckily, he wouldn't find out.

The ties that pulled him to Vivie were strong and undeniable. When he moved across the country, he'd have the space he needed to break them. She didn't welcome his advances and he shouldn't be making them.

Simple.

He glanced at the empty seat beside him, imagining Vivie there. Who was he kidding?

There was nothing simple about him and Vivie.

CHAPTER TWELVE

A FEW DAYS LATER, Vivie stood on the edge of her charred property, her spirit as fractured as the destruction she surveyed. Why had this happened? How? She and Liam had worked so hard. They'd done everything possible and it still hadn't been enough.

A broad hand settled on her shoulder and she leaned back against Liam's solid comfort. For once, her internal alarm didn't shriek at a man's touch. Liam had proved he was more than just any man. He'd fought by her side and respected her wish not to evacuate until they'd had no other choice. It had restored some of the trust she'd lost after her attack. All men wouldn't force their will on her. Not Liam—this incredible person she'd come to care about deeply.

"You can rebuild." His gruff voice sounded a breath away from her ear, sending shivers of awareness through her. If she could muster the courage, she'd turn and slip her arms around his waist. Bury her head in his chest and hope for his embrace in return. But what if she panicked? Rejected him again as she had the day they'd gone berry picking? It wasn't fair to send mixed signals. His tender concern made her wonder if maybe, just maybe, he cared for her, too—ugly secrets, phobias and all.

"It's all gone," she said, unnecessarily, studying the skeletal remains of her burned-out farmhouse. The roof and sides had collapsed into the foundation. As for Button's enclosure, it'd been decimated. Its tree resembled a charcoal drawing of itself, minus many of its limbs. A giant hand seemed to have twisted the metal fence and tossed it to the ground…proof that the world could marshal forces far stronger than she could stop.

Her insides quivered as she absorbed the implication. After the attack, she'd thought that if she changed her life, made it insular and secure, she'd protect herself and those she loved. Now she saw that safety was an illusion. For the first time in years, she felt scared. Vulnerable. Exposed. She tried repeating her survivor-not-victim mantra but the thought fizzled and died.

"You haven't lost everything." Liam rested his chin on top of her head and his arms encircled her. She waited for the familiar fright to take hold, but relief filled her instead. His touch silenced the screams within.

"What do I have left? Look at this place." She gestured at the remnants of her garage, the scarred forest around her property. It was a graveyard.

Liam's grip tightened and she snuggled against him, inhaling his clean male scent rather than the acrid air.

"You still have Button, Scooter and Jinx. They're okay."

True. She breathed easier as she pictured them secure in their temporary homes. But where would they go next?

"And you still have your diner. Maggie."

The blanket smothering her spirits lifted slightly. Liam was right. She still had her accomplishments, her pet family and her best friend. Could she also count Liam in the mix? As a friend, mentor, or something else? She wished it could be more, but the scars crisscrossing her heart went too deep. He deserved more than she could ever give.

Maybe a friendship with him would be enough. "I still have you, too."

Liam turned her in his arms and his eyes blazed. "Yes, Vivie. You do. You have from the day we met. I know this isn't the right time to tell you, but—"

She put a finger to his mouth, stopping words he might regret saying later, thoughts she shouldn't know. They'd torment her whenever she considered all of the might-have-beens between her and Liam.

"There's a lot to figure out." She forced herself to leave the warm circle of his arms and pick her way across her front yard.

His hand cupped her elbow when she tripped over a burned piece of siding. "Your insurance will cover this," he said, his voice low.

She glanced up and noticed he'd taken on a guarded expression. Had she hurt him by not letting him speak? His bleak eyes suggested it. Her heart squeezed. She could barely accept her own feelings. Hearing his, whatever they were, would be too much. Especially when her entire life lay in rubble and ash.

"But it won't be the same." She reached down and picked up the bent picture frame of last year's Christmas pet photo. Amazing that the picture, although scorched on the edges, had somehow remained intact. She studied her pets as they antagonized the Santa. Would Button be in next year's picture? It seemed possible given her jaw hadn't healed straight. They'd have to take the snapshot at home...

wherever that'd be. Where could she live that would make her feel safe again?

Her lungs burned as she examined the area. She couldn't shield herself from all the evils in the world.

If she rebuilt, another fire could sweep it all away. A flood might do the same. An ice storm had severe outcomes, too. She'd once believed danger lurked mainly on dark city streets. Now she saw that it flourished in the country as well. No escape.

"Do you want to go through it? See if there's anything salvageable?" Liam's concerned eyes searched hers.

"No. There's nothing left for me here."

Liam nodded. "Are you ready to go?"

Her eyes stung. "Go where?"

"Back to Maggie's? The diner? The rehabilitation center?"

"You know what I mean."

They considered each other, his expression thoughtful. "I'm sorry, Vivie. I know this is hard."

A bitter laugh escaped her. "No one knows how it feels to lose everything until it happens to them. Have you ever lost it all?"

He lowered his eyes. "That's a story for another day. This is about you."

Instantly, she regretted her accusatory question. So much about Liam remained a mystery. What had he suffered? Survived? And how had he gotten through it? She filed her questions away. She'd ask him later—when white noise didn't fill her buzzing mind.

"What place would accommodate Button and me? And if I can't find one, what will happen to her?" Surely they were beyond Liam's threats to put the young bear down... Button had made such progress. Was happy living with Vivie and spending time with her and Liam in the forest.

Liam tapped his chin. "Bill Bisso's selling his farm. Wants to move to Florida to be with his grandkids. He might consider renting it to you until he has a buyer. With some modifications, his barn could hold Button until she's let go."

The thought of another loss knocked Vivie flat. Not after all this. "She's not being released this fall. Not with her jaw the way it is. She'll need until next spring—at least—to fully learn how to compensate for it."

Liam blew out a breath and adjusted his hat. "Let's not dwell on that now. Would you like to see the Bisso place?"

She followed him back to the SUV. "Did the fire go near it?"

"Not this time, Vivie." He reached for her

hand, holding it gently as he stared at her beneath the brim of his hat. She knew what he wanted her to understand.

Only she didn't need the reminder. Catastrophes weren't isolated events. They struck without rhyme or reason and she could do nothing to safeguard herself against them.

"I'M REALLY GLAD we're doing this. Thanks for inviting me."

Liam returned Maggie's smile as they hiked then glanced back at Vivie, who trailed behind. Her rounded shoulders and jerky gait made her resemble a sleepwalker, and lately that was how she had behaved.

"Mount Marcy's been on my list. I want to climb all forty-six high peaks someday," Vivie's talkative friend chattered. All signs of wildlife had fled the area, warned away by Maggie's nonstop conversation. Funny how the quiet he and Vivie normally shared packed more meaning than this small talk.

"I heard this is your forty-fourth. Congratulations." Maggie retied the leather string beneath her canvas hat and smiled again.

"Thanks." Liam gestured to her pack. "If that's getting too heavy, I can take more. Same for you, Vivie," he called.

Vivie's head rose but her eyes focused on

something over his shoulder. "I'm fine," she said, looking anything but.

If Maggie hadn't been there, he would have pressed the issue. Gotten Vivie to open up about how she was dealing with losing her home and moving into a new one. Given her monosyllabic answers and hermit-like existence these past two weeks, he knew she suffered. Since she'd stopped wanting to take Button out, both she and the bear had seemed listless.

But he needed Maggie along. Asking her to join them had convinced Vivie to agree to this overnight camping trip. Now, how could he get Vivie to relax and remember her experience on Poke-O-Moonshine's summit? She'd been exhilarated there. Hopefully this trip would help her recapture that feeling. Remember that life held joy as well as sorrow. You couldn't have one without the other. And hiding away from it, as she did, wasn't living at all. "How much longer before we reach the campsite?" Maggie leaped over a couple of stones.

"We should get to the dam soon. We'll have time to set up camp and make dinner before nightfall." He glanced back and noticed Vivie had fallen farther behind. "Let's slow up a bit, Maggie."

She followed his gaze then shot him a concerned look. "Okay."

He propped his foot against a tree, fiddling with his laces while waiting for Vivie. What could he do to make things better? To take her pain away? Time was running out and he still hadn't told her about his move for fear of upsetting her further. In six weeks he'd be across the country, leaving her on her own without even Button to comfort her.

When he imagined how she'd hate him for the bear's release, he winced. He'd give anything not to be the bad guy in Vivie's life. But what other role could he play? Not hero. Especially not a romantic one.

He'd come close, the day they'd viewed her burned house, to confessing his feelings. If she hadn't stopped him, he would have opened the door to a future together. One he couldn't guarantee.

She passed him without turning her head, her limp hair obscuring her face. Clearly she wished she hadn't come, and it stung. Still, he had to think of her. What was in her best interests rather than what he wanted. A no-strings-attached, short-lived relationship wouldn't give Vivie the security she deserved. He didn't trust that his feelings for anyone, even someone as amazing as Vivie, could quash his inevitable need to move on.

"Wait up, Vivie." In two strides, he'd reached her side. "I'll come by Friday to fix the dripping shower. Will that work?"

She shook her head. "Rowdy did it."

He reached ahead and pushed a branch aside for her. "How about the circuit breakers?"

"He replaced them."

"So you're all set on the farm then?"

"Yep."

He sped up, passed her, then stopped, blocking her way. "Vivie, I'm trying here."

For the first time since morning, her eyes met his and he flinched at the pain in them. "I'm done trying, Liam. I wish you would, too. With me, anyway."

She angled around him and marched up the trail, her gray shirt disappearing around a bend.

Did she think he'd quit that easily? He'd get through to her. For Button's sake as well as hers. The bear wasn't neglected, but Button clearly missed her lively companion. As did he.

He shouldered his slipping pack and followed Vivie. Somehow, tonight, he'd find a way.

THE CAMPFIRE CRACKLED and sparked beneath the diamond-studded sky. Liam stretched out on his back, one ankle crossed over the opposite knee. He listened to Maggie explain the nuances of obtaining a golden versus a burned marshmallow and heard Vivie's occasional "Uh-huh." Was Maggie fooled into thinking Vivie listened? Or did she suspect, as he did, that she'd tuned everything out... even those close to her.

A full moon crested Mount Marcy, its pale reflection glimmering on the calmer waters downstream of Marcy Dam. A steady rush of water mingled with the sound of frogs and the faint laughter and guitar strumming from distant campsites. For a moment, his fingers itched to play—a phantom ache from another life. Tonight, the mood was festive, the evening expectant. Yet instead of enjoying himself, he felt restless and stifled. Vivie had shut him out and he wanted in.

He'd grown used to knowing what was on her mind, in her heart. What she planned and what she worried about. Now he'd been left in the dark and was groping for a way to help. But he couldn't do that if she wouldn't open up.

At long last, Maggie quieted and stood with a yawn. "The hike wore me out. I'm turning in. Won't be able to climb that beast tomorrow if I don't get my rest. Night."

She raised an eyebrow and scrutinized him over Vivie's head, as if to say, "Now go for it, fool," then turned and disappeared inside the tent she and Vivie shared.

He sat up and stared at Vivie, who sat expressionless. Flame-cast shadows pooled beneath her gaunt cheeks and sunken eyes. She'd lost weight since the fire and he noticed an uneaten s'more on a napkin beside her. Was she remembering to take care of herself? Guilt pinched. He should have asserted himself sooner instead of giving her space.

"You asked me once about things I've lost," he began without preamble, watching with satisfaction when her head turned sharply. He had her attention now. As tough as this would be to relay, if it helped her, it was worth reliving.

"Yes." She wrapped her arms around her knees and leaned forward to face him.

"I've mentioned that my father died when I was seventeen. My mother's Alzheimer's worsened after that and in a sense, I lost her, too."

Vivie moved closer and her leg brushed his. "Does she remember you?"

He squinted at the dark sky, the glittering spots of light brighter than Manhattan. "Sometimes. Though mostly she thinks I'm my twin, Niall. Or even my dad." He'd be seeing his mom next week for Mary Ann's wedding. Would she recognize him this time?

Vivie's small hand twined in his and a deep tenderness took hold. How was it possible that she felt both fragile and strong?

"That's hard. I'm sorry, Liam."

Her face looked otherworldly in the golden flicker of the campfire, the silvery moonlight crowning her brow.

He tightened his fingers in hers, glad for every moment she didn't pull away. "You mentioned you and your mother weren't close."

Her lashes fanned her cheeks and he waited as she seemed to struggle for the right words.

"My mother was only ever interested in one thing. Her happiness. Didn't matter if I'd gotten used to my new stepfamily, school, made friends, had a pet. If she wanted out of her marriage or relationship, off we'd go, sometimes in the dead of night. No goodbyes. No taking things that we couldn't fit in one suitcase."

Understanding dawned. "Even pets?"

"I never got to keep one longer than a year." She sighed, a soft, yearning sound.

Suddenly her fierce attachment to Button made sense. She'd been forced to give up animals all her life. Letting go of the bear wouldn't be easy.

"That must have been difficult."

"I used to dream about someday putting down roots. A place that no one could make me leave. After the attack, I wanted that place even more. Somewhere I'd always feel safe."

"And then the fire."

Another sigh.

"Yeah."

He put his arm around her and she rested her head on his shoulder. His breath stopped as he waited for her to move away. Instead she stayed, and pleasure, sharp and sweet, filled him. In the distance, lanterns glowed and bobbed in the woods as campers made their way to their tents, calling their goodnights. Soon, all was quiet again and it felt as though he and Vivie were alone in the vast wilderness, finding their way in the darkness, to each other.

"Houses are temporary. Families—loved ones—they're what counts."

He felt her nod. His thumb circled the soft flesh of her palm and she shivered against him. Was she as aware of him as he was of her? Or could she be frightened, not wanting such intimate contact? Impossible to know, but she hadn't pulled away...yet.

"After the attack, I moved here because I thought terrible things probably didn't happen in places this remote. My house, the diner, they were where I felt secure."

"A building doesn't make you safe." At his harsh tone, she lifted her head and studied him.

"Are we still talking about me? Because it doesn't sound that way."

His chest expanded, the old dread seizing him as his memory skimmed back ten years.

"I lost fifteen of my battle buddies when under siege in Kunar."

She clutched his other hand, her eyes wide. "Liam. That's awful. I didn't know."

He tightened his fingers around hers and shook his head. "I don't talk about it."

Her nose scrunched. "Ever?"

"Not until now."

"Why are you telling me now?"

He had a lot of reasons, but the deepest truth of all escaped him.

"Because I want you to know me."

He saw her swallow hard, but her gaze didn't waver.

"I want that, too," she said at last, and his

tense shoulders dropped. He wasn't alone in his feelings. "Tell me."

"We'd recently retaken a contentious area in Kunar. It'd been in insurgent hands for over six months. The location made it a prime spot for drug and weapons smuggling."

A shudder passed through her and he drew her back to his side, slipping an arm around her waist. She stiffened, but didn't move away. "Sounds dangerous."

"I'd had assignments like that before. Hold an outpost. Defend it. Keep back insurgents... Nothing about this seemed out of the ordinary."

"Yeah, spending every day with a gun in your hand, waiting for the next ambush, that sounds fairly humdrum to me," she exclaimed.

He wondered if she thought of her own attack and tightened his grip around her waist. Didn't want her getting spooked.

"Out of context, I guess that doesn't seem normal, but it was war. That was how we lived...and died."

"What happened to your friends?"

His pulse pounded in his ears, louder than the humming crickets. "About a week in, we started taking sniper fire. Recon pairs went out but never returned. Other groups went out after the missing and vanished, too. That's when we knew we were in trouble."

"That's terrifying."

"Yeah. We were all scared. Any combat soldier who tells you he wasn't is either lying or a fool."

She touched the side of his face and the caring gesture nearly undid him. "You're neither of those."

"I'm a lot of things, but no, not that. Later that day the return fire increased. Our commander, not long out of officer training, with little combat experience, told us to keep our positions. Hold the post. He refused to call for help. Thought we had the man power to do it."

"Didn't he request, I don't know, eyes in the sky or something? That's what the traffic reporters call it."

"We thought he did. He gave the orders and we had no choice but to obey, even when he sent out more recon missions."

"Your friends."

"They disappeared. Presumed dead." His voice was gravel, sharp stones that slashed as he spat them out. "And then the snipers got more accurate as they closed in. Started picking us off when we patrolled the outpost walls."

"Did you see someone die?" Her fingers

slid along the scar on her neck and he hated that he brought back her own trauma. Should he stop?

"Did you?" she repeated, louder now.

"Three of my bunk mates. One died next to me. Could have been my head that got blown off. A few inches. That's all the difference there was between life or death."

"He must have been more exposed."

"No. I was. I'd dropped my goggles and Jim leaned down to get them. When he straightened…" His voice trailed off, the impact of that memory exploding in his mind. He'd had his eye on the horizon. Should have spotted the sniper that got his friend.

"That doesn't make sense. You were the clearer target."

He cupped her lovely face. "Bad things happen. There is no logic to it."

Her mouth worked, her features contorting. "How can you live like that? Not believing that you have control? Or even that another force is guiding all of this?"

"Like the one that allowed those men to attack you? Or burned your house?"

Her eyes shimmered. "Maybe I did something wrong. Deserved it."

"Jim and his wife fostered children with AIDS. You think he deserved it?"

Her head drooped. "No," she whispered at last.

"And neither did you. But that shouldn't make you shut yourself away. Hide. What good is life if you're too afraid to live it?" He put a finger beneath her chin and raised it until their eyes met. "In the military, we call a near-death experience our Alive Day. Some even celebrate it…remembering to be grateful that we survived."

"I like that," she whispered, her eyes shining. "My Alive Day is October 15."

"Mine is December 31."

Her brows met. "You almost didn't live out the year. How did you escape?"

"We were overrun. A few of us managed to get out. Hid in American-friendly towns until special ops picked us up. But those couple of weeks trapped in that outpost, nowhere to go, waiting to die, were the lowest point for me."

"Is that why you became a conservation officer?"

"Huh?"

She smoothed her hand along his jaw then slid it to the back of his neck. He tensed, wanting to feel her sweet lips on his. The comfort and pleasure he knew he could find in her kiss.

"Because you could be outside, not trapped

in a building like the outpost in Kunar? Do you even like your home?"

He pictured his empty fridge, the blank walls and bits of furniture he'd accumulated while he'd rented it.

"It's a place to sleep."

She nodded, a knowing look creeping into her eyes. "Then it's not your home. Have you ever had one as an adult?"

"I usually move every two to three years."

"Why?"

He shrugged. How could he describe the feeling that urged him to leave when he stayed still too long?

"You're reliving the war," she observed.

"What? No. That was a long time ago."

"So was my attack and I'm beginning to see that maybe I'm not handling it as well as I thought, either." Her eyes filled with surprise and wonder.

He struggled to follow her logic, unsure of where it led. Or if he wanted to pursue it. If she was right, he'd run from his outpost in Kunar and never stopped. It floored him.

"That part of my life is over," he said, though he didn't sound convincing, even to himself.

"How long have you been in the Adirondacks?" She swatted at a buzzing mosquito.

added up to a beauty only nature could take credit for. Bathed in the strengthening sun, she seemed made of gold.

Button, larger than Scooter, muscled out the Labrador and butted the ball down the grassy field. Vivie flashed in from the side and kicked the ball out from under Button's muzzle to Jinx who stopped grooming herself long enough to bat at the ball. She scampered away the minute two four-legged beasts descended on her.

This time, Scooter reached the ball first and nosed it farther down the field with a happy bark. But Button galloped after it, her black rump rising and falling as she grunted and knocked the ball into an overturned trough.

"Yes! Good job, Button!" Vivie grabbed a large dog biscuit out of a pouch around her waist and passed it to the grunting, stamping bear. Scooter plopped on his haunches and whined, earning him an ear scratch.

"I know you can't hear me." Vivie dropped to her knees and wrapped her arms around her dog. "But I love you. And you'll get the next one. Look for my pass."

Button muscled in on the hug and the three of them fell over, Vivie's giggle infectious.

She sat up fast at Liam's answering laugh. "Liam! I never let Button out here on her own since it's not secure, and these biscuits are okay for her digestive system. I checked with the vet."

He held up a hand to stop her nervous babble. "Hey. I'm not here in a professional capacity."

She stopped talking, and her white teeth caught her full bottom lip.

Behind her, the game resumed. Scooter nudged the ball out of the trough and shoved it up ahead, Button huffing hot on his heels.

"Looks like quite a matchup." Liam unlatched the gate and eased inside, pausing a moment as the animals thundered by.

Her eyes followed the pair, a small smile appearing when Jinx cuffed Button as they passed her.

"They're each holding their own."

"It's good exercise for Button," Liam said, breathing in Vivie's wildflower scent as he drew near. When he came this close to her, his heartbeat skidded fast and light, no traction.

She shoved her long hair out of her eyes. "For all of us. I haven't seen Scooter this fired up in years. Button's good for him."

"One of the family?" He cocked an eyebrow, wanting her to deny it. Knowing she wouldn't.

Her eyes met his squarely, the light brown color deepening. "I hope so. The vet said if her jaw hasn't set properly by now, then it won't."

"That won't stop her release unless it's ruled debilitating," he warned, not wanting her to get her hopes up. He'd seen her relationship with Button grow through the weeks, knew how difficult letting her go would be.

"We don't have that ruling yet, do we?" Her chin rose and he met her challenging look.

"No," he admitted, "But—"

Her shoulder bumped his. "You said this wasn't an official visit. Can we not talk about this right now?"

Although one side of her mouth curled, the sheen in her eyes told him not to push it. She'd finally emerged from her depression after the fire and he wouldn't give her more sad thoughts. Not today. Not when they could play soccer instead.

He took off after the bear and dog, calling over his shoulder, "Button's on my team!"

She flew by him and swatted the ball he'd been about to kick. "Scooter's an old hand at this. Looks like you're going down."

He twisted and blocked her next move, zipping the ball to Button who knocked it into the trough.

When he turned, he met her frown, the line between her brows and her irritated flush making her more adorable than ever. What he would give to pull her into his arms and kiss that pouting mouth.

She stomped over to Button and fed the bear another biscuit. Scooter barked madly and circled. "Don't get used to that—it'll be your last."

He leaned against a post and crossed his arms. "I just want to know what I get when I win."

Her small nose scrunched. "Not happening."

Shoving off the fence, he stepped close enough to make her head tilt up. "You still haven't given me an answer about the wedding. If I win, we'll go together."

The flash of panic on her face nearly made him take back his words. It'd be hard for her to return to the city. He hadn't thought of that. But he'd keep her safe. Wouldn't let her out of his sight.

He stumbled back in surprise when she shoved his chest and sprinted after the ball Scooter had liberated. "If I win, Button stays at least until spring."

"Can't promise that." He dodged the bear

who seemed more intent on tripping him than helping. Not much of a teammate...

"You're with the DEC," she huffed as their feet tangled, fighting for ball possession. "Fill out some paperwork. What's another few months to make sure she's gotten through the winter and can fend for herself in better weather?"

He took control of the ball and snaked down the field, hearing her right behind him. She wasn't being completely unreasonable, but the longer she kept Button, the harder it'd be to let go.

"I can't make any promises," he repeated, groaning when Scooter descended on his feet and knocked the ball away. Button looped after him but was too late. The dog shoved the ball into the trough and turned with an excited bark.

"Good boy!" Vivie waved her hands and waggled her fingers, the gesture revving up Scooter even more. She tossed him a dog biscuit and he backed away from an advancing Button.

The bear parted its mouth and a muffled growl emerged.

Vivie bent at the waist, holding her sides and breathing deep. "You see? How can her injury not be debilitating? She can't properly open her mouth, or growl. What if she needs to defend herself against other bears?"

He held in a sigh. Exasperating woman. "Thought you didn't want to talk about this."

"Now I do. It's about a bet."

He considered her for a long moment, then shrugged. "Look. If the vet says she's unsafe in the wild, I'll do what I can to help."

"What if I say she's not safe?" Vivie planted her feet wide apart, her mouth set in a firm line. "I'm her caregiver. I know best."

The tip of his sneakers touched hers and she blinked up at him. "You've done a wonderful job with her, Vivie. But there's still a ways to go before those decisions are made. We can spend the next six weeks going over it or enjoy this time. How about we get on with our bet?"

A playful smile appeared on her lovely face, twisting his heart. "You mean the one you're about to lose?"

She broke away and chased after Scooter and Button, calling over her shoulder, "Game on!"

CAR EXHAUST. HONEY-COATED roasted nuts. Day-old trash.

Vivie covered her nose and mouth, trying not to breathe much of the city air. Attempted to shut it out. Everything. Especially the memories that crept from dark corners and seized her.

She glanced at the cabbie's open window as they crawled along the packed avenue. The murmur of rushing crowds and impatient traffic closed around her and she slid lower in her seat. There was no blocking out a place as insistently alive as New York City. It pulsed with menace, electric with dangerous possibilities. If only she hadn't lost that bet to Liam. Her eyes drifted to his handsome profile. She wanted to spend time with him... just not in Manhattan.

She pulled out her cell and glanced at the text from her support-group leader.

You can do this, Vivie. Face your fear. Stop by the meeting tonight if you have time.

She slipped the phone away, wishing the words would erase the foreboding that twisted through her gut.

Liam reached for her. "Feeling okay? Your fingers are like ice."

She nodded, a quick short jerk of the chin that made his eyes narrow. His thumb stroked the backs of her knuckles. "We can leave. Grab the next train home if this is too much."

"You can't miss your sister's wedding." When she glanced out the window, an alley between two buildings caught her eye. Suddenly she felt as if she were being dragged inside. A wave of helpless terror shuddered through her.

Liam's arm slid around her shoulders and he pulled her near. "You're not okay. I shouldn't have asked you to come. Made that bet." When he leaned forward to rap on the plastic partition, she pulled his hand back.

"No," she whispered. "This is good for me." *You're good for me*, she corrected silently.

Liam stroked the side of her face and she rested her cheek against his palm. She'd come a long way from the woman who'd panicked at his touch. Now she relished it. Wished he'd do it more, although that would only complicate their tenuous relationship. They'd begun as strangers, turned into enemies, worked their way to friendship and now this...a no-man's-land of romantic entanglements as snared as barbed wire.

Hearing about his narrow escape in Kunar, how she might never have met him, drove home how much she cared. Crazy that she'd finally opened up and fallen for a man who'd never be content to have a home, put down roots. He'd leave in a month and once again she'd lose someone she cared about. Her life on replay.

His lips moved against her temple. "My family can be a lot. Just to warn you."

"Growing up, I met all kinds of families."

"Do you ever keep in touch with any of them?"

She thought back to a particular stepsister, one who'd shared her music and an impressive flip-flop collection. "No. We usually left too fast and not on the best terms."

Regret tugged at her. If she'd stayed in contact, despite her mother's wishes, she might have had a family to call after the attack. At least she'd had friends who'd let her stay with them when she'd been too afraid to sleep at home. Then she'd found her support group and, eventually, Maggie.

She glanced at the tall man beside her, his shoulder above hers, level and solid. And now there was Liam...

Since their Mount Marcy trip, she'd mulled over his observations and realized that he was right. Just like the fire, bad could find her, wherever she hid. So why lock herself away? It'd been good to get out again and resume their hikes with Button. And the occasional soccer game.

"I hope Steve doesn't mind searching out skunk cabbage every day."

Liam's mouth curved. "I think Button's gotten addicted. Lately that's all she eats. That and corn."

"Catkins, too." The cab jerked to another halt and her purse fell to her feet. "She'll plow right by them for skunk cabbage, though." Vivie grabbed a lipstick before it rolled under the front seat. "I wish she wouldn't forage so far."

"It's her nature." His eyes lingered on her mouth as she freshened her makeup.

She rubbed her lips together, feeling warm under his scrutiny. "At least she always finds us again. I'm getting used to it."

"Good. You can't manage everything. Control her all the time."

She nodded, pleased that she could let go that much. It felt like progress. Lately, she'd begun questioning how much of her life was in her control...even the night she was raped.

She'd always berated herself for not splurging on a cab ride home at that late hour...for taking the dark shortcut, for staying past her shift to learn a new sauce recipe. Any of those choices could have changed the course of her life and she'd hated herself for not making even one of them.

She squeezed Liam's hand and felt his fingers tighten around hers. Had she taken any of those paths, however, she wouldn't have moved to the Adirondacks and met Liam...

Did she have any right to intervene and stop his move to Yellowstone? Convince him to stay with her and Button?

She dropped the impossible thought. Liam's past drove him, even if he didn't see it. If she changed his mind, he'd eventually see her as his jailer—he'd feel imprisoned by her need to put down roots.

They turned down a cobblestone street filled with quaint, three- and four-story brick buildings.

"There it is!" Liam leaned forward and pointed at a black oval sign with bronze-carved letters spelling out The White Horse Tavern.

The cab swerved to the side. Liam quickly paid the driver before ushering Vivie out of the cab and through the massive oak door.

"What's a guy need to do to get some service around here?" he hollered, his voice lighter, less serious than she'd ever heard it.

She glanced around the large, homey room, taking in the black-and-white pictures adorning the walls, the scuffed floor in front of a dartboard, a wrought-iron chandelier tipped with carved horse heads and a brass-trimmed bar that ran along one half of the room. A Bob Dylan tune played in the background, the folksy song fitting this informal space perfectly.

A man with thick, wavy dark hair and green eyes emerged from behind the bar, a keg firmly in his grip. When he lowered it, he caught sight of Liam and strode toward them.

"Liam! How are you?"

The men clapped each other on the back in a one-armed bro hug and stepped apart, grinning.

"Great. This is my—" Liam's eyes slid toward her, a question in them.

She extended a hand. "I'm Vivienne Harris, Liam's friend. Please call me Vivie. And you must be one of the infamous Walsh brothers."

The man's eyes crinkled at the corners, his open, friendly expression disarming. "Guilty. Aiden Walsh, Liam's oldest brother."

Aiden's eyebrows lifted when Liam wrapped an arm around Vivie's shoulders. She peered up at him in surprise. Why was he sending his brother mixed signals? Acting possessive. Proprietary. He'd said he didn't grow attached to people or things. Didn't want to be tied down, but he'd latched himself on to her, anyway... Not that she was complaining. Still. They seemed like a couple when she'd just called them friends.

"Liam!" A young girl, who looked around nine or ten, flew down the stairs behind the bar. Her fine blond hair streamed behind her.

"Ella!" He caught her in his arms and swung her until she squealed and thumped his back. He set her on her ballet flats.

"Knock-knock."

Her bright eyes gleamed and dimples appeared in each cheek, giving her an impish look.

Liam ran a hand over her crown. "You know I can't resist a good knock-knock joke. Not too old for it yet, Ella?" Tenderness tugged at Vivie's heart at the twinkle in his eyes.

Ella shook her head. "Never! And you haven't heard this one before. Promise."

Liam arched a brow, an indulgent smile twisting his lips. "Who's there?"

"Cowsgo." Her cheeks puffed out as she tried and failed to hold in a giggle.

When Liam's eyes lifted to Vivie's, his amused expression stole her breath. There was no other word for it. He was gorgeous— a gentle warrior.

"Cowsgo who?"

"No. Cows go *moooooooooo*." Ella cupped

her hands around her mouth, drawing out the vowel before flinging herself into Liam's arms and burying her head in the crook of his neck. "Why don't you come home more? I miss you."

"I miss you, too, Elly-Belly." He tickled her ribs and she giggled, squirming in his arms until he let her go. She sprinted back to the stairs screeching, "Liam's here! He's here!"

"Coming up," he called after her and linked his fingers with Vivie's. "Are you ready for this?"

She smiled, remembering how much she'd always wished for this kind of a family.

"Yes. It's nice to meet you, Aiden."

A customer at the bar waved at him and he turned. "Better get back. Great to meet a—a—friend of Liam's." Aiden observed Liam for a long moment until he shifted beside her. "Sure we'll be seeing lots of each other over the next couple of days."

Liam tugged her toward the staircase. Halfway up he turned and gazed down at her. "Thank you for coming. My family has some crazy idea that I'll never settle down because of all of my moving. You'll stop a lot of nagging from Mary Ann."

Stung, Vivie snatched her hand away. So that's what she was doing here. Fooling his family into thinking he was all right. Why had she imagined he wanted her for himself? She shouldn't have let herself believe the impossible.

His brows crashed together. "What's wrong?"

"Nothing we can talk about now." She remembered her wild-eyed mother and that restless driving need to find someone or someplace better. How much was her parent like Liam?

A muscle in his jaw leaped. "If you didn't want to come you should have told me."

She'd climbed a few stairs when he caught her wrist, stopping her.

"Why are you pushing me away, Vivie?"

His vulnerable expression softened her. "Why would I need to? You're already leaving. Remember?"

His pained eyes searched hers. He opened his mouth when a voice boomed from the top of the stairs.

"You two coming or what?"

She glanced up and saw a man who closely resembled Liam.

"Guess we've got no choice now," Liam grumbled good-naturedly and climbed after her.

"I'm Liam's handsomer, slightly younger twin brother, Niall. You must be Vivie."

She returned the man's handshake and turned with a smile to the dark-haired woman beside him—her silver eyes were startlingly beautiful.

"I'm Kayleigh, Niall's fiancée."

"And business partner," her future husband put in, giving her an indulgent look that grabbed Vivie's heart. How wonderful to have someone who wanted to spend their personal and professional life with you. True love. No question about it.

"Nice to meet you."

"Liam! I'm in Mom's room. Come see me," called a voice from deeper inside the small apartment.

Liam shrugged. "We'll catch up later, bro." His eyes slid between his twin and Kayleigh. "Glad things are going so well and congratulations on winning the Shorty for best app this year."

A wide smile lit up Kayleigh's face. "Our start-up's doing better than I ever dreamed." Her adoring gaze fell on Niall and an adolescent boy made a gagging sound.

Liam turned to the teen leaning against the wall. "Connor. Good to see you, bud."

"Yeah. I bet. Must be why you come home so much, then." His voice dripping with sarcasm, the kid turned on his heel and disappeared through another doorway off the living room.

Niall shook his head and the twins seemed to hold some silent conversation that involved brow lifting, a frown, shaking heads and a shrug.

Ella raced from another room and skidded to a halt in front of Vivie. "You're pretty."

Vivie smiled. "Not as pretty as you. You are beautiful."

Ella lowered her head for a moment and fiddled with her locket. "That's what my brothers say, but they have to, right?"

Vivie glanced between the twins, noting their indulgent expressions. "Nope. Brothers can be beasts…so it must be true."

Ella's eyes widened and she smiled. "I like you. And Mary Ann says come right away."

Liam nodded. "Got it."

A pre-teen boy a few years older than Ella passed by and yanked a string of licorice from his mouth. "Better hurry. She's acting kinda crazy."

Liam pulled the youngster into his arms. "Hey, Daniel."

"Did you hear what I said? Hurry."

Liam nodded. "Going." He turned to Vivie. "Ready to meet the bride-to-be?"

"Bridezilla is more like it. Maybe I'll make

her into one of my cartoon characters." Daniel stuck his candy back in his mouth and sauntered away.

"Liam!" cried a female voice—Mary Ann, Vivie supposed.

"Coming!" he hollered and Vivie followed him through the maze of furniture, toys, books and lounging pets. A cat cuffed her ankle, making her jump.

"Knock it off, Grinch." Liam picked up the cat and held it overhead before he kissed its nose and lowered the squirming animal to the ground. "That'll teach you to mess with my lady."

His glowing eyes warmed her. Was she his lady? For this weekend, or longer? Her temples throbbed as she pondered the possibilities, what each of them wanted versus what they could handle.

They rounded the frayed end of a couch and stopped inside the entrance to a sunlit room, a bumped-out window letting in the afternoon sunshine. In the middle of the room stood a redheaded young woman garbed in white lace, a sheer veil attached to the back of her curls with a crystal barrette. A woman stood behind her, measuring tape in one hand, a pincushion in the other.

"Liam!" Her smile flashed white against

her freckled, pale skin. "Can you believe I'm doing this?" She gestured to the dress belling around her bare feet.

"Weren't you and Michael engaged in junior high?"

She stole the seamstress's tape measure and chucked it at him, only her aim went wild and it smacked Vivie's arm.

"Oh. I'm so sorry! Gosh. What a first impression I'm making. I'd come over and hug you, but I don't think Brea wants me to move. I'm Mary Ann by the way."

Brea shook her head vigorously and continued pinning the wedding dress's waist tighter.

Vivie closed the space between them and extended a hand. "I'm Vivienne but—"

"Everyone calls you Vivie." Mary Ann peered over Vivie's shoulder at Liam. "My brother told me."

Her curiosity piqued, Vivie almost asked what else Mary Ann had heard.

"It's so good to hear he's dating. We were worried when Niall got wind of him moving to Yellowstone. Glad that's off the table."

Liam raised one eyebrow at Vivie and she closed her mouth. So he wanted her to play along. Pretend, for the sake of not upsetting his sister, that he wasn't moving cross-country, running as usual.

She was a smoke screen. Nothing more, and the thought burned away the growing confidence she'd felt lately. Suddenly the city noises penetrated the windows and wove around her heart, squeezing it until it leaped and bumped in her chest. Perhaps she would attend the support-group meeting tonight.

When she pulled out her cell to text them, it clattered to the floor waking an elderly woman napping on a daybed.

"What? Why is everyone in my room? Who are all of you? Where's my husband?"

Mary Ann rushed to the bed and took the woman's hand. "Mom. It's me. Your daughter, Mary Ann."

Liam's mother sat up and smoothed her short white curls with a quaking hand. "I don't have a daughter. Just a baby son. Aiden." Her voice rose. "Has something happened to him?" White showed all around her irises. They darted around the room before landing on Liam. She blew out a long breath.

"There you are, darling. Is Aiden okay and why have you invited so many people over? Are we having a party?"

Liam started forward but Mary Ann held out a hand, checking him. Hurt flashed between the siblings and Vivie's heart ached that Liam's mother didn't recognize him again. This should be a joyous moment, but was, instead, a difficult one.

His mother hadn't asked for this condition and neither had the family, yet they accepted what fate gave them.

She needed to learn to do the same.

VIVIE WATCHED LIAM's bent head as he spoke earnestly to his mother. All through dinner, she'd caught his pained expression as his mom hadn't recognized him. Yet now, just as she prepared to leave for her support group, his mother had realized who he was and asked to catch up with him.

How could she drag him away from that? He'd vowed to go with her when she'd mentioned her plans. If she told him she needed to leave now, he'd insist on coming. She'd feel safer with him by her side, but couldn't ruin his chance to talk with a mother who recognized him.

Fear rose as she forced herself to stay silent and walk to the door. Mary Ann was in the kitchen with Ella. Niall and Kayleigh were cleaning up, and Liam's other brothers were in their bedrooms. So no one would notice her leave, especially with an Ella Fitzgerald tune blaring.

Vivie hoisted her purse, picturing the can

of pepper spray inside. The support group met in a familiar part of the Bronx. Still, she was taking precautions.

She'd been to that well-lit neighborhood plenty of times since the assault. Knew it well. As long as she followed the usual bus route, she should be able to navigate her way back. Granted, she'd have to catch the bus from SoHo, but she'd manage. She had to try new paths or she'd never grow stronger.

She eased open the door, raced downstairs and sprinted along the shadowed street until she caught a bus on a main thoroughfare. She banged on its closed doors and the driver opened them, gesturing impatiently for her to climb in.

She thought she caught a glimpse of Liam jogging up the sidewalk as they pulled away from the curb. But she turned back toward the front of the bus. As her support-group leader said: time to face her fears.

Alone.

THREE HOURS LATER, after her support group, Vivie boarded a bus and double-checked her map for the next connection to SoHo. She yawned and rested her forehead against the window, eyes heavy. How nice that she had twenty minutes until she left this seat. It'd been a long day...

Suddenly, the bus hit a bump and her eyes flew open. Had she fallen asleep? Fear fluttered in her stomach. She glanced at her watch, then out the window. Everything looked dark and unfamiliar. She'd been asleep for almost a half hour.

A groan escaped her. How had she made such a colossal mistake? Granted, this had been a tiring day full of travel, meeting people and working with her support group. Still, she should have been more vigilant. Leaving Liam behind had been a mistake.

"Excuse me?" she called and walked up the aisle of the empty, swaying bus. "What stop is this?"

"Coming up on Castle Hill."

She shook open her bus map and groaned. Four stops too far. And Castle Hill...not a Bronx area she knew. Was it safe? It wasn't anywhere close to SoHo. She peered at the outlines of connected stone homes, what looked like a playground and a kid's bike on a stoop. Children. That had to be a good sign. A family neighborhood. Not a threat. Not even at this hour.

"Can I catch another bus here soon?"

The bus driver took off his hat and

scratched his ear. "Running about every twenty minutes or so. You could get lucky."

"Thanks." She pulled the wire and a chime sounded.

The doors opened with a pressurized hiss and the driver grunted. "Take care."

"I will." She forced a smile and stepped out into the warm air. When the bus drove away, she turned in a slow circle, her heart beating fast.

Now that she was closer, the houses loomed tall and scarred. Some of the windows were cracked or boarded over. Neon graffiti shone dimly in the gloom, covering several of the walls. Gaps appeared in a chain-link fence around a small playground, the bottom pushed in or cut away in sections. Needles, food containers and beer cans littered the weeds around it.

What had she done? She should never have gotten off that bus, but now it was too late.

Her mouth went dry when a wailing police siren sounded in the distance. It practically screamed danger. She scurried toward the stop across the road and up a ways, praying a returning bus would appear at any minute.

Her hand rose to her neck and she felt her scar. Had the knife extended another inch, gone a bit deeper, it would have nicked her carotid artery and she would have bled out on the spot. An Alive Day if ever there was one. Would she be so lucky if attacked again? She passed by a dented sedan with cardboard duct-taped over a passenger-side window. Another car lacked its hubcaps. Sweat beaded her forehead.

She thought of calling Liam. Like most people in the city, his family had only one vehicle. Mary Ann had complained it was in the shop, but he could call for car service... though a bus would get here sooner. It was pointless to worry him. Especially since she'd already phoned before leaving the meeting and, despite her short nap on the bus, wasn't overdue by much...yet.

She pulled out her pepper spray and forced herself to walk at a normal gait, to not appear panicked despite her struggle to breathe. The night of her attack had been like this. She'd been so certain then. So naive. Sure that nothing bad could happen to her. Not something so extreme, anyway. But that innocent belief had been ripped from her, and with it her ability to live life to the fullest. Her assailants had killed her spirit.

Up ahead she noticed a gap between houses, much like the one she'd passed that long-ago night. The hair on the back of her neck prickled as she imagined ominous eyes watching her. Assessing. When a cat fled across her feet, she jumped. Her pepper spray fell from nerveless fingers, rolled over the curb and into a sewer grate. She dropped to her knees, grabbing for the can, but missed. It vanished, and fear, dark and thick, poured through her.

This was it. She was defenseless. Completely unprotected.

On wooden legs, she forced herself forward. The bus stop stood just past the alley. If something terrible lurked, she'd have to face it. She pictured Liam, Maggie, Button, Scooter and Jinx. For their sakes as well as hers, she would defend herself. Fight back. Whatever the outcome, at least it wouldn't mean returning to her bubble of an existence.

Across the street, a muscular man ambled, his gait unsteady, his shaved head shining as white as the moon. When he spotted her, he stopped and grinned, looking much too happy to see her for comfort.

"Hey, pretty lady," he called. "You new here? Haven't seen you around. I would have noticed."

She shook her head, every muscle tensing as he crossed the road toward her. Behind her the alley loomed black and impenetrable.

A feeling of déjà vu overcame her, and her knees dipped.

"You solo or what?"

She smelled the booze on him before he attempted to scale the curb. His hands gripped a car's back hood when his foot slipped. She pictured Liam. Wondered if he worried about her. If he could see her now...

A stream of expletives escaped the man and he pointed at her. "Better not be laughing."

She was anything but amused. It took everything she had to stay calm and not to give in to tears. She'd cried the last time and it hadn't made a difference. According to Liam, nothing would have. She rubbed her bare arms and forced herself to stay where she was. Stand her ground. She had a right to be safe, wherever she was, and she'd defend it. After the fire, she understood that walls, things...didn't matter. Hiding behind them hadn't helped her fully heal.

He conquered the curb and sauntered closer, hitching his slipping pants. They seemed weighed down by something heavy in his pocket. A gun?

"What do you want?" she asked, her voice as steady as she could manage.

His gray teeth flashed, years of hard living turning his face masklike. "What are you offering?"

"Got a picture of my bear." She clapped a hand over her mouth. What a crazy thing to say. But in this dangerous moment, her loved ones ran through her mind and Button sat high on the list.

The man steadied himself against the broken street light. "No kidding? You have a bear?"

She nodded and fished out her wallet, realizing, belatedly, that was the dumbest thing she could have done. But she forced herself on, pulling out the snapshot of her pushing Button on her tire swing. Liam had taken it…

The man yanked the snapshot away and held it close to his face, taking his time studying it.

"You raise these things?" he asked at last, passing the picture back.

"Just got certified." The conversation felt surreal. As if she watched it from a distance, assessing her performance, unable to intervene or guide it.

The man reached into his pocket and she froze. Here it came. A knife, a pistol, something to punish her for tempting fate…not being vigilant on the bus… But instead he retrieved a pack of cigarettes and held it out.

She nearly collapsed at the reprieve. Didn't they offer that to death row prisoners? A final smoke? When she shook her head, he lit one, blew out a stream of smoke and pointed the glowing end at her.

"You are one tough lady. Heard some dealer supposedly got a tiger guarding his stash, but I stay away from that. Don't do drugs. Wish I could kick these."

He waved his cigarette, his rheumy blue eyes wide. "Wild animals, man. Dangerous."

Vivie almost laughed. Wild animals scared him and he petrified her... Maybe, like everything else, fear was relative.

"Her name's Button." She craned her neck. Where was the bus?

He exhaled slowly, smoke curling out of his nostrils and drifting up to his red-veined eyes. "I like that. Button. Could be one of my kids' stuffed animals."

Hoping to keep him talking until the bus, or someone else appeared, she asked. "How many do you have?"

He tapped his chin and she noticed a deep scar running through it. "Five now. One on the way. Old lady kicked me out, though. Don't appreciate me. Girls will be lining up when they find out this is available."

He gestured to himself and grinned.

"I see." Please, oh please, don't let him imagine her on that list. If he did, if he forced the issue, she wouldn't freeze this time. Wouldn't cry.

"Want to hang out more? Been crashing at a friend's. Not fancy, but it'll do."

"Uh. No thanks. Though I appreciate the offer."

His hoop earring swung as he angled his head and studied her. "You got nice manners, lady. I appreciate that. What are you doing in this place, anyway? You're alone. Right?"

She met his eyes and her fingers tightened around her wallet, picturing her animals' pictures inside. He had no right to them or anything that belonged to her. She would never surrender a part of herself again. She couldn't—wouldn't—accept that.

"I'm waiting for the bus."

He flicked his cigarette to the ground and its embers trailed into the sewer grate.

"Just passed a couple minutes ago." He stepped closer, his eyes narrowing. "Ain't safe to be out here alone. Waiting. Don't know who's going to show up." His voice lowered and felt like a threat.

A sudden calm swept through her. She'd heard that kind of voice before. Once she'd been at its mercy, but never again.

She stepped close, near enough that the tip of his sneakers touched hers. "I'm not afraid." She pressed her finger into his grimy T-shirt. "And I don't care about being alone. I can handle myself."

Exhilaration pulsed through her, filling her with a strange mix of hysteria and power.

He threw his hands in the air and rolled his eyes. "Hey. I believe you. But still. Why don't I sit with you at the bus stop? Got some shady characters around here I don't think you'd like to meet...or maybe *they* should be afraid." A phlegmatic laugh rattled out of him and she stared at him in astonishment.

"You want to make sure I'm safe?"

"I know. You got this. But I'd feel better seeing you get on that bus. Don't want that bear missing you now, do you?"

Astonishment and relief rushed through her, making her sway on her feet. When she stumbled, he cupped her elbow and steered her to the bus shelter. He swept debris off the bench inside, pointed for her to sit, then dropped beside her.

"Th-thank you," she stammered, meaning it on many levels. More than he knew.

"You thought I was going to do something bad, didn't you?"

She opened her mouth to deny it, but nodded instead. No lies…especially to herself. Not ever again.

"I'm sorry." She smiled into his grizzled face. "It's just—"

He held up a hand. "Hey. I know how I look. Been stopped by the cops enough times I call them by name. Not everyone like me is a bad guy. I drink a little too much sometimes, but that's it."

She nodded slowly. No. There were a lot more good men than bad. The weight of fear she'd carried all these years dropped away, leaving her buoyant. A relieved chuckle escaped her, and suddenly a dam burst inside. Laughter poured out, carrying with it the dread she'd buried deep.

"No offense, but you sound a little crazy, lady!" He chuckled to himself, then shook his head. He pulled out a pair of glasses before picking up a paper off the ground and popping it opening.

Her laughter subsided at last and she grinned. She'd never felt saner in her life.

CHAPTER FOURTEEN

THE SMELL OF RICH buttercream frosting filled
Liam's nose as he cut another slice of wedding cake the next day. He tipped it onto a
plate and laid it on the serving table beside
him.

"Got any pieces with a rose left?" He
glanced up at Vivie's teasing voice and the
knife slipped from his hands to the platter.
In a strapless blue dress, with her hair up in
a curling mass, she looked even more beautiful than usual.

"Pink or purple?" Forcing himself to stop
staring, he pointed to the uncut middle tier.

"Pink. No. Purple." Vivie laughed, en-
chanting him. "How about both?"

He lost himself in those glowing, light
brown eyes. "You got it."

"Liam?"

"Yeah?"

"The cake?"

He gave himself a little shake and picked
up the triangular cake cutter. "Right."

When she cocked her head, her dark gold ringlets bounced around her long neck. "Are you okay? You've seemed off all day."

Off? He was lost. Floundering. Struggling with emotions for her that he couldn't deny or admit.

"Tired, but I wanted to wait up for you yesterday. You still haven't said why you got in so late or left without me." He passed her the plate, knowing he sounded like some jealous boyfriend. It'd been hard to hold back his questions last night, but the exhausted, breakable look about her had kept him from pushing it.

A strange expression crossed her face. "Trust me, it wasn't planned."

"Did you meet an old friend? Someone from culinary school?" A man? he added silently. His fingers mashed one of Mary Ann's silver-bordered napkins.

"I'll tell you later." Her lips curved again and she peeked at him over her shoulder before strolling away. He watched her rejoin his family on the edge of the tavern's impromptu dance floor. A hunger to follow her took hold. To hold her close. But when he caught her, what would he do? He couldn't keep her.

A trio of musicians rocked some fast tune. His brother Daniel spun on the floor while

Ella, dressed in a pink replica of Mary Ann's gown, twirled with her hands overhead. Close friends and extended family joined in the clapping and cheering. He surveyed the transformed pub. Flower arrangements with candle centerpieces and lace tablecloths gave the room a vintage, elegant feel. Gleaming silver platters and warming trays filled a laden buffet table. White tulle covered the exposed-beam ceiling and gathered in the center at the White Horse's famous chandelier.

If he ever got married, he'd want something small and intimate like this, though it'd be on top of a mountain. Nature's beauty to decorate. His hand stilled, midcut. When had he ever considered marriage before? His eyes sought out Vivie again, his heart knowing the impossible answer.

She fit in perfectly with the Walsh crew. Daniel dragged her onto the dance floor and she nimbly copied some elaborate robot moves, making the crowd howl in approval. His chest squeezed to see her so relaxed and happy, surrounded by family…children…a home…everything he couldn't give her. Exactly what she deserved.

Yet the need to hold her, to kiss that soft mouth, pounded through him. He'd never regretted parting ways with women before.

They'd always been casual relationships. Had an expiration date. But with Vivie, he didn't trust himself to let go so easily. She'd crept under his skin and into his heart.

A small line formed at the cake table and he passed out more plates, his eyes staying on the captivating woman he wished he could truly call his date...or more.

He'd fallen for her, he realized with a jolt. Loved her for her headstrong ways, though he could throttle her for them, too. Admired her determination to help those who couldn't help themselves, like Button. Was undone by that big heart that accepted his chaotic family and even him at his worst.

This weekend together had dialed up his emotions. Watching her interact with his family—teaching Ella elaborate braids, convincing Connor that ties were cool, going through his parents' wedding album with his mother—had made him want a life he'd never imagined. One with Vivie. But would she be happy moving on whenever his surroundings closed in around him?

Her bell of a laugh rang out as she flapped her elbows, shook her backside, then shimmied to the ground alongside some of his elderly aunts. The "Chicken Dance." A family staple. Of course she'd love it along with everything else she'd missed during her nomadic childhood. How could he inflict the same future on her? It would be unfair and he loved her too much to do it.

"She's a keeper," said Mary Ann beside him. He tore his eyes from Vivie and flinched at his sister's observant gaze.

"Yes. She'll make someone happy someday." Though he spoke casually, the thought tore through him. Vivie with another man. A partner who would be content with the stable life she needed.

"Not you?" His sister's sharp brown eyes found his. "Let's go outside," she said abruptly. "I could use some air." She tugged on his arm and led him through the front doors to the small fenced-off sidewalk seating area.

"You look beautiful, sis," he said, meaning it. Against her white lace gown, her hair shone red as a warm blaze, her freckles accentuating her uptilted nose and round cheeks.

She kicked off her shoes and propped her feet on the seat next to her. A group of tourists clattered by, snapping pictures and stopping when they saw the Closed sign on the tavern's front door.

"Thanks, Liam. But you're not getting me off topic. We're talking about you and Vivie."

"There is no me and Vivie," he admitted. Now that the wedding was winding down, it was time to come clean. "We're just friends."

"Thought so. When you were playing with Ella yesterday, your cell phone screen lit up with a message from park services out in Yellowstone. So you are moving again."

"You're reading my phone messages?"

She lowered her chin and looked at him from beneath stern brows. "I'm your older sister. It's a given…"

He shook his head. "What was I thinking?" He loosened his bow tie. "I should have told you, but I didn't want you worrying on your wedding weekend. Wishing I'd settle down."

"You also lied about just being friends with Vivie." Mary Ann unpinned her veil and folded it on her lap. "Stop deceiving yourself."

He shifted in his metal seat. His older sister saw too much. "I'm not."

"Uh-uh. Not buying it." When she shook her head, her pearl earrings swung.

"Even if I do care, there's a lot about Vivie and I that can't work."

"Not from my perspective. You two were adorable together last night at dinner. She loosens you up. Makes you laugh more than you have since the war." Mary Ann put her elbows on the table and leaned forward. "She's good for you, Liam. From the way she looks at you, I can tell she cares about you, too."

"I'm not good for her," he confessed.

Mary Ann moved to the seat next to him, wrapping an arm around his shoulders. "That's not true, Liam. I know that whatever happened to you in Afghanistan changed you. Made you on edge. But the rest—the kind, caring, smart, funny, strong brother I love— is still the same."

The backs of his eyes pricked and he rolled them skyward, to the setting sun. Mary Ann had no idea how it felt to watch your best friends die. To know that there was nothing he could have done to stop it. No matter how much Vivie made him believe he could forget, he'd never shake the past. That helpless trapped feeling wouldn't leave him, no matter how far he ran.

"I'm a survivor. That's all I am." Funny how, until this moment, he hadn't realized that Vivie's description of herself matched his own. She was right—pulling up stakes before he got too attached wasn't really living, either.

Mary Ann's floral perfume folded around them when she dropped her head to his shoulder. "You are so much more. If you'd stay still long enough, you just might see it."

She squeezed him around the middle, then turned when her groom poked his head through the door. "It's time to throw the bouquet," he called.

"Be right there."

Mary Ann straightened and studied Liam, her mouth firm. "When we go in, I want you to ask Vivie to dance."

He suppressed a groan and nodded, glad, at least, that his sister's playful smile returned. She didn't need to worry about him today. Shouldn't think of anything but her happy future.

Following his sister, he ducked inside and headed for the assembled pack of single women by the back corner. Vivie slouched in the middle of the group, as if someone had shoved her there. He guessed Ella, who bounced on her toes beside Vivie, was the culprit. His pulse picked up when he envisioned holding Vivie as they danced in a few minutes. Would he be able to keep his feelings in check? It'd be a Herculean task, but he'd manage. For both their sakes.

"Five. Four. Three. Two. One!" The group chanted and Mary Ann flung her flowers over her shoulder and turned. Feminine squeals filled the room and a scuffle broke out. At last one victor emerged—Ella, who grinned as she held the arrangement aloft, then passed it to Vivie.

"I got it so you'd marry Liam and be my sister someday."

Vivie brushed her wet lashes and stooped to hug Ella. He strained to hear what she said, but the band started up another tune. The slow, romantic song quieted the group and couples drifted out onto the dance floor. Mary Ann narrowed her eyes at him, then jerked her chin at Vivie. Aiden stood behind the bar and nodded at Liam. Were his older siblings conspiring against him?

He squared his shoulders. Nothing for it. It was his sister's day, and what she wanted, she got, no matter how difficult the demand. And when it came down to it, he wanted to hold Vivie.

"Care for a dance?"

Vivie lowered the bouquet from her nose and handed it to Ella.

"I'd love to." Her wide smile drove out his breath. It took him a minute before he stepped forward and swept her into his arms.

The feel of her licked through his blood, driving him senseless. Her intoxicating scent, something wild and fresh, reminded him of home…only he couldn't call the Adirondacks that much longer. The jarring thought sent a chill of regret through him. This was exactly why he avoided connections, ties. But something about Vivie felt inevitable, unavoidable, meant to be…only she wasn't.

"Having a good time?"

"I love family weddings. So personal." Her eyes shone up at him and his arms tightened around her slender waist as they swayed to the song. She was lovely, and totally unconscious of it.

"They definitely like you."

"Ella's adorable. They're all wonderful, but I expected that."

Their eyes met and held. "Why?" His voice rasped. He could hardly hear himself over the steady pounding in his ears.

"Because you are, too."

Her words exploded inside him. He rubbed his hands along the back of her neck, feeling her shiver. She stood on tiptoe and pressed her cheek to his and he groaned, low in her ear.

"This feels nice." She wrapped her arms around his waist and nuzzled close.

"You don't mind being held?"

She shook her head. "Not by you. And not after last night."

"What happened?"

She took his hand and pulled him to a side table when the song ended.

"I've got something to tell you."

"AND THEN HE called me crazy." Vivie grinned as she wound up her story, pleased all over again. Only Liam's face was dark, flushed. He didn't seem to share her excitement.

"You spoke to some stranger past midnight in an unknown neighborhood?" His fingers drummed on the wooden tabletop.

"Not willingly."

"You should have called me." She'd never seen anyone actually speak through clenched teeth, but somehow Liam managed it.

"The bus would have gotten there faster."

"Or called the cops."

"Oh. Sure. What would the 911 call be? A man is talking to me? I'm sure they would have rushed right over since nothing else important was happening in the city." Her excitement transformed into agitation. Couldn't Liam see what a giant step forward she'd taken? What it meant in terms of working through her past?

He yanked off his tie and pulled open a couple of his shirt buttons. He looked devastatingly handsome in his tux today. All broad shoulders, square jaw and tall, dark good looks. Yet now, he resembled a charging bull, or a fire-breathing dragon, as anger singed the air around him.

"Tell me again how you wound up there?"

She sighed. "I missed my stop. Must have fallen asleep for a few minutes. It'd been a long day and I wasn't familiar with the transfer."

"Well you should have been, Vivie. Or brought someone along who would have kept you safe."

"Like you?" Her temper rose to meet his. "I don't need a knight in shining armor. Or a gun-toting man in uniform. As it turned out, I only needed myself."

"You got lucky." His eyebrows met over his nose and his nostrils flared. "You could have been hurt again or—" his eyes dropped to her scar "—worse."

She swallowed hard, imagining the possibilities. But wasn't that the very thing that kept her house- and diner-bound, stopped her from leaving the areas she'd designated as "safe" and enjoying her life?

"I was lucky. That guy could have attacked me. But he didn't. Maybe I had something to do with it and perhaps I didn't. What matters is that I didn't back down. It was the best thing that could have happened to me."

Liam shook his head at her, shocked. "It could have been the worst."

"I didn't go looking for it, but like you said, bad stuff happens and we can't control it. What's important is that I got through it. I'm not just a survivor anymore, Liam. I'm a—a—"

"Conqueror."

They both gawked, startled to see Connor loitering nearby. He shrugged at their stares. "What? Nothing else interesting is happening at this lame wedding."

"Stop eavesdropping, Connor."

The teenager slipped in his earbuds and slouched away. "Whatever."

Vivie turned the word over in her mind, liking how it felt. Connor was right. She had conquered her fears and would never see herself, or her life, the same way.

She leaned forward and grasped Liam's hand. It tensed in her grip, then gradually relaxed until his fingers twined in hers.

"I don't want anything to happen to you."

"I can't live in a box. Not anymore."

Liam studied her from beneath his thick lashes. "No. But I won't always be around to make sure you're okay."

The harsh truth pierced her joy. "I know." She wouldn't be afraid anymore. But without Liam, she'd be torn apart, a piece of her missing...one she hadn't known existed. What choice did she have, though, but to let him go? She loved him, she realized, but it made no difference.

"Let's have all of the bachelors up here for the garter toss!" hollered Aiden.

Giggling, Mary Ann extended her leg while her groom slid off the scrap of cloth and twirled it over his head. A rowdy beat pulsed in the room. The attendees stomped their feet and whistled loudly enough to turn Mary Ann's cheeks a bright pink as she yanked down her skirt.

"Aren't you going up there?"

Liam peered up from their joined hands. "No point. I won't steal a chance from a guy who wants to get married."

She lifted her eyebrow, unable to stop herself from teasing him, despite the painful reminder of his words. "So you believe in superstitions? Guess that means I'm getting hitched, then."

His fingers gripped hers, hard. "Not you, Vivie. Not a chance."

Pressure built in her chest. Since her attack, she'd written off marriage, believing she'd never let anyone close enough. Now, after conquering her fears yesterday, she knew better.

"What do you mean? I have no chance of getting married? Wouldn't make someone a good wife? Am—am I damaged goods or something?" Her ragged voice sounded as ripped up as she felt. For so long she'd felt that way about herself. Was it possible he saw her that way, too? She closed her eyes, wishing she were home again, her pets huddled beside her. She loved Liam, but he'd never feel the same way.

He scooted closer and wrapped an arm around her. "Vivie. I'm sorry. That came out wrong. Anyone would be lucky to have you."

"Just not you."

He tipped her chin up and his eyes searched hers. "Would you want to be married to someone like me?"

She thought about his traveling. How no sooner would she get settled, start another business, then he'd uproot them again. It was the life she'd led growing up. One she'd vowed never to repeat. Liam might not want to grow attached to things, but she needed connections. Not to keep her safe anymore, but to make her complete. She desperately wished Liam could be part of that.

When she shook her head, his mouth tightened, the hopeful light in his eyes fading.

"Then we understand each other."

"Too well," she murmured, wishing with all her heart that they didn't.

The ringing of a utensil on glass hushed the exuberant group. Liam's twin, Niall, lowered the garter he'd just caught and all turned to Liam's mother, Agnes. She waved a goblet.

"Shouldn't we have a song from Liam?"

Heads swiveled their way and Vivie turned to face a motionless Liam, the color drained from his face.

Mary Ann hustled to her mother and led her to the kitchen, the double doors swinging closed behind them. When the guest chatter resumed, Vivie shot Liam a sidelong glance. He seemed far away, his thoughts inward, taking him to some disturbing place.

She touched his tense biceps.

"Hey. What happened there?"

He seemed to return to himself with a start, peering at her fingers, then back up to her. "I used to sing. Now I don't."

His silence pressed around them, heavy and thick.

"So that's it? No explanation?"

"It's not something I talk about. Let's leave

it at that. Would you like a soda?" He half rose and she pulled him down.

"No. You opened up to me about Kunar. Why do I think this is related? That you left something out?"

"It doesn't make a difference." He untied a gauze bag filled with candy-coated almonds and held it out to her. "Want one?"

She grabbed the candy and dropped it on the table. "Why are you avoiding my question?"

"Why are you pushing it?" He stared at her, hard, but she wouldn't look away. Wasn't backing down. Somehow this was important. She could sense it.

"You said once you wanted me to know you. This is part of it. Good or bad."

After a long, tense moment, his head lowered and he released a pent-up breath. "After my dad died, I took odd jobs and saved up for a guitar so I could teach myself to play. Music was the only thing, in my big family, that was just mine. It took me away from our problems for a little while. Let me stop thinking about my mom's health, our money issues, missing my dad. It was an escape."

She waited for more, holding her tongue. The pink and purple flowers in the table arrangement had started to droop and she plucked one, twirling it in her fingers.

At last, he continued. "When I was deployed, I sang for my unit. It helped take us away. Forget our fears. Missing home."

She traced his arm with her fingers, hoping her touch would reassure the courageous veteran. "It must have comforted them. You, too."

"It did."

"Until…"

He grabbed the water pitcher on the table, filled a glass and drank. After a long gulp, he set it down and ran his finger around the cup's rim.

"Kunar. The siege. Eventually nothing helped. Made any difference."

"You sang there."

He lifted haunted eyes to hers. "Yes, when we weren't taking fire, being picked off. It was the only thing that kept us going. Out there, we were scared of not going home. We didn't know if we'd see tomorrow. But I had to be brave for myself, for my country, for my family, for my friends. When I was afraid, music was there."

She rubbed his arm, feeling the bumps that had risen on his skin. "And you shared it with your fellow soldiers, too."

He sipped more water and she noticed the liquid tremble in the glass.

"That gave them some peace, Liam. Don't you see that?"

"They still died. Almost all of them."

"Isn't it better that they at least had some songs from home—during their last days?"

His hazel eyes shimmered, a kaleidoscope of color and pain, before he slid them away. "They liked it when we sang 'Born in the USA' really loud, hoping the insurgents could hear. It was Jim's idea."

She smiled at him. "I bet it gave them courage. You gifted them with that, Liam. Your singing wasn't pointless. It moved people. Affected how they felt and thought. You made a difference. Maybe not with your gun but with your voice."

His gaze flashed to her. "That's what you think?"

"That's what I know. When I almost—" She paused and reflexively drew away from remembering the pain. But she was surprised to find those memories held a bearable ache, not the deep hurt she'd expected. "On my Alive Day, I only heard myself crying and the men. Terrible things I would never want to be my last memories. But you, you gave your friends music and that is the most beautiful thing you could have done for them. I would have given anything to hear music. Sung instead of screamed."

He pulled her to him roughly, burying his hands in her hair so that the pins came loose and the mass tumbled down her back. "Vivie," he began, his voice hoarse. "There's a lot I want to say to you—it's impossible, I know, but—"

A flash of lace appeared beside them.

"Sorry, guys. Mom's having a meltdown. She went upstairs, found Liam's old guitar and keeps insisting he sing."

In the far corner, Aiden and a woman who resembled Agnes talked gently to Liam's agitated parent. She clutched the guitar to her chest and tears flowed down her lined cheeks.

"I know it's a lot to ask, but is there any way…" Mary Ann's voice trailed off and Liam's chair scraped back.

"Yes. On one condition."

"Anything," Mary Ann said, looking shocked and elated.

"Vivie sings with me."

LIAM KISSED HIS mother's damp cheek and eased his guitar from her grip. Her clear-eyed happiness soothed the deep burning inside. Vivie had a point. His music did make a difference. If it made his mother feel better, smoothed over this bump in the reception, then it was worth reliving the past. And maybe the past was something he needed to face, as Vivie had last night.

When he and Vivie approached the band area there was brief applause followed by an attentive hush.

He plucked two notes and felt the audience lean toward them. He touched a string and began to tune the instrument. It was not the finest guitar. He hadn't been able to afford a better one at the time. Its neck was nicked. One of the pegs was loose and prone to going out of tune, he recalled.

He brushed a soft chord and tipped his ear to the strings. As he glanced up, he glimpsed Vivie's face, clear as the moon. She smiled excitedly and the soft light in her eyes made his heart squeeze.

He touched the loose peg gently, running his hands over the warm wood. The varnish was scraped and scuffed in places, but that didn't make it less precious to him.

So, yes. It had flaws, but what did that matter when it came to things you treasured? Vivie had called herself damaged goods and he could say the same about himself. Yet, did that mean they couldn't be loved…find love…together?

Anyone could love someone perfect. Whole. That was easy. But to love someone scarred. Wounded. To know the flaws and love them, too. That was rare and pure and perfect. Could he and Vivie share that?

He adjusted another string and pictured his old bunk mate, Roger, asking him for some Bon Jovi, Pete wanting more Journey. How both of them, and the rest of his unit, had sung along or closed their eyes, remembered better times. He had brought them peace at the end and the thought soothed a jagged part of him that had scraped his heart raw.

At last, he moved a finger and the chord went minor in a way that sounded a bit sad. He moved his hands again and this time two chords sang with each other. Then, without a plan, he began to play.

The strings felt foreign to his fingers, like old friends meeting up again. He played soft and slow, sending notes to the edge of the circle gathered around them. Fingers and strings worked together carefully, as if this tender bond might be broken at any moment.

Then he felt something inside him open and music poured into the quiet. His fingers danced, intricate and quick. The music moved like a maple key spinning to the forest floor, dandelion fluff floating on a summer breeze. It felt as if it carried his time in Kunar with it, along with the anguished waiting, the heart-stopping fear, the despair that he'd never make it out.

At last, he slipped into a familiar tune, a love song Mary Ann had played endlessly when they'd grown up. Her eyes smiled at him and Vivie joined him in a duet. Her voice was honey smooth, a light soprano that complemented his baritone perfectly. They sang as though they'd done so together forever, each one taking turns weaving harmonic lines, supporting the melody and sometimes carrying it for the other. The moment was the sharpest, sweetest he'd ever known.

He felt the heat of her beside him. Breathed in the summer-rain and meadow-flower scent of her. Listened to the tender fluttering of her voice. It was beautiful. His eyes kept returning to her as she sat on a stool, arms hugging her knees.

At last the song ended, the final chord ringing in the silence, and after a bit, it slowly began to dawn on Liam that he'd been staring at Vivie for an awkward amount of time. But she didn't seem offended or amused. She studied his face, as if she was waiting.

He wanted to take her somewhere private. Brush her cheek with his fingertips. Tell her that she was the most beautiful thing he'd ever seen. That the sight of her was enough to drive the breath from him. How sometimes he missed out on what she said for the soft lilt of her voice. He wanted to say that if she were with him, then nothing could ever be wrong in his world again.

In that moment, he considered asking her to come with him to Yellowstone. He felt the question boiling up in his chest. He drew in air, then hesitated. What could he say? Come with me? Leave your work, your friends, home, everything you know and love?

No.

Sudden certainty tightened in his chest. He couldn't promise her anything. He closed his mouth and smiled instead at the applauding crowd and his beaming mother.

Whatever he said couldn't guarantee her permanence or stability, and after all she'd been through, she deserved at least that.

CHAPTER FIFTEEN

LIAM PROPPED HIS feet on a milk crate and leaned back in the spindle chair that made up the only furniture in his rental house's living room. When the music playing from his docked iPhone shuffled to another tune, he glanced at the lit screen—3:00 a.m.

Another sleepless night.

Given his upcoming morning shift, he should be snoozing. Since Mary Ann's wedding, however, a driving restlessness kept him up most nights. He couldn't stop thinking about his duet with Vivie, the feel of her when they'd danced, how well she'd fit in with his family. Most of all, he mulled over his Yellowstone move. Three weeks from now he'd be across the country. Wouldn't be responsible for her or Button.

The thought should have calmed him. He needed distance to stop his growing attachment. Yet, whenever he imagined his unencumbered future, emptiness filled him. He'd miss her. No doubt about it. She'd become an important part of his life. He wouldn't be whole without her.

A coyote called in the distance, its lonely cry hanging in the dark.

Extra Pickles picked up her russet head and whined.

"Big baby," he murmured affectionately, then leaned down to rub her soft ears. "Soon you'll be listening to wolves in Yellowstone. But I'll be with you."

Her long pink tongue flashed and wetness smeared his palm.

"Thank you, sweetheart."

He wiped his hand on his sweatpants and paced to the window. Outside, a quarter moon rode on waves of clouds. A breeze blew through the screen, colder than it'd been in months. Bright eyes flashed in the oak tree beyond the front stoop, an owl looking for a meal in the rustling grass. Now that August waned, animals scurried and flitted more, anxious to migrate, hibernate, weather the harsh winter ahead.

Change.

It was part of life, if only Vivie could accept it. Would he want her to move with him if she was up for it? Before the wedding, he'd rejected having anyone permanent in his life. Now, he wondered.

No one understood him the way Vivie did. Maybe her own tragedy helped. Or her caring, gentle nature. She understood his past and how it influenced him today. Before her, he hadn't examined his old wounds. Didn't want to bleed again. She made him see things differently. Know himself better.

But was it enough? Could he be tied down? Vivie deserved nothing less than a true commitment, and until he knew for sure, he didn't dare speak his heart. It'd kill him to go, but better that than risk hurting her. He cared about her too much.

He continued to stare aimlessly and found himself singing along with a Springsteen tune, the familiar lyrics making his eyes sting. Still, he belted it out until the song finished and saluted his fallen friends. He hoped they heard him. Had sung along, too, the way they had in the old days.

He waited for memory's crushing weight to bury him. Instead, light filled him. He pictured his battle buddies hollering off-key, grinning, as a taste of home took them from their nightmare. Vivie was right. His singing had helped. Maybe he hadn't saved them in the traditional way, but he'd made a difference. Eased their lives…

He ambled to his fridge and studied the

near-empty shelves. A carton of milk, eggs so old he didn't remember buying them and a jug of soda. He grabbed the pop, poured himself a glass and leaned against the counter. Taking a gulp, he contemplated the bare floor, imagining the kitchen table he'd never purchased. Just as well. Less to move. Just his bedroom furniture, belongings and...

And what?

What else did he have?

The thought made him wince. Strange. It had never bothered him before. He hadn't wanted things weighing him down. Vivie was right, having nothing made leaving easier. Yet now he wasn't so sure it was material goods that mattered. Leaving Vivie felt impossible.

He polished off his drink, rinsed the glass and headed back to the living room, Extra Pickles hot on his heels.

"You don't need to go everywhere with me, you know."

A damp nose nudged into his hand again for a petting. He stroked his collie's long fur, his fingers trailing through the silky strands on her back as her tail thumped. Needy dog. She trailed him the moment he got home. Loved hiking with him. Fishing. He felt bad he'd neglected her lately because of Button, but he couldn't risk her spooking the cub...

or worse, have the growing bear hurt his pet. But he missed her when she wasn't around.

He was capable of one attachment at least.

That'd been enough before. Now…he didn't know what to think…his thoughts and feelings tangling in a knot he couldn't unravel.

A pile of envelopes by his front door caught his eye. The mail. At least he could be productive while awake. Pay some bills. That was enough to put anyone to sleep.

He grabbed the stack and nearly tripped over Extra Pickles as she dodged in front of him on his way to the bedroom. He stopped and crouched, cupping her narrow face.

"You are too much, tonight. What am I going to do with you?" He scratched the sweet spot above her left shoulder and her back leg jittered. "Now lie down. I'm doing some work."

She followed instructions, lying across his feet beneath his computer desk.

"Great. Who needs slippers?" he mused out loud, but kept his toes under her warm, heaving side. There was no denying Extra Pickles. Pointless to even try.

Fifteen minutes later he'd paid his electric and phone bills but hesitated about notifying them to turn off service at the end of next month. Time enough for that.

Yet an urgent sense seized him. A need to know. Now. Was he going or not? Could he stay...for Vivie?

The writing on the next envelope caught his eye. Mary Ann. He tore it open and discovered a politely worded thank-you note for his wedding gift followed by a more typical missive at the bottom. "Check your email, jerk."

Nice.

She had to mean the private account she'd set up for him last year. The one he rarely used. He had his work account. The people who needed him got to him through that. Personal emails... He never thought much about them since his family wasn't big on communicating except though Mary Ann, who called...often.

What had she sent him?

Sure enough, her message appeared among a bunch of junk emails. The subject line: "Check you out!"

He clicked on her attachment and his heart sped when a picture of him and Vivie singing at the wedding popped up.

Her beautiful face glowed up at him as he played, her cheeks flushed, eyes sparkling. There was no mistaking that look. Or at least he hoped not. Love. It had to be...because his own face held the same, intense, passionate expression as he gazed down at her.

She might love him. Want him, flaws and all.

The thought pinged through him until it settled into his chest. How could he have imagined tiring of her company? Feeling claustrophobic with a woman who knew him so well and cared about him still? For a moment, he pictured a life without her and it terrified him. He wanted her to look at him that way again. Always. Wanted the feelings she brought out in him. Wanted her. And that wouldn't happen if he and Extra Pickles left the Adirondacks alone.

But would her affection change if she moved to Yellowstone with him? Without Button to bring them together, would her feelings last? How would she cope with leaving her friends, her business? He didn't want her to resent him or regret being with him. But it could happen. How to know?

The music in the living room shuffled to another song, reminding him that he hadn't turned it off. In a few steps, he grabbed the iPhone out of the docking system and scrolled to his contacts list. He clicked on Vivie's name to see another picture of her and studied her gorgeous smile, hoping for clarity.

Nothing. Just the same longing that filled him each time he saw her.

His thumb slid across her cheek and he imagined her soft skin.

A familiar voice stopped him as he reentered his bedroom.

"Hello? Liam?"

He'd been thinking so much about Vivie. Was he dreaming up her voice, too?

"Liam? Are you there?"

Her husky voice reached out to him. A warm hug when he needed one. He glanced down at his phone and nearly dropped it when he saw he'd called her.

An accident?

Probably not. But he wouldn't have imagined she'd answer his call since she didn't get cell service up at her house.

"Liam?"

He brought the phone to his ear and gently pushed Extra Pickles, who'd wrapped her paws around his legs, away.

"Vivie."

"Why are you calling so late?"

"An accident. Maybe. I don't know. How did you get this call?"

He sat in his desk chair and gazed at their picture.

"I'm actually outside. Once in a blue moon

I get a signal out here. Glad my phone was in my coat pocket or I wouldn't have heard it."

He glanced out his window at the quarter moon and imagined Vivie under it. Alone. Unprotected.

"You shouldn't be up so late. Go inside. Lock your door."

Her soft laugh sent a shiver across his skin.

"I'm not afraid anymore, Liam. Remember? Plus you said the poachers were rare out here."

"That doesn't mean you're safe, Vivie. Go inside."

A sigh sounded through the phone. "Fine."

He heard a door open, then close.

"Happy?" she asked after a moment.

"No," he admitted, the truth rushing from him too fast to stop.

"What's going on? Why are you up so late?"

He stared into her beautiful amber eyes on the screen. "I can't stop thinking about you."

Silence stretched and his palms grew damp. "Vivie?"

"Yes," she said faintly. "I'm here. I can't sleep, either, for the same reason."

"Thinking about yourself?" He couldn't resist.

"Exactly," she said drily, then sighed. "I wish it were that easy."

"Maybe we're making this too complicated."

She said something indecipherable, the call breaking up. An image of him struggling to reach her, thousands of miles away, gripped him. He felt himself dissolving along with her words, imagining a day without her voice. The thought struck like a blow.

"Liam? Are you there?" she asked. Her voice clearer. Stronger. As if she was close. The way he needed her to be, he realized.

"Always. Or I want to be."

Silence hung between them again, briefly. He could almost feel her soft exhale before she said, "Liam. I don't know what you want."

An idea struck and the dim room seemed to brighten around him.

"My shift starts in a few hours, but I'd like to pick you up later, for a date. Say—seven thirty?"

"I'll be ready, though I'm not sure for what…"

"That's what we're going to figure out."

"I— Okay," she said. "Seven thirty, and—"

Static filled his ear and he glanced down at the empty screen. Call dropped. Not that it troubled him. What he had to say, he wanted to say right. Stolen moments before heading to work weren't nearly enough.

Not when he wanted to spend forever with her.

"WHERE ARE WE GOING?" Vivie heard the tremor of excitement in her voice later that evening, felt it in her body. She gazed out the tinted window of Liam's SUV and marveled at his transformation. Never before had she seen him so…so…carefree.

He laid a warm hand on her knee and squeezed, sending a jitter of excitement flooding through her. His lazy smile lifted the right side of his mouth and he took his eyes off the road for a moment to peer at her.

"Whiteface. We're going to the castle."

She returned his irresistible smile and settled back in the seat. "I've always wanted to go there. Maggie says it's beautiful." A thought occurred and she frowned. "But don't they close the building at eight?"

Liam nodded. His eyes slid toward her again, hazel depths sparkling. "Got it covered. Called in a favor from a friend with Park Service."

"Oh. So we'll have it to ourselves?"

His mouth curved up again. "Yes."

With that one word, her senses flipped

on and suddenly everything around her—the rising, winding road, the tree-covered mountains, the birds wheeling in a purple sky—looked brighter, more vibrant than she'd ever seen them. Her lungs expanded and she breathed deeply, filled with expectancy...but for what?

She cared about Liam, loved him. The depth of her feelings had become clear when she'd spotted him pacing by his family's apartment window, anxiously waiting, the night of her near mugging. Who else but Liam worried about her like that? Cared and supported her? He didn't want to get attached, yet he stayed beside her through everything, big and small, from studying for a certification test to fighting off a fire.

Since they only had a few weeks before he left, she didn't dare hope for anything other than a pleasant evening with the man she'd fallen for. Still—her heart leaped every time she glanced at his handsome profile. The sensation of his strong hand on her leg, his thumb brushing her knee, filled her with an electric awareness.

When they reached the tollhouse, a bearded man leaned out.

"Hey, Liam. See you've got your date with you."

She felt heat spreading up her neck and into her cheeks. She wished she was his girlfriend, not a casual date.

"Looks like a clear view today." Liam nodded toward the narrow road that rose, then disappeared around a hairpin turn.

"Had a lot of visitors, but they're mostly gone now. Should have the place to yourselves by the time you get up there." The man turned a sign over, the words Memorial Highway Closed visible.

"Thanks, Joe. I owe you."

The man grinned, sheepish. "Aw. If you hadn't found my Hermione, don't know what I would have done. This evens the score." Joe tipped his cap. "Have fun, you two."

Liam waved and they roared up the steep incline, a rocky cliff wall to their left and bedrock boulders interspersed with wildflowers to their right, the world dropping away beyond it.

"Hermione?" She raised an eyebrow, imagining what Liam had done to save this damsel in distress.

"His pet hedgehog. She disappeared while he was cleaning her cage and we searched half the day before finding her curled up in one of his slippers."

Liam, rescuer of hedgehogs…and her…

She shuddered as she thought of the fire and how he'd saved Button. Rescued them all. The house didn't matter compared to that. She'd told him she didn't need a hero, but it was wonderful to have one around. If only he would stay. When she sighed, his hand tightened on her thigh and she glanced from it to the dangerous road they careened over.

She placed his fingers back on the wheel. "Two and ten, mister."

His mouth twitched. "That's for kids."

"And people with sense. Do you see this drop-off?" The car whizzed by a sign that proclaimed 2,500 feet.

"I could drive this road in my sleep. Plus that stone wall will stop a car going at this speed."

She relaxed against the seat. "I want to live through my first date with you."

His eyebrows lifted and his gaze swerved her way for a heart-stopping second. "First? Does that mean you've already agreed to more?"

She opened her mouth and closed it, unsure how to handle this flirtatious version of Liam. It messed with her head and her heart. "Just get us up there in one piece," she managed.

He lifted a couple of fingers from the wheel and cocked an eyebrow. "This okay?"

She swatted his shoulder. "Knock it off, Liam."

He shrugged. "For now," he said, and the low baritone promise in his voice tiptoed down her spine.

A string of cars passed them, going in the opposite direction as they neared the summit. Suddenly a medieval-replica castle loomed into view, complete with gothic arches, glinting stone walls and leaded glass windows. A lone station wagon backed out of the now-empty parking lot and the driver gave them a cheery wave.

Vivie gazed around her in wonder when Liam pulled into a space. "It's like something right out of fairy tale. I love it." She scrambled from the car and dashed beneath the arched porticos to a waist-high fieldstone wall behind the castle. Another sign read 4,865 feet.

Smaller mountain peaks jutted around her and she turned slowly, taking in the breathtaking panoramic view. The sun rode low and heavy in the sky, a deep yellow ball that smeared the cloud drifts pink and orange.

"It's gorgeous," she exclaimed.

"You're more beautiful," Liam whispered in her ear, his arms encircling her, holding her tight against him.

She curled around. "What are we doing, Liam?"

His mouth twisted but his eyes remained serious. "Having dinner."

"Right." She gently eased away, not wanting to push this fragile moment. "Are we eating out here?"

He extended a hand and she grasped it, loving the weight of their joined fingers swinging between them as they walked. A girl could get used to this.

They reached a large arched door, and he held it open, gesturing for her to precede him. Inside, it was cool and dim and the light filtered through tall, narrow windows.

"We're eating up there." Liam gestured to a metal spiral staircase. He looked a little dangerous tonight in gray dress slacks and a black dress shirt that set off his vivid eyes. "After you." He bowed slightly at the waist. His full lips curved into a smile when he straightened.

"Fancy," she murmured, smoothing the yellow maxi dress she'd donned, glad her silver sandals dressed up her outfit even more.

When her head cleared the staircase, she gasped and rushed the rest of the way into the candlelit room. Her heart beat fast as she surveyed the large space. Flames sputtered in every corner, a long buffet table laden with sushi, fruit and salads dominating a far wall. Fresh flowers spilled out of a clear glass vase on a round table by one of the oversize windows.

Her heels clattered on the stone floor as Liam cupped her elbow and led her to the table. He pulled out her seat, then took his own. "What do you think?"

"How did you manage this?" she asked, though what she really wanted to know was *why*? He couldn't have decided to stay here. Want a relationship…could he? Her heart swelled and she knew instantly that her answer would be yes if he asked.

She trusted him like no other. He'd done so many supportive things, large and small, these past two and a half months. After dancing to her mother's restless tune growing up, then clinging to her home after her attack, she'd finally had the courage to open up, to believe again, thanks to Liam. Deep down, she knew she'd always want him near…if only he'd stay.

Liam poured something fizzy into her fluted glass, his handsome face shining above the flickering candle. "Sparkling grape juice, okay?"

"Perfect."

He filled his glass and raised it. "'May we have those in our arms whom we love in our hearts,'" he quoted.

She studied him for a long moment, not sure how to take his beautiful words. Did he love her?

They clinked glasses and their eyes clung as each sipped.

"I hope you like sushi. There's also some local cheese. Bread from the bakery. Hummus, cucumber salad…"

She raised a hand. "This is amazing. How did you get it all up here?"

He grinned. "Had it delivered. Joe oversaw everything. Had his nephews set up the food and room. They don't use this except for special occasions and since this is one… I rented it."

She sipped her drink and set it down on the white linen tablecloth. "He must love Hermione."

"Everyone needs someone to love." The passionate flare in his eyes made her pulse race.

"Let's eat," she said when the silence stretched to its breaking point.

They filled their plates and returned to the table. "Yellowfin tuna. What a treat." She dipped the fish in soy sauce and brought the chopsticks to her mouth. The tart, gingery flavor exploded on her tongue and her eyes closed in appreciation. "Wow. So good."

When she opened her eyes, Liam was gazing at her, his expression warm and appreciative. "You look like an angel."

"I clean up okay." She deflected the compliment, feeling awkward, not knowing where this was going.

"Even when you're mucking around on a hiking trail, Vivie. You're the most beautiful woman in the world to me." When he reached for her hand, she slid her fingers between his, her breath quickening.

"It's been quite a summer."

A tortured expression flitted across his face and vanished. "It's almost over."

"Soon you'll be gone."

His fingers tightened around hers and she nearly winced at his grip. "Vivie, I've done a lot of thinking. Since Kunar, I've been careful not to get attached. I'd lost too much and couldn't bear to lose another person I cared for."

The hair on her arms prickled. "And now?"

His thumb brushed the center of her palm, sending frissons of electricity through her.

"Now I know that I am attached. To you."

"Oh," her breath hitched and she couldn't find the words to say anything more.

"You've changed me and I can't go back to how I used to be. I don't know how it happened. Or when. Maybe it was our work with Button, the fire, the wedding, or all the moments in between. But I know I'm a different man. A better one, I hope."

"You're perfect to me," she found the courage to say and his eyes searched hers.

"No. Not perfect. But I'm crazy about you. Vivie. I don't want to leave and always wonder how you're doing."

Her mind stuck on one thought, replaying it over and over. He was going to tell her he'd changed his mind. Wasn't going to Yellowstone. Would stay here for her.

"I want you to come to Yellowstone with me."

She stared at him, uncomprehending at first, her mind too full of bliss to absorb the blow. When it hit, however, it hit hard. She jerked to her feet and walked to the window, watching, without seeing, as the sun sank behind the mountain range.

He gripped her shoulders and gently turned her to face him. "Vivie. Will you come with me?"

Despair clogged her throat. Of course she couldn't leave her home. She was no longer afraid. That wasn't the issue. But she had responsibilities, people and animals who depended on her.

"I can't. There's too much for me here."

The hope in his eyes dimmed. "I could give you so much in Yellowstone. All that I am. It's yours."

"And how long before you'd want to leave Yellowstone? Maybe move us to Alaska? Nova Scotia?"

He scrubbed a hand over his eyes. "I can't guarantee that we'd settle down permanently, Vivie, but I would never leave you."

Her shoulders slumped. "It's not enough. I can't give up everything I've built here. And there's Button."

His head rested atop hers and he gathered her close. "I haven't heard official word about Button, Vivie. The vet report should be in soon. If she's cleared for her jaw, then one of the refuges may take her or she'll be released."

Her muscles tightened as she imagined the impossible...letting Button go. But wouldn't she have to do the same with Liam? Both were options too terrible to contemplate. She'd seen Button's curious side-chewing motion. There was a chance she wouldn't be approved for release and would stay in her enclosure. Become a permanent part of Vivie's family. If only that family could include Liam, too.

"Is there any possibility you'd consider staying here?"

She glanced up at him and found it hard to look away from his soulful eyes.

He carefully brushed an eyelash from her cheek, then rested his palm against the side of her face. "I've been here long enough. I'll only be miserable if I stay."

"And I'd feel the same if I left." She broke away and wandered to the buffet table, staring at the flickering candlelight. Deep down, she knew that Liam was the only man she'd feel this way about, but it wasn't meant to be.

She smelled his outdoorsy scent before she felt his hand slip into hers. She turned to face him.

"You don't know you'd be unhappy if you left. Yellowstone could be a new beginning for you. For us."

Her lips twisted and she snatched her hand away. "Staying put could be a fresh start for you, too, but you don't consider that. You only took me to the wedding to fool your family into thinking you're stable. Doing all right."

His brows crashed together. "I am all right."

"Moving all the time, never allowing yourself to care about anyone, to build a life? That doesn't sound okay to me."

He paced away to the long, narrow window near the top of the stairs.

"I wanted you at the wedding with me. End of story."

"No, it's not. There's more. Your family worries about you. Wishes you'd settle down."

He turned and their eyes met across the shadowed room. His chest rose and fell. "They do."

"Then stop putting this all on me."

In a few strides he closed the distance between them and gathered her in his arms.

"You're right. It's both of us. Let's take this one day at a time. See if you feel differently in the next three weeks." With his head lowered, his words flowed over her lips.

"You might be the one to change your mind… But either way, we can at least enjoy the time we have left together," she whispered back, and in an instant he was pressing his firm mouth to hers, sucking gently on her lower lip before capturing it fully. She breathed in his scent, the fresh pine smell that made her head swim. She clutched his shoulders as his kiss strengthened, her fingers twining in the thick hair that brushed his collar. He moaned low in the back of his throat and his hands slid up her back, cupping her head as he deepened the kiss until they both gasped for air.

His heart drummed against her chest and an electric lightness rolled through her. She'd never felt so vulnerable, yet empowered, in a man's arms before. Intoxicating. When his mouth trailed down her jaw, her head lolled back. She shivered when his lips nibbled along her neck, lingering at its base.

"You feel so good," he growled when he pulled away at last.

She grabbed the back of a nearby seat, feeling dizzy. "So do you."

"Have I convinced you yet?" The excitement in his eyes was infectious. But how could she be anything but honest? Yes, he made her feel things no other man could. Still...it was a big decision.

"I need time."

He lifted her off her feet and gave her another breathless kiss before setting her down again. "We have three more weeks and I'm making the most of them. You see...I love you."

Her breath evaporated in her lungs and her

heart somersaulted. He loved her. It was beyond imagining. Wishing. Did she dare say it back given her doubts about their future?

She put a hand against his chest. "Liam. I don't want you to get your hopes up." There was so much to consider…and would a refuge in Yellowstone be available for Button? One she could volunteer at perhaps? Would she be able to keep her family together? So many questions to work through. Three weeks might not be enough. But the thought of losing this…these moments with Liam… it hurt, too.

"Too late." His mischievous grin was contagious and she returned it, pushing him away to return to her dinner.

"Impossible. That's what you are." She pointed her chopsticks at him before scooping up a California roll, her heart full to bursting.

"It's all part of the charm," he said with a wink before picking up his chopsticks.

And it was… That strong, thoughtful man who'd entrusted her with his deepest hurts, his hidden insecurities. It only made him more special to her.

She brushed away the last shred of her doubts. They had three weeks together and a lot could change. Better to enjoy this time and worry about the future when it happened. For now, she'd let go and live—for Liam, for her pet family and most of all, for herself.

CHAPTER SIXTEEN

LIAM LAY ON his side and eyed the beautiful woman sunbathing next to him on the long wooden dock. A moist northern wind blew, rustling and fluttering leaves as a few early turners floated in colorful bursts. Another sign of approaching fall. The end of their idyllic three weeks together.

A heaviness drummed inside him. Vivie still hadn't agreed to go to Yellowstone. Since their evening at Whiteface, they'd been inseparable. He envisioned driving west alone in three days and a ripping sensation tore through him—a rending inside if he left her behind.

He twirled a yellow leaf and peered at Vivie. They belonged together. Why hadn't she made up her mind to see things his way?

A splash sounded from the bank and a large black animal paddled out to join them.

Button.

Of course Vivie struggled to leave when she didn't know her bear's future. As her certification supervisor, he'd been ordered to share that news with her today. He dropped the leaf in the water and watched it drift, wishing he could do the same...avoid telling Vivie the DEC's decision.

"Hey, sweetie," he heard Vivie croon, as the young bear's large head appeared by the wooden platform. "Ew!" she squealed when a half-eaten fish flew over her stomach and landed between them. He tossed the rank object overboard.

Button snorted and Vivie sat up to stroke the animal's wet fur. "Sorry. Just wasn't expecting such a nice—uh—gift. Do you want your turtle?" Vivie reached into her bag and pulled out the mutilated rubber toy. It was barely recognizable, but Button reached eagerly. She got a paw on it, then went under when she lost grip.

"Button!" Vivie squealed and Liam grabbed her before she leaped into the river. It would be all kinds of dangerous to get close to a thrashing, nearly grown bear.

Button's head broke the surface after a heart-stopping moment, the turtle in her mouth.

"Yay! You got Turtle." Vivie laughed and her relief and excitement charmed Liam. How she loved that bear. She knelt and touched her nose to Button's, leaning over the dock's edge. "Did you eat some nuts?"

Liam scanned the bank of oaks and spotted a haughty pheasant strutting slowly by, nibbling at the grass and peering cautiously in all directions. They'd brought Button here to show her how to plunder squirrel hoards and forage for acorns herself. It was the last survival skill they needed to teach her. Since she'd remember her mother's hibernation spot, the fattened bear could find a cozy sleeping spot without their help when snow fell.

Not that Vivie envisioned Button anywhere else than her sleep stall, he knew. She'd even mentioned wiring the barn for heat. Liam held in a sigh. Button would make her own warmth this winter. The department had slated her for release in a few days.

A spray of water splattered him and he watched Vivie splashing Button. Her giggles rang out as the bear swam in circles. Button swatted her large paws, sending plumes of liquid over both of them. He glanced away. Their joy in each other was painful to watch now that it had to end.

He didn't doubt Button would thrive in the wild. Vivie, on the other hand, might not do as well, even though she'd grown so much stronger since he met her. Would she be able to eventually forgive him when she found out the plan? Understand that he was doing his job and what he knew was best for Button?

Suddenly, a lithe body snuggled close and he peered down at the woman he loved. Her autumn eyes sparkled up at him, her mouth too close to resist.

After a moment, he pulled back and traced her face. A crow's rasping caw sounded far above in the sky.

"What are you thinking?" she asked.

"How happy you make me."

She smiled. "These past three weeks have been perfect."

"I don't want them to end." He touched his forehead to hers and her eyelashes brushed his.

"They don't have to."

He straightened, hope springing through him. Had she decided to join him? He'd steered clear of the topic, not wanting to spoil their time together, but with his departure near, it couldn't be avoided any longer.

Still, he had to share Button's news before they made plans. Make sure Vivie didn't end up regretting it if she agreed to come with him before learning about the bear.

"My boss met with me this morning about Button."

Her face tightened and she sat up, her arms

crossed over her stomach. She glanced at Button who stood on the bank and watched them, shaking her wet fur.

"What did he say?"

"The vet report indicates there's no serious feeding issue from Button's jaw dislocation."

Vivie's eyes stayed on the bear. Button stuck her snout beneath a pile of rocks and gobbled nuts, oblivious to a chattering, agitated squirrel beside her.

"That's good news. It means more refuges might take her. We're still on waiting lists and I'll keep her until we find a safe spot." Her voice quavered and he wrapped an arm around her rigid back, her skin cool in the Indian-summer heat.

"They're releasing her on Friday."

The words felt heavy in his mouth, crushing as stone.

She didn't move and her glistening eyes remained on Button. "But you said we'd try to find a safe place for her."

"None of the refuges have space. They give priority to injured animals and Button can fend for herself."

Vivie jerked from his arms, her angry exclamation making the bear lift her head and stare at them.

"What if she's attacked? Her mouth doesn't

fully open. She couldn't defend herself. She needs me."

Hating himself for what he needed to say, he pushed on. "No. She doesn't. Her food is out here. Her body is designed for the weather. Her instincts and memory will tell her when it's time to hibernate. As for defending herself, the vet doesn't see that as a problem given she's at the top of the food chain and black bears aren't aggressive, so she's unlikely to be attacked by another bear."

"But she won't have love," said Vivie in a watery gulp.

"Not from a human. No."

"I'm her mother."

"She's almost an adult now. It's time to let her go, Vivie, like any mother would do when it's time for her child to leave home."

"Something could happen to her and I won't be able to stop it."

"You can't protect her forever. She'll have to learn to fend for herself. You overcame all odds and it made you stronger. Button will do the same."

Vivie shuddered and wrapped her arms around her knees, laying her cheek against them.

"I don't want her going through that. The

answer's no, Liam." She shook off the hand he placed on her shoulder.

"It's not your call."

"She's my responsibility," Vivie cried, her voice breaking over him like shattered glass.

"You've prepared her," he said, trying to soothe her. "Trust in that and don't hold her back."

A tear dripped off her chin followed by another. "She's happy with me." Something lay across her voice, a long shadow.

He pulled out a handkerchief but she ignored it. "Of course she is. But it's not natural. Button needs to be with her own kind."

Vivie peered up at him, her expression both wounded and furious. "And you agree with this? Believe I'm not enough for Button?"

Here it was. The easy way out. He could blame it on work and still get the girl. But what kind of man used deceit to win another's affections? Not him.

"Button needs freedom. You can't keep humanizing a wild animal, imagining that she thinks like we do. She'll need to come and go on her terms, not yours."

Vivie pierced him with a look. "Why do I feel like we're talking about you as well as Button?"

He jerked his head from side to side. "Not a chance. I want you with me. In Yellowstone."

Her laugh sounded bitter. "Then why haven't you pushed for my answer? Didn't you think I'd need to make arrangements by now?"

"I didn't want to pressure you."

"You didn't want to pressure me or yourself?"

Each word was a stab to the chest. Realization detonating in his gut.

"You're not coming with me."

Her hair fell across her forehead when she shook her head. "Neither one of us would be happy. I'll never understand why freedom is more important to you than love."

"I want to be with you," he exclaimed as she stuffed her belongings in a tote.

Her anguished expression nearly undid him. "If you really loved me, you'd want to stay."

He pinched the bridge of his nose. "You know that's impossible." The pressure in his chest built to an unbearable ache as he imagined the claustrophobic feeling he'd experienced in Kunar, the sense that he was trapped. He didn't want that associated with Vivie.

"Then we don't work," she whispered, tears in her voice. "I wish it could be different."

He held her limp hand until she pulled

away. "Will you at least think it over? I don't leave until Friday."

"The same day they're coming for Button. How convenient for you," she said, her voice broken.

He nodded slowly, guessing it would appear to her as if he'd orchestrated everything.

Her mouth turned down. "I should have known."

"I never planned on this."

"But you hoped for it." She pointed at him, her face white. "Admit it."

His head bobbed and her eyes narrowed. "I always wanted Button where she belonged."

"And you never imagined that could be with me...no wonder you can't see yourself staying, either."

"Vivie, that's different."

"Is it? My business, my pets, my home... that is me. You have to care about all of it. I don't come piecemeal. I'm not some doll you can put in a box and truck around the country whenever the mood strikes you."

He opened his mouth to protest, but wasn't that, in a way, how he had pictured their life together? Pulling up stakes whenever the urge to leave returned, Vivie by his side? He knew she'd lived that life with her mother, but he wouldn't have made her leave things behind in the dead of night, uproot her without closure. It would have been different, if only she'd let him prove it.

"You can't take Button from me, too, Liam. Please. Stop the DEC."

He shook his head slowly. "There's nothing I can do."

Her head dipped and he saw her brush her cheeks. "There has to be something."

Helplessness swept over him. There was no way to fix this. He'd been wrong to think he could prevent casualties, even when it came to his own life...or Vivie's.

"There's nothing."

She stood up and the wooden platform rocked. "I see." Her eyes resembled dead brown leaves. "Then there's nothing left for us, either."

She turned on her heel and strode away. Button joined her when she stepped back into the forest and out of his life.

THREE DAYS LATER, Vivie woke with a start in Button's pen. Her head rested on the bear's side, which was softly rising and falling. She glanced at her watch—8:00 a.m. The DEC would be here any minute and would take this beautiful animal away from her. Worse, Liam would be leaving, as well. As betrayed as she felt, it hurt to envision her life without him.

Everything inside her recoiled. Soon they'd haul away a member of her family and dump her in a strange location, leaving her frightened and alone. Button would be as scared as she'd been the day she'd lost her first mother. As for Liam, he'd be starting over without Vivie.

Tears formed in her eyes and she blinked them away. How could she stop this? Liam had made his own decision, but for Button, Vivie's home was all she knew. Remembered. How would the bear manage on her own? Protect herself? Even though the vet and the DEC believed Button would be safe, Vivie knew the forest was a dangerous place—look what had happened to Button's mother.

Vivie shuddered when she imagined Button wounded. Bleeding. Possibly dying alone in the wilderness. The life Liam thought she needed. Bile rose in her throat when she recalled their last conversation. She'd hoped once they'd started a relationship, he'd change his mind. See a life here together with Button.

How wrong she'd been. He was as wild as the animals and countryside he supervised. How stupid to think she could change him, or heal the war wounds hidden inside. He'd always reject feeling penned in and wanted Button to be just as free.

She swiped at her nose and buried her face in Button's warm side. Where would her sweet bear sleep tonight? On rocks? Under a tree? It'd be nothing as soft and secure as a hay-filled barn. Worse, Button wouldn't know where she was. How to get home. The DEC was dropping her miles away. Would she think Vivie had abandoned her?

A sob tore from her throat. Button's snores stopped and she lifted her head, her brown eyes rolling back to meet Vivie's.

"Hey, babe," she whispered, her voice thick with emotion. Vivie sat up and ran her hand over Button's silky ears, her pointy snout and moist nose. Was this the last time she'd see her bear? Touch her? Was today the last time she'd ever see Liam?

The thought tore through her heart and she gasped at the pain of it.

Button lurched to her feet and nosed Vivie's hands, sniffing for a treat. Vivie pulled out a bag of strawberries, Button's favorite. The bear's soft lips swished across Vivie's palm as she gobbled the snack. Their last meal together.

"They're not in season, but still pretty good, right?" Vivie babbled, hardly knowing what she said. But what sense could she make when she was about to lose what felt like her child along with the only man she could ever love? There were no words.

Button snorted and sniffed Vivie's pockets then up her sides. "That's all I've got," she croaked, wishing she had more. The DEC officer had given her strict instructions not to feed Button breakfast. Something about incentivizing her to leave the drop-off area in search of food.

Vivie shivered. Button loved to eat, but she cared about companionship more. No matter how hungry the bear felt, she'd be confused and disheartened once the men left her on her own. Vivie couldn't picture Button galloping off to some random bushes once released. She'd search for the caregivers who loved her…and whom she loved back. That was the reason Liam couldn't oversee the drop-off.

Dazed, Vivie looked around the barn, feeling as though someone had shaken her world like a snow globe and nothing was coming down in the same place. Would Liam miss her and Button when he'd settled in Yellowstone? Or would she be forgotten? Another trap he'd escaped?

Vivie hugged Button's neck and the bear

rested her chin on Vivie's shoulder, her warm breath rushing by Vivie's ear. Suddenly, Button jerked away.

"Where are you going?" Vivie called, though she already knew. The bear nosed through the hay until she'd sniffed out her turtle and grabbed it.

"You love Turtle, don't you?"

Button rolled on her back, paws in the air and chewed on what was left of Turtle's head.

"I love you, too," she murmured, her vision blurring as she realized she'd never said it to Liam. If she had found the courage, would it have made a difference? Convinced him to stay? She'd never know.

As for Button, this amazing cub had changed Vivie's life. Saved it as surely as she'd come to Button's rescue. How could their tie be cut?

Horns tooted in the driveway. For a moment she eyed the back door of the barn, imagining letting Button out, escaping to some distant spot where the DEC couldn't find them. What she would give for even one more night with her bear. Another day with her man.

Shoving herself to her feet, she trudged to the barn door, unlatched it and slid it open. Liam and two other officers stood by a van and something within her crumbled when she glimpsed the large crate inside.

Vivie froze, her thoughts a howl. *No. No. No. No. No.*

She glanced back at Button. Did the bear have any idea how much her life was about to change? Did Vivie?

Liam approached, his face serious. "I'm sorry, Vivie, but we need to take Button."

"You don't need to take her," she cried, anger temporarily evaporating her despair. "You're following policy. Or your own 'life rules.'" She stuffed her shaking hands in her pockets.

"Either way, it's time for her to go," he said softly, his voice hoarse. Was he putting on some kind of act? Pretending that it hurt him to see Button leave? Or did he ache inside like her, a raw wound?

She stared at him until he flinched, wanting to know how he really felt. Maybe he'd realize how wrong he was and take everything back. Maybe he'd stay...

"Please step aside, Vivie."

"And if I told you no?"

"It wouldn't change anything."

Despite her best efforts, her lower lip quivered. "Then do it," she cried and turned away.

Liam whistled to Button as he did when

they hiked. Immediately the bear bounded after him, eager for the day's adventure. Only this time, she'd never come back and neither would Liam.

Vivie wiped away a tear and felt Scooter butt against her legs. What would she do without Button and Liam? How would they do without her? A weight settled on her chest, making each breath a struggle.

Steps receded behind her and suddenly all was quiet in the barn accept for Scooter's panting. When an engine sounded, she shook herself out of her stupor.

Button was leaving and she hadn't even said goodbye.

She raced outside to see Liam and another officer lift Button into the crate and slam it closed. Before she reached the van, they'd secured the hatch.

"I didn't say goodbye!" she sobbed, heedless now of how she sounded. The officer exchanged a glance with Liam, then joined his coworker in the front of the idling vehicle.

"Liam. Open the crate. Let me kiss her one last time. Please."

"We were lucky to get her in as easily as we did. I'm sorry but it's too late."

She shoved by him and peered through the window at her bear. Button pushed her narrow nose through the wires and butted against the glass. Vivie pressed a kiss there, wishing Button could feel it. Know her mother cared.

She cupped her hands around her mouth and shouted, "I love you. Be safe."

Button raised a paw and batted at the cage door, her head twisting from side to side.

"Don't forget me," Vivie choked out. She leaned her forehead on the hatch, then stepped back when the van drove away. Button's wide brown eyes peered at her until they turned onto the road and rounded a bend.

Vivie's legs gave out and pebbles cut into her knees.

"It'll be okay, Vivie."

She shoved Liam's hand away, craving and rejecting his touch at the same time.

"None of this is okay. Please leave."

No...stay...

Love me enough not to go...

A deep sadness filled his eyes. "I'm on my way to Yellowstone now."

She glanced at his U-Haul truck, his collie, Extra Pickles, squeezing her head through the open passenger-side window.

"Goodbye, Vivie."

Not trusting herself to look him, she jerked her head. Her pleading thoughts might rush from her, a torrent that would drag them under and carry them nowhere.

He shuffled his feet, hesitating before he walked slowly to the van.

The wheels kicked up dust as he drove off...leaving without her saying goodbye or telling him that she loved him. She jumped to her feet, her instincts telling her to chase after the truck, flag him down, jump in beside him after all. How could she let him go?

But in a moment he'd disappeared down the road. Too late.

Scooter trotted to her side and dropped something at her feet.

Turtle.

A sob tore from her throat followed by another and another.

It was over.

Once again, she'd lost everything.

CHAPTER SEVENTEEN

LIAM DROPPED HIS pack and lowered himself to the rocky summit of Factory Hill. A gust whistled around the jagged edges of the peak, flapping his hat brim and ruffling his Windbreaker. He blew out a breath and wiped his brow with a handkerchief. His movements were automatic, thoughtless, his mind farther away than Heart Lake below or distant Mount Sheridan.

Instead of seeing the burned umber spikes of Yellowstone's Red Mountain range, he pictured the lush Adirondacks, their sides blazing in color, a few barren trees in the mix. Snow might even dust Whiteface's pinnacle. Weather in upstate New York could be unpredictable in October and caught many campers unprepared. He'd rescued more than a few.

A screech ripped him from his thoughts. An eagle soared overhead, gliding in circles on wind currents before swooping to the valley nine thousand feet below.

He'd thought he could climb far enough

to leave his hurt behind. Now, after losing Vivie, he realized he couldn't outrun pain. It would follow him wherever he traveled. Perched here, on what felt like the top of the world, it echoed through the emptiness that yawned within him.

He unzipped a pocket on his pack and pulled out a bag of trail mix. At the sight of the chocolate chips mingled with the granola, he smiled. Vivie would approve. In fact, she might have demanded more. If only she were here...

Chewing a salty-sweet handful, he leaned back on his elbows and surveyed this part of the park. It was massive. Expansive. Its wilderness extended as far as he could see. No man could feel trapped in a place like this. Yet he didn't feel comforted. In fact, he felt miserable.

Why had he let himself get attached to Vivie? He'd known the risks. Should have expected the closeness that'd happened once he'd opened up. Talking about Kunar had broken through his walls. Left him vulnerable. He didn't know how to repair his defenses and stop the longing that dogged him. He missed her with a relentlessness that beat the air back in his lungs.

A scorpion skittered up a rock beyond his

hiking boots and he pulled his knees to his chest, watching. Its tail curled over its armored back, ready to sting at first threat. Once, he'd been like that. Impenetrable, ready to keep others from getting close. The animal scurried across the stone, then disappeared. It preferred isolation, as he had before Vivie.

He wished for another meal at the diner with her. A hike together. An afternoon reading on her back porch. Until now, he hadn't realized how much he'd grown used to having her in his life. Her absence felt like an amputation. A missing limb that he sensed but could no longer see.

His eyes scanned the vast space. He had everything and nothing. At least, not what mattered.

Love.

It'd liberated him. Freed the chains of his past. He saw that now.

Love had no borders or boundaries. It could never tie him down. Why had he been afraid of staying in one spot? As long as he had Vivie, he'd never feel restricted.

Fool.

He'd run across the country only to realize his shackles were still there, fear holding him hostage. He had to get rid of it to truly escape and find his way home.

To Vivie.

Would she forgive him if he returned? Apologized? He pictured Button and he dropped his head into his hands. She might never absolve him of that. Still, he had to try.

He stood and donned his backpack. Luckily he'd gotten an early start. If he hustled, he could make it back to base before sunset.

Time to chase after what he wanted instead of running from what he feared. Once he'd given his notice, he'd call James. They'd been in touch and his colleague had mentioned they'd been using overtime to cover his position. Better let them know he wanted it back before they hired someone. In a couple of weeks he'd catch a flight to New York.

He glanced at the light brown rocks, the color reminding him of Vivie's amber eyes. If he timed it right, he'd be home to celebrate an important day for her. Would she be glad to see him or push him away?

His feet slid as he hurried down the trail. There was only one way to find out.

"SWEETIE, WHAT ARE you still doing here? I'm glad you brought the pies, but we've got enough staff coming in for the first shift. No need to stay."

Vivie stopped stuffing napkins in a holder and turned. "I'm helping."

Maggie grabbed the overloaded dispenser and frowned. "You need more care than the diner. Have you seen yourself lately?"

Vivie caught her distorted reflection in the chrome side of the napkin holder. Her hair looked flat on one side, tangled on the other, her eyes sunken and dark.

"I don't care about that."

"I do. You've been miserable for weeks." Maggie steered her into the kitchen and held both her hands. "I'm sorry about what happened with Button. I know you miss her, but will any of this bring her back?"

Or Liam? Vivie added silently, before pushing the traitorous thought away. She wouldn't wish for his return. Freedom mattered most to him. He probably had exactly the life he wanted— unencumbered and without expectations. She'd been naive to think she could make him feel differently. Want other things…need her.

Rowdy backed in through the screen door holding a tray of tomatoes. Brett followed, bags of produce slipping in his grasp.

"These are the last from my garden. Frost will kill the rest tonight most likely."

The container thumped to the counter and

Brett dumped his vegetables into bins. "You okay, Vivie?"

"Of course she isn't," grouched Rowdy. His knife whizzed through the tomatoes, dicing them in seconds. "Lost her bear and her fellow."

Brett shrugged and sniffed an onion. "Maybe it was meant—"

"Shut it!" Vivie clamped a hand over her mouth, as shocked by her outburst as her wide-eyed staff and partner. "I'm sorry, Brett," she called and fled back into the restaurant's empty seating area, Maggie on her heels.

"Go home, Vivie. Or better yet, don't. Go somewhere different. Get out. You've been holed up for too long."

Vivie shook her head. "What's the point? I have no one to go with me. No one I love."

Maggie hugged her. "I love you and if I didn't need to be here, I'd take you dancing in Montreal or for a bobsled ride on Mount Van Hoevenberg. But in the meantime, there is someone who'll be with you that you love… or should… Yourself."

Realization jittered through her. For so long she'd been closed off. Had she shut herself out, too? She loved her animals and Maggie, and had finally let Liam in, too. But what about her? Didn't she owe herself that same affection? Believe she was worthy of it? Liam and Button were gone, but so was the old fearful Vivie. In her place was a woman unafraid to face life.

Maggie was right, even if Liam didn't care about her enough to stay, she should love herself. Needed to crawl out of the hole she'd fallen into when Button and Liam had left. She glanced at the wall calendar and stiffened.

October 15.

"Okay. I'm out of here." She scooped up her purse and headed for the door. She knew what she had to do.

"Where are you going?" Maggie called.

"Not home," Vivie assured her, then turned the Closed sign over and strode to her car.

She backed out of the parking lot and turned left, heading for Poke-O-Moonshine's trailhead. As always, her mind returned to Button and worry gnawed at her. It'd been over a month now. Had she gotten used to being alone? Vivie hadn't. Scooter and Jinx did their best, cuddling with her on the couch as she watched reality-TV marathons. But it wasn't the same. They didn't need her to raise them as Button had. Now the young bear fended for herself in some distant part of the Adirondacks. Was she safe? Lonely? Missing home?

Was there any chance Liam felt the same? Pain squeezed her heart as she remembered his decision to leave. How he'd turned her down when she'd asked him not to go. She loved him so much. Had trusted him with her flayed heart and he'd splintered it all over again.

The sign to the rear trailhead to Poke-O-Moonshine appeared and she pulled into the small parking area. The engine ticked quietly as she stared at the blur of red, yellow and orange beyond her windshield. Squirrels raced across the branches in front of her, acorns bulging their cheeks. They prepared for winter, not sure how harsh it might be. As Liam said, you couldn't prevent bad things from happening and she was living proof.

Her mind snagged on her last thought. Living. She'd lived through so much. Survived it. As Liam's brother Connor had said, she'd conquered it. Was there a chance she'd one day be stronger for this loss, too?

She wouldn't find out by hiding in her home or her car. No. Instead, she'd celebrate her troubles. How she'd come through them. This was a special day. The anniversary of her attack.

Her Alive Day.

She scrambled outside and glanced down at her sneakers. Not as good as hiking boots, but they'd do. The dim forest surrounded her as she plunged onto the trail.

Her feet slipped on the steep angle and she pulled herself up on exposed roots at times. The more roundabout trail that passed along the back of her property was easier, but she didn't want easy. She needed to push herself, as Maggie said, jump-start her life again.

October 15.

Once this date would have filled her with dread. A time of year she'd want to forget. Now, she would remember it in a different way. Be proud of all that she'd accomplished and overcome.

It wasn't just the day she'd been raped. Or the moment she'd nearly lost her life.

No. From now on she'd celebrate it as one of the most important times of the year.

Neither Liam nor Button would come home. She needed to make peace with that. Accept her life as it was and find happiness. Liam had coaxed her from her protective shell of an existence and she'd been wrong to slip back, wouldn't do it again.

In fact, why had she been so determined that Liam needed to stay? Given how far she'd come, she should have taken the next step and traveled with him.

It stung that he cared more about his freedom than staying with her, but if she loved him, shouldn't she have accepted it? Understood? She should have loved him for who he was, not the person she wanted him to be.

Regret weighed her steps and gradually she slowed, her breathing labored. A flash of black caught her eye at the bottom of a distant ravine and her heart slammed against her chest. Hugging a tree, she leaned over the ledge for a better view. A bear about Button's size ambled out and she nearly lost her grip.

She opened her mouth to call, exaltation and a profound relief flooding her. Button was back. Had found her. It was a miracle.

Before she could yell, a second young bear emerged. A larger bear followed and the three animals meandered through the clearing far below, sniffing and eating as she watched, stunned. A family. The casual, familiar way they interacted, their halfhearted cuffing and bumping, made it clear. All three stayed close, their affectionate play mesmerizing.

This was what a bear family looked like.

It was exactly what she would have denied

Button if she'd kept her in the pen. Her chest squeezed. The group seemed so peaceful. Happy, perhaps. At one with their environment and each other.

Seeing them was the best present she could have gotten on her Alive Day. She'd survived and Button would, too. The bear would one day have cubs of her own. Know the joys of motherhood. Would be a great caregiver because Vivie and Liam had taught her that, as well. Her heart filled and overflowed as she pictured Button and her future offspring.

In a flash she understood what Liam had explained all along. This was Button's world. Vivie had been wrong to try and keep her from it. Vivie's reasons had been for her own good rather than Button's.

She was the thoughtless, heartless one. Not Liam. He'd put Button's needs first. Had given her the freedom she deserved. Why hadn't Vivie done the same for Liam?

Tears seeped from beneath her squeezed eyelids. She'd made so many mistakes. Had pushed Liam away when she should have gone with him. Why had she acted so selfishly?

Suddenly, a hand fell on her shoulder, the touch instantly familiar and impossible...

She whirled, lost her footing and was hauled

up over the embankment before fear of the long tumble took hold.

"Liam!" Her eyes ran over the tall, handsome man, his face creased in concern. "What are you doing here?"

"I could ask you the same." His hazel eyes scanned her face and body as if searching for injuries. "I was driving to your house and spotted your car. Thought you'd taken this trail."

"Maggie said I needed to get out."

He nodded at the steep ravine. "That might have been too far."

She jerked her head sideways. "Do you see them?"

Liam peered over her shoulder. "See who?"

When she glanced back, her shoulders slumped. "They're gone. There was a bear family."

He smiled. "Must be doing some foraging before scouting out a den. Button will be doing that, too."

Vivie waited for the blow of his words, but found comfort in them instead. "I'm glad."

His brows lifted, his anxious expression clearing. "You are?"

She nodded, feeling surer by the second. "Seeing the bears together made me want that for Button. You were right about setting her free."

His eyes closed for a moment and when he opened them, his warm expression made her head spin. They held so much affection. Was he thinking of Button or her?

"I shouldn't have tried holding you back, either," she added. "I'm sorry I didn't go with you to Yellowstone."

"I'm not." His quiet words shocked her into silence.

His fingers laced with hers and he pulled her close. "If you'd come, I wouldn't have learned that I needed to stop running."

Excitement swam through her bloodstream. "Are you moving back here?"

"If you'll have me. Wherever you are, that's home. I don't need freedom. I need you."

She threw her arms around him. "I'll always want you and if you try to leave, I'm coming with you. Guess you're stuck with me."

His breath rushed by her temple as he laughed. "Sounds good."

"Not feeling trapped?"

He placed a finger on the soft underside of her chin and tipped it up to stare into her eyes. "Never. I love you, Vivie."

Fireworks of joy lit up her heart. "I love

you, too, Liam. I never want to be apart again."

Air rushed from him, his eyes dancing. "We won't."

His mouth lowered and gently slid along hers. Instantly her body tightened, loving the feel of him against her as he crushed her close. Their chests rose and fell together and their breaths synchronized in the still forest. The familiar male scent of him wove around her and she burrowed her hands in his thick hair. With a groan, he deepened his kiss, pulling her nearer still until she stood on her tiptoes.

He invaded her senses, filling her with an awareness that obliterated everything but him…this incredible man she loved.

He stroked the sides of her face and rained kisses along her jaw. "You're beautiful," he murmured a few minutes later when he pulled back.

"I've been terrible," she admitted, needing to remind him of the ugly side of her, too. Know that he loved her—damaged goods and all.

"No. Never that." His eyes sparkled down at her. "Stubborn, maybe. Cautious. But the same could be said about me. So what does that make us?"

She smiled. "A pair."

He nodded and lowered his mouth again. "Happy Alive Day," he murmured before capturing her lips in another searing kiss.

EPILOGUE

TWO SUMMERS LATER, Vivie snuggled beside Liam on their back porch swing, her head resting on his broad shoulder. Jinx stretched across both their laps and Scooter, at their feet, snored louder than the goldfinches' warbling. Wind moved through the oak branches, a slow, soothing hush. The sky glowed pink and orange, a frail full moon rising as the sinking sun hovered over the mountaintops. The vivid sunset stole her breath as always. No matter how many times she watched it, it would never stop dazzling her, like the man beside her.

"I'm glad the builders convinced us to make this wider." She gestured to the freshly painted structure and looked up, her heart expanding at the loving expression on her husband's face.

Liam rested his hand on the curve of her stomach. "We're going to need the extra room."

She returned his smile. "I still can't believe it. Twins."

"It's a good start," he answered, his eyes twinkling. The color matched the new trees and bushes that had sprung up since the fire. With a newly rebuilt house and nature doing its own remodeling, she'd hardly know flames once raged through here...if it wasn't for the large, empty space that'd held Button's enclosure. She stopped her sigh. Today was a happy day. Their first ultrasound. And what news it'd given.

"Only 'good'?" She drew back and raised a brow.

Liam pulled her close again and she settled against his warm, solid chest. "We'll go for triplets next time."

A laugh escaped her. "Are you trying to kill me?"

He stroked her cheek, the feather touch of his fingers sending a shiver dancing through her. "Just making sure we have the big family we want."

"You've given me so much." She glanced down at their entwined hands and the matching gold bands that glinted in the weakening light. The warm, late-summer air smelled sweet, the flowering bushes sending up clouds of perfume to the treetops. In a few weeks, leaves would start to turn and weather would grow crisp. She'd spotted her first V-shaped

flock of migrating geese just this morning.
Animals were getting ready for winter. For a
moment she pictured Button's frantic face as
the DEC had taken her away two years ago.
Had her little girl found her way?

"Not as much as I have planned." His
mouth curled up again, happiness lighting his
face. "I love you." He brushed his lips over
hers in a kiss that spoke his feelings louder
than his words.

"I love you, too." She touched her forehead
to his, their eyelashes brushing. "I was broken
and you were the only one who could fix me."

"And you're everything I needed, but didn't
know I could have. I'm thankful every day
that we wake up together." He cupped both
sides of her face and his features sharpened,
his eyes intent. "I'd made it out of the war
alive, but you showed me that wasn't enough.
Building a life—with you—that's what's
made me a survivor."

"No more restlessness?" She turned and
pressed a kiss into his palm.

"Only when we're apart."

"It's the same for me. That old fear is gone.
There's too much love to give it any room."
She touched the dimple in his chin, her heart
as full as it could be.

A rustling sounded at the edge of the

woods. Something large skulked along the scrub brush. Liam angled his body so he shielded her, and Scooter's nose quivered before he lifted his head and sniffed the air.

"Let's get the animals and you inside," Liam said in a low, serious voice that set off her alarm bells.

Before Liam could grab Scooter's collar, the Labrador scrambled to his feet and bolted off the porch steps toward the swaying bushes.

"No! Liam, he's after something. We've got to get him."

"Stay put," he commanded over his shoulder and ran after her wayward dog.

Heart pounding, she watched Scooter bark and turn in circles. Even Jinx slunk toward the woods, making her pulse hammer hard at her temples. Usually her pets knew better.

Liam managed to corral Scooter, but Jinx hunkered low, looking ready to pounce.

Orders or no, she had to get her cat.

She hustled off the porch, earning a frown from Liam and stopped cold when a large black bear emerged.

Liam turned back to the woods. Without moving, he said. "Vivie. Take Scooter and head into the house now. Jinx will stay out of its way. Do it quick."

Yet there was something about that bear… the way it stared at her…and when it turned its face to look behind it, she knew. The sideways jaw…

"Button!" she screamed, racing toward her bear.

"Vivie! Don't—" Liam yelled, but she didn't slow. She needed to get closer to her sweet cub, all grown up and as beautiful as ever. Majestic, even. Her heart beat a wild rhythm, her eyes drinking in the sight.

"You came home," she choked out. "I missed you so much, Button."

Button bobbed her head and snorted. When she galloped at Vivie, Liam let go of Scooter and intercepted her.

He and the bear went down in a tangle of fur and limbs and when he got to his knees, Button butted his chest and licked his cheek.

Liam laughed, the rich sound ringing in the cleared property. "She hasn't forgotten us, Vivie."

Vivie brushed a hand across her stinging eyes and felt two paws descend on her shoulders. A familiar, furry cheek pressed against her own.

"Button!" She wrapped her arms around the bear and let the tears fall where they would. Button's warm pelt covered her like a childhood blanket. "Where have you been? How did you find us?"

The bear wriggled, finding places to lick Vivie that made her giggle—her ear, her cheek, her hands. Then Button pressed her snout against Vivie's stomach the way she had always done as a cub. She exhaled long and loud against Vivie's shirt.

"I'm having a baby, Button. Twins. There's going to be two more to our family so that makes..." Her eyes took in Scooter, Jinx and Liam. "That'll be seven of us counting you. Can you believe it?"

Button butted her softly, then lurched to her feet and tromped back into the brush.

Dismay and loss filled Vivie. "Button! Come back!" She stood to follow, but Liam grabbed her hand, then stepped close.

"She's wild now, Vivie. We're lucky she stopped by at all. Must have heard us talking and decided to take a look."

Vivie struggled to answer but her throat swelled and pinched off the words. She'd never stopped wanting Button in her life. She was a member of the family and it wouldn't be complete without her. Pain dampened her happy day. Once again, she'd lost her bear.

"Let's get inside. I promised you a pancake dinner, didn't I?" Liam put an arm around

Vivie and steered her to the house. Scooter raced to the side of the new woodshed and disappeared.

A noise stopped them before they reached the steps, louder than before. They whirled and to Vivie's shock, Button appeared again, followed by one black bear cub, and then another. Twins!

Exaltation made her head swim. She pressed a hand against the lightness in her chest. It was everything she could have wanted for Button and more.

And then, blinking through a cedar sapling, a third small face appeared.

Button pawed the ground and snorted until the littlest of the brood tumbled out and landed in a clumsy heap by Jinx. The cat flipped back, then recovered fast enough to sniff the animal, head-to-tail puff.

"You're a mom," Vivie gasped. "Triplets. Congratulations, Button."

Button stared down at her offspring until they gathered close. At last she looked back at Vivie, her head high, eyes gleaming.

Vivie fought the urge to whoop, not wanting to scare the quivering cubs. This was exactly what Liam, Dr. Vogel, the Reeds and even the DEC had wanted for Button. A chance to live in the wild. If Button hadn't faced the risks, she would never have had the joy of raising her own family. Vivie's hand rested on her stomach as she glanced at her beaming husband. And neither would she.

Scooter bounded up and Vivie held her breath, afraid of a protective mother bear reaction. But the dog held something in its mouth that made Button step forward. A nearly unrecognizable rubber toy dropped to the ground.

Turtle.

Button grunted and pawed the grass beside her old companion. She sniffed it, then caught it between her teeth. Like a cub, she rolled on her back and held the object in her claws, gnawing on what was left of it. It tugged at Vivie's heart to see a glimpse of the baby bear she'd raised.

At last Button got back on all fours, nudged her progeny away from Jinx and bobbed her head at Vivie and Liam. After a long, final look, she turned and disappeared into the forest, Turtle in her mouth, her cubs scampering after her.

Vivie turned in Liam's arms and rested her wet face against his chest. "I can't believe it, Liam. This is more than I ever imagined for her. She's happy. Really happy. It's the life she was meant to have."

"And now we're having it, too, Vivie," he said softly, his voice rough with emotion. He looked up at the color-streaked sky, his arms encircling her, his hands resting on her stomach. "We're not riding away into the sunset. We're staying here, where we can enjoy it together, always. I owe you my life and my heart. I love you so much and I'm going to tell you that every day." He cupped her face, and gazed into her eyes. "I promise you that."

Moved beyond words, she stared up at him and touched his face. His skin was warm. His expression tender. She'd never imagined her days could be so full of joy until a tiny bear cub had raided her kitchen. And now she and Button both had the lives they were meant to lead.

Bringing her lips to Liam's, she felt her heart expand. This was exactly where she wanted to be, with Jinx, Scooter, Button, the babies who would soon join them and most of all with Liam, the man who'd shown her how to trust and love and live.

* * * * *

LARGER-PRINT BOOKS!

GET 2 FREE LARGER-PRINT NOVELS PLUS 2 FREE MYSTERY GIFTS

Love Inspired®

Larger-print novels are now available...